RÍO GANGES

RÍO GANGES

David Theis

WINEDALE PUBLISHING
Houston

Published by Winedale Publishing Co.

Published in the United States by Winedale Publishing Co., Houston

www.winedalebooks.com

Library of Congress Cataloging-in-Publication Data

Theis, David, 1951-
Rio Ganges / by David Theis.
p. cm.
ISBN 0-9701525-6-6 (alk. paper)
1. Americans—Mexico—Fiction. 2. Mexico City (Mexico)—Fiction.
3. Runaway wives—Fiction. 4. Photographers—Fiction. I. Title.
PS3620.H45 R56 2002
813'.6—dc21   2002000636

Manufactured in the United States of America
2 4 6 8 9 7 5 3
First Edition

Book design by Harriet Correll
Jacket design by D.J. Stout and Julie Savasky

Dedication

*In memory of my mother, Alice,
my father, Joe,
and my big sister Joey.*

Acknowledgments

Deepest thanks to Paula Webb and her writing group, Stella Lillicrop, Eric Lawlor, Jessica Greenbaum, Terry Demchak, Maureen LaMar, Janice Rubin, Tom Cobb, David Kaplan, and—the last shall be first—Joe, Rose, Gabo, and dear Susanne.

Río Ganges

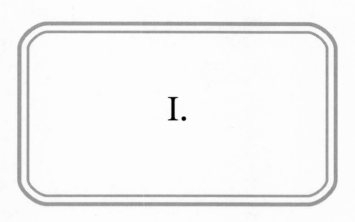

I.

1.

The last time I heard my father's voice, it was night and I was driving south toward the border. Jane was with me, and so was May, our daughter. We were beyond the reach of most radio, and our hand-me-down car didn't have a tape player. My in-laws could afford almost any accessory they wanted; they just hadn't wanted to play tapes.

"You see this?" my father-in-law, a music professor at U.T. Arlington, had once said to me as he held a cassette in front of my face. "Mahler doesn't belong on a strip of ribbon like this. It's nothing but musical dental floss."

Why it was more acceptable for Mahler's profound art to emanate from a dashboard radio, he didn't say. And I didn't ask. My in-laws no longer intrigued me. They were just two more Dallas suburbanites.

Their daughter and I had been on our best behavior since the early winter darkness covered us on Highway 59, near Victoria. Regret and hope kept us calm and silent in the Olds 88 that her parents had given us as a moving present. They were being good sports about my taking their daughter and granddaughter so far away. "You're not going to sneak into Mexico in that cruiser," my father-in-law warned me when he handed me the keys. "The natives will take notice. Try to get some pictures of farmers gawking at my car." This last was a nod toward my profession, photography. Or my art, rather, since I didn't make any money at it. In Mexico, I would make my living as an English teacher.

And I did get a kick out of the idea of blasting through Mexico's remaining chunk of the great Sonoran desert in a ten-yard-long American gas hog. But I wished we had some consistent music, so that Jane and I could just surrender to the road and not have to think about the thick purple scar on my cheek.

The radio static got on her nerves not long after we entered the brush country south of Beeville. "If my parents can give us their car, couldn't we at least afford to put in a CD player?" she asked. She'd swallowed the rest of what she'd wanted to say, and I could sense her reaching deep for tonight's portion of patience. And it was only right that she do a little bitter swallowing. We were moving to Mexico in part because of things she had done.

There's another way of putting that. Things she had done—mostly having an affair with a partner in the modern dance troupe she had joined after college, a man I hadn't even perceived as heterosexual until she gave me the bad news—had given me the leverage to move us to Mexico. I wanted to take pictures in the same country as Graciela Iturbide. That seemed like a plan, that and teaching English for a living while I photographed naked, beautiful Jane; elegant, spiky cactus, and sad, leathery men for the sake of both my soul and my portfolio.

My dried-up hometown lay only thirty miles to our north as we passed Beeville. Maybe that's why I was thinking about my father.

Had my mother's nervous breakdown started after my father left us? Her, me, my younger brother, and our deeply, if rather charmingly, retarded older sister. Or had her wild imaginings in fact driven him away? I was only ten when he left, and my mother can't remember anything right, so most likely I'll never know.

When we passed the Beeville Naval Air Station, I looked back to my right in the direction of my family's home, clenched my teeth at the thought of both my mother and my father, and pushed south toward George West. How peaceable the Olds was, how long and quiet and embarrassing to a man who had just finally given up on his Honda Civic.

I leaned forward to turn the radio dial, but didn't come anywhere near Jane, who sat at the far end of the car's long, daunting bench seat. All the radio gave me were crackles and dead air. I didn't look at her. This was not a good time for us to look at each other. But I sure sensed her, tense against the passenger door.

She was a little afraid of Mexico, and our trip to Monterrey last Christmas hadn't helped. Her eyes had burned from the smog, and she wanted to cry because of the poverty. I knew she was mostly going this time for May's sake, that she wanted to keep our fragile family intact for our 18-month-old, who could sleep for hours in a moving back seat. But she was coming for me, too. She told me that she hoped I would find myself in Mexico, that in a foreign country I would somehow reinvent myself and actually become the extraordinary man she had thought she was marrying. She never added: the man she had given up so much for, the G.I Bill guy she had stepped down for.

She got plenty in return, in my opinion. No one appreciated her great beauty as much as I did. No one would ever photograph it as much, or as well. I'd touched her plenty too. For years we fucked almost every day. But it was the photography that really won her for me. The whole routine. The tripod. The portraiture lights. The dark room. The sex in the dark room.

I showed her how her creamy brown skin both absorbed and reflected light. I showed her the formal perfection of her wiry, sculpted hair, and of her delicately tapered face. And of her dancer's body. She already knew, of course, that she was beautiful. But she'd come to that knowledge late, maybe because she was nearly the only dark-skinned person in her suburban high school. And so she was thrilled when I showed her to herself.

I looked at Jane in profile, and turned the dial at the same time. She stared straight ahead into the dark brush country, and the beams of a rare, oncoming car bathed her face in light.

I would never get my fill of female beauty. Five years of Jane had only left me greedy.

"Sorry," she said. "I guess it was actually my idea not to buy a CD player, wasn't it?"

I cleared my throat, and said, "I don't remember."

Just past Freer, with its "Welcome Sportsmen," and "Welcome Deer Hunters" signs, and heading toward Encinal, we were now so in the middle of nowhere that the radio didn't always register static. The stations clear enough to tolerate were from Mexico. *Mariachis*, accordion-driven *conjuntos*, passionate *rancheras*.

"Would you find another station?" Jane said as I lingered over a crackling *mariachi* lament. As I worked the dial delicately, like a safecracker, I knew it wasn't really the music that bothered her. If it was, it would've been cruel of me to drag her across the border.

No, Jane could get into a snappy *norteño* number. Trained dancer that she was, she could even look good at it. We'd polkaed to Flaco Jiménez just a couple of months before in a country dance hall, not far from Austin. On one song we'd held May between us and spun around as if we knew exactly what we were doing.

The bandages had just come off my cheek then, and I must have looked pretty raw. But the star-shaped scar—my "red dwarf," I'd called it, by way of lame apology for having tried to kill myself—was part of the reason I'd wanted to dance that night. The way I'd gagged on my little .25, twisting it and blowing open the wrong part of my head, had taught me some important lessons. Like how May needed a living father, which I should have already understood, after my own years of living with a ghost. The ghost of a living man, maybe. Nobody knew where my father was, or if he was still alive.

Dancing a *cumbia* that night, Jane melted against me. She had raised the level of my own dancing considerably, and I sometimes felt like I was stepping and shuffling inside of her. When the song ended and Flaco lowered his accordion in his dreamy, satisfied way, and the Mexican and Chicano couples returned to their tables, we lingered in the middle of the dance floor, and she touched my cheek for the first time since it had been stitched together.

"You're actually learning to dance," she said. Then we picked up May from the kindly couple who had offered to hold her.

The radio crackled, then a station came into focus. The language was English, but hick—the broadcast of a high school football game, from Freer or Three Rivers, or some other brush country outpost. So I left the volume down, and hoped it would serve as acceptable background noise.

There's a service station up ahead two or three miles, I started to say. But before I could speak, the broadcaster shouted, "he's got the first down" in a way that made me look at the radio.

When the broadcaster gasped, "We got two more minutes of football!" as if he were announcing the end of the world, I reached for the knob and jacked the volume up. "It ain't over till it's over!" he crowed, and some undigested part of my life rose up out my stomach, where a second before I hadn't felt a thing, then caught in my chest and bulged.

"It ain't over till it's over," the broadcaster repeated, and a sound that started as a groan came out of me as a gurgle.

Jane jerked and looked at me. Through the corner of my eye I could see the alarm on her face as I put my foot to the brake and ground the Olds to a halt in the middle of the empty road.

"What the fuck are you doing?" she said, but all I could do was stare at the radio, and finally pound my fist against the dashboard above it.

"It ain't over till it's over," I said to her. "We ain't beat yet."

For the second time in three months I had really scared her. Jane's eyes widened and she braced herself against the passenger door. She felt an entire first down away.

"Jacobs is back," the announcer said in his amateurish, nasal voice. "Jacobs is back."

"Uh," I stammered. I don't have an actual speech defect, but sometimes words catch against my teeth. "That's my dad. On the radio. That's him."

Jane's eyes narrowed. "Get us out of the road," she said.

That wasn't too much to ask, so I put the Olds back into drive, eased us off to the shoulder, and put on the emergency blinkers.

My hand shook as I reached for the knobs, but the pressure in my chest had eased. "I'm not crazy," I said. "It's really him."

Jane looked suspiciously at the radio. Her doubt seemed to interfere with the reception, as now my father's voice crackled.

8

"This could be the ball game," he said, and my distant past, the part of my life I thought I was better off forgetting, washed over me—my mother telling us Daddy had packed in the night and left in the afternoon, right after his broadcast shift. He had announced the prices at Foster's feeds one last time, read the farm-and-market news one last time, wished his listeners a pleasant afternoon one last time, then he had driven south, according to neighbors who had seen him and assumed he was on his way to a quail shoot in Pawnee.

I wanted to explain how clearly I recognized this voice to Jane, to make her believe me that this was him, but I couldn't talk.

A ball carrier for my father's team was tackled near the goal line, then the reception broke and pumped-up static filled our car.

"Ah," I cried, forcing out a sound. Then I knelt on the seat and reached back for the still sleeping May.

"Dan," Jane said, "please don't wake her up."

I've got to, I thought. I turned with her carefully, making sure I didn't bump her against the seat back, then sat with her nestled into my lap. The radio roared at us wordlessly.

I put the car in gear again, looked behind me to make sure no cars were coming, then eased back onto the road, turning us back north, toward the spot where I'd last heard his voice. I drove slowly, holding the sleeping May in the crook of my right arm.

"Let me have her," Jane said. "Please, Dan."

But I pressed May against me. The two-lane highway was completely empty. We were in no physical danger. I drove slow, extra careful, and remembered riding with my father in his pickup, going out to gather watermelons from my mute uncle's farm. His brother didn't have a voice box of his own. He had to talk through what looked like an electric shaver. *Your uncle's sort of a broadcaster himself,* my father said once, and laughed. *Just like me.*

I laughed too, though I didn't get the joke, and felt vaguely guilty afterwards, as if I'd laughed directly at the hole in my uncle's throat.

My father talked for a living, but he didn't even tell me goodbye. I wanted to say this to Jane. I was hopeful. I felt some talk coming on. But no, it was tears, rather than words, that came out.

Then with a crackle his voice returned, in an excited jumble of words.

Where was he calling the game? If he would just say the name of the team, I would know where to find him. The Rattlers or the Longhorns or the Bulldogs or the Coyotes. Encinal, George West, Three Rivers, Freer. Just one word and I could track him down, present him with his granddaughter, knock him on his bony ass.

"This is your grandfather's voice," I gasped, but May only stirred against my side, and didn't wake up.

"I told you," my father boasted, "it ain't never over till it's over."

My longing for my father suddenly turned hard inside me. I couldn't stand to hear him crow out that line one more time. I handed May toward her mother, who snatched her away. I drove to the shoulder of the road again, then pulled over and got out of the car.

The December cold hurt my wet cheeks. I tried to dry them with the backs of my hands, but my knuckles didn't sop up any moisture.

I remembered the Christmas when he gave me a Brownie camera, and the pictures of him that I'd taken. I remembered his hawk nose—"my beak," he called it—in black and white. His close-set eyes, in black and white. His mouth, appropriately wide for a man who made his living talking, in black and white. I didn't remember the color of his eyes, or even his hair. Just black and white.

The car door opened, and when I turned to look, Jane was easing around the car's long trunk toward me. From the tail-light's glow, I couldn't tell if she was angry or sympathetic or full of pity, but at least she would still come to me, as pathetic as I no doubt looked.

She crossed the space between the car and me in two long strides and stood right in my face, almost up against my stupid scar. But she didn't throw her arms around me. She just looked into my eyes, and inside her I saw anger, fear, and love, and something else that I didn't recognize, something that scared me.

"Let's go find him," she said emphatically, as if she were fin-ishing, and not beginning, a debate. "How far away can he be?"

That was not what I expected or wanted from her. "What?" I said.

"Go find your father. You have every right."

I looked away from her and up to the stars. It was a clear, bril-liant, winter night. The heavens had pitched a tent of glory over my little drama. Between Jane's beauty and the stars, my heart slowed.

"My job starts in three days," I said. "It's a two-day drive."

"Call them. Tell them you had car trouble."

I had already met my new bosses, the school principal and the department head, and my new co-worker, an English teacher also from South Texas, via Brown University. I'd even met *el patrón*, the big man who owned the school and everything else in that corner of the world. They had let me pick my own starting day. If I came a week later, no one would care.

Jane touched me for the first time all day, but it wasn't a caress. She balled the shoulder of my flannel shirt in her fist and pulled my face toward hers.

"All you ever do is look for this man," she said. "Now you've found him."

I shuddered from fear and cold, pulled myself away from her and him, and stumbled toward the barbed wire fence between me and the empty land beyond, aware as I always was of my lack of physical grace. I grabbed the wire, careful of the little spikes, and looked straight ahead. In the starlight I saw how the scrubby land dissolved into total darkness. Nothing more. The emptiness calmed me and I could turn to face my wife.

She and I had a chance to make it. We had a chance to grow old together, to do great things together, to love Mexico together. And the thought of my father's face made me feel cold inside, even dead.

"Fuck him," I said. "Let's get going."

We backtracked to Freer and checked into the first motel on the strip, one with a "Welcome Deer Hunters" sign on its marquee. We put May in a single bed, then showered together, washing each other's bodies, scrubbing and touching until we couldn't take it anymore.

We'd only made love once since I shot myself. There'd been no passion to it; we only wanted to see if we could still manage the motions before moving so far away.

This night was different. Even though we were in the kind of crummy, soulless room that usually tightened Jane up, she loosened for me, and I felt a whole bad year melt away. We had needed a break from sex, it seemed. We were better that night, smarter than ever before. We kept adjusting to each other's motions and body angles, finding the way to get me deeper inside her. Everything I did was right, except for the goofy sound I made when I came, something like the bark of an unidentified animal. I wanted to laugh when I got my breath back, but she wouldn't let me. She held me too tight against her.

2.

I had assumed that because we were going to central Mexico, we would have to pass through Mexico City, as if *el D. F.* was a magnet that sucked in all travelers within 100 miles. I was up for a trip to the great city, but didn't look forward to navigating its streets in the Olds. And Jane emphatically did not want to begin our life in Mexico with a visit to the biggest, dirtiest city on earth. "I'll have to work my way up to it," she told me before we ever left Austin, and I remembered her unhappiness in Monterrey. Of course, on that trip I had taken her away from her lover for a few days; maybe that was why she seemed so unhappy.

But even now that she felt so guilty, to get her to move I'd had to promise that the school was out in the country, and that we'd be surrounded by sleeping volcanoes and bathed in clean air. That's how Carlos Valparaíso, the industrialist who owned the school—it was somehow part of his manufacturing complex—had described Polotitlán to me when I'd met him in Houston during the job interview. According to the Houston woman who had actually hired me (she was the coordinator of the Polotitlán English program), Valparaíso's appearance at the interview was just one sign of how important the English program was to him.

I was still confused about the job. A very rich man had hired me to teach very poor children. Why? Apparently they were growing up in the shadows of his industrial complex and hacienda, and would one day be working in his factories. Still, did that explain why he would take the trouble to show up for a teacher's interview?

Jane slumped in her seat as we entered the desert south of Matehuala, and passed through stretches of Joshua trees. I didn't want to catch their oddly human quality in a photograph—the bent, tired looking trunks, the rasta-man thatches of leaf on their crowns. These trees were so blatantly ghostly that they didn't need any coaxing to give up their secrets. As a ten-year-old with a Brownie I could've captured a Joshua tree just fine.

Still, they were fun to talk about. May and I gave them names as we whooshed by. A particularly tall one very near the highway we called Big Ben, even though May didn't know anything about the London landmark. She named a short, stumpy Joshua 'Fritz,' in honor of our Austin neighbor's mutt that had nipped at her once and terrified her ever after. In our old apartment, the bogeyman came to be named Fritz. That May wasn't afraid to invoke that demon in Mexico seemed like a confirmation of my decision to move us here. Mexico was no place for cowards, and living here was going to make us all braver.

"Fritz," I repeated, as casually as possible, and glanced at Jane, who was bent over our Sanborn's map. Which she then dropped on the seat between us.

"We don't have to go to Mexico City at all," she said. "We can turn just past Querétaro. It'll save us a hundred miles."

It didn't surprise me to learn that I had missed our turning point on the map. "Great," I said, sharing in her irritation with me. I wasn't a good map reader. Unless I was calculating the level of available light, or evaluating the visual texture of a backdrop, I generally didn't pay enough attention to detail.

"Aunt Doris!" May shouted from the back seat, and pointed toward a short, squatty tree. Doris was my retarded older sister, who had never grown out of her baby fat. In her perpetual innocence, Doris had once asked Jane if she were a nigger. This was on an early visit to my family, but Jane took the question well. It wasn't the first time Doris had asked her an embarrassing question. "I don't know, Doris," she'd answered. "What do you think?" Maybe Jane had really meant, What does Dan's hick, redneck brother think? But she hadn't put it that way. After she got to know Will a little better, she had dropped redneck, but still thought hick was just about right.

But I was pissed. "Shut your mouth," I had said to my sister, and glared at my brother and mother, who wore equally shocked expressions. "Jesus Christ," I said to them both.

"Hey, she didn't get that from me," Will said. He was younger than me by three years, but taller and stouter and meaner. More competitive, at least.

"It's okay," Jane had said, putting her hand on my shoulder to calm me. "When I was little I used to ask myself the same question."

After that show of kindness about my family, I had started thinking of marrying Jane, and on our drive back to Austin the next day I proposed to her. I tried to be casual. When we hit that stretch of Highway 123 between Stockdale and San Marcos with the woods on either side—woods that deer sometimes emerged from on suicide missions, bursting out of the trees onto the highway where they smashed against pickups—I just cleared my throat and blurted it out. "Do you want to get married?" No more artfully than that. It was winter, and the empty gray deerless trees slid by us as I drove.

Time seemed to stop, or to slow supernaturally, after I spoke. I'm normally in favor of stopping time. That's partly why I take pictures. But when she didn't answer right away, I wanted to not just stop time, but to run it backwards—just five or seven minutes to the instant before I'd made a fool of myself. But I screwed up my courage, and instead of apologizing, rested my hand on her knee. Jane put her left hand on top of mine, and then her right hand too, but still didn't say a word.

While we were making love that night, utterly locked into our rhythm, I had proposed again. "Marry me," I whispered as we rocked. "Let's do this for the rest of our lives."

"Yes," she murmured, almost distantly, like she had something on her mind. But then she reached behind me and grabbed the backs of my shoulders, pulling on them to increase her traction. "Yes," she said again.

After we had finished and rolled apart, she breathed deeply, as if I'd fucked the wind out of her. "I won't hold you to it. That can just be our way of talking dirty."

I think that was supposed to be a joke, but I was still too far outside myself to laugh. "No way," I answered. "You've already said yes."

Jane could have insisted then that we weren't really engaged, but she didn't. She inched across the bed and put her head up on my chest. I took that as a yes, without ever asking myself why I was so anxious to marry her. That would have seemed a ridiculous question.

I turned the radio on, and when I couldn't find a station, I turned the crackle down to a low hum, to have a little noise. I started to think about my father, but pushed the image away.

"I'm going to miss Doris," Jane said. "She always tells you exactly what's on her mind."

That rebuke was probably aimed at me, since supposedly I'm just the opposite. I tend to calculate and weigh and parse everything I say, except for marriage proposals. But maybe Jane would be the same way if she'd grown up with a perpetual three-year-old who always said exactly what she thought.

"I guess you want me to be more like Doris," I said. Jane laughed hard, as if letting off pent-up tension, tension we should've already fucked away these two nights on the road.

"What's so funny about Aunt Doris?" May asked, and Jane and I laughed together. My cheek throbbed as the Olds hummed through the desert.

On a pocked, crowded, two-lane "highway" about thirty-five miles north of Toluca, I pulled over at combination roadside café and service station. A young man in greasy blue coveralls approached to ask if I wanted Nova or Super, and once again I felt strangely liberated when I asked for the more expensive gas. Back in Austin, I almost always got the cheapest of everything. But after crossing the Sonoran desert, the Olds deserved Super, and so did I. Even though I didn't have to pump my own gas, I pushed my stiff body out of the car and stretched. Just across the road stood a tree-covered, cone-shaped mountain, which I later learned was the spent volcano that gave its name, Polotitlán, to the small town that spread across a section of its base.

Just behind the service station, the ground was cracked with erosion, and beyond the deep crevices ran fields of corn. The stalks bent in a sudden gust of wind, which lifted some dust. A small plane flew above a distant cornfield and went into a gradual descent.

I pulled out the letter of instructions that Valparaíso himself had given me at our interview, looked at it blankly, unable to concentrate, then asked the attendant where *la hacienda de Polotitlán* was.

"Where that airplane just landed," he answered, gesturing toward the horizon. "On the highway, you'll see a big gate of stone on your left. Turn there."

Jane took May to the restroom while I went into the café for some bottles of mineral water. My eyes went straight to the Bohemia bottles in the front of the drink case, but I had promised Jane—and myself, too—that after the shooting, I wasn't going to drink for a while. A couple of men sitting beside a big dirty window rolled and ate tacos, and a burly man stood behind the counter, watching the television in a far corner of the café. The reception and sound were both bad, but still the man seemed engrossed in whatever program it was, and oblivious to me. I tapped at the counter with the edge of a ten-*peso* coin. Probably this was a coincidence, but just as I tapped, the jukebox against the far wall lit up, and mariachi trumpets began to blare.

The man behind the counter looked at me then, and nodded as if he somehow recognized me. "You're looking for the *patrón*," he said. "For Don Carlos."

I paused and wondered if my Spanish had gone haywire, and was making me think I'd heard things that people couldn't possibly have said. Then I answered, "That's right."

The man behind the counter stepped toward me. "He's waiting for you. Very anxiously, too. I'll call the hacienda, to tell them you are here."

"No," I stammered. "We're fine. We'll be there in just a minute. I just wanted to get some drinks."

I heard the door open behind me, and looked back to see Jane walk in carrying May, whose wide-open and alarmed eyes bore straight into me.

I was going to ask what the matter was, but Jane cut me off. "The toilets were full of turds," she said. "To the fucking brim."

May had started to imitate Jane's language, and sometimes I cautioned Jane to be careful how she talked around her. But this time I swallowed my words. I felt as if I was responsible for the traumatic sight and smell, that I'd left all that unflushed shit behind myself. So instead I murmured, "We'll be in the hacienda in five minutes."

"Never mind the drinks," I said to the man behind the counter. But I couldn't leave until I'd asked one question. "How did you know it was me?"

He pointed to his cheek, and my fingers went automatically to my scar.

At the stone gate, adorned by two carved eagle heads, one facing the other, two uniformed guards waved us through. They wore rifles slung across their backs; one guard's barrel pointed up, the other's down. They didn't stop me to ask my business, they just gestured toward the caliche road which curved to my left, around a field of trees that did not look particularly Mexican. As I followed the curve, and saw that the trees looked like a jumble of forms, some short, some tall, some tropical, some pine, I wondered what new world of vegetation I was bringing my family into. But as I took the curve, the pine-covered volcano stood straight in front of me, and its blanket of familiar-looking green comforted me. Pines are one of the five kinds of trees that I can name. In my rearview mirror, I saw the white cloud of caliche dust that the Olds was raising, and I heard the crunching of little stones beneath our tires.

The road curved for what seemed like a mile, but when we

came onto a straightaway, I still didn't see any hacienda. The exotic-looking trees had been replaced by a field of *magueyes*. When I imagined myself taking pictures in Mexico, I always included a *maguey* cactus with its broad leaves and long thorns and that metallic shade of green that I didn't know the name for. I felt my heart speed up and I drove a little faster too. I felt that I was only now entering Mexico, that the desert had been a preamble.

We hit another curve, and then I saw a red radio tower, just as tall as the tower of my father's old station back home, poking up out of a row of thick tall trees whose bottom thirds had been painted white.

"That must be the hacienda," I said, "where the tower is."

May stood up in the back, and leaned forward between Jane and me. Instead of telling her to sit down and put on her seat belt, I tried to slow the car to below thirty. But I couldn't make myself hold the speed down. I felt both hurried and afraid to arrive at my destination.

"Tell me again about Valparaíso," Jane said. "Who is this guy?"

"Well," I said. "He's shorter than us. He's blonde. When he speaks English he's got this guttural accent that doesn't seem very Mexican."

"Is he smart?"

"He hired me."

"But, is he smart?"

That made us both laugh.

"Did you take his picture?" May asked.

"Not yet," I said, though in my mind I had already started to frame the formal, well-paid portrait that he had promised to commission.

"I used to take pictures myself," Valparaíso had told me as our interview, which had only touched lightly on the job in question, had wound down. "When I was a kid."

"He seems okay," I added to my description of the man. "Pretty easy going for a rich guy." As if I had some personal knowledge of how uptight rich guys usually were. I was probably calling on my knowledge of how stern Jane's merely upper-middle-class mother could be. "After Houston he flew to Canada with his father, to have lunch with the prime minister and talk a little business."

"I have to go to the bathroom," May said. "Really bad."

"We're almost there," I said. The radio tower looked to be just around the next curve, which I took. And then the tires of the Olds vibrated across a patch of cobblestone pavement, and a long white windowless building with a merely functional looking door smack in its middle appeared before us.

"Is this it?" Jane said. "It's big."

I didn't mention my disappointment at the building's plainness. "Where's the bathroom?" May said in a voice that approached all-out whine.

Then the unappealing door opened and another uniformed guard stepped out. At least he didn't have a gun strapped across his back. He waved at me to keep going and so I did, bouncing lightly across the stones until we'd reached the building's edge, which I curved around and saw Valparaíso pacing in front of another unimpressive door. He was smoking a cigarette that he threw down and ground against the cobblestones with his heel as I pulled up in front of him. The red radio tower stood just to the side, and I glanced up at it as I got out of the car.

"Daniel," he said, pronouncing my name in Spanish, which pleased me very much. "You made it."

He took my outstretched hand and pulled me toward him for an *abrazo*. "Nice car," he said. Then he let me go when he saw Jane opening her door. He scurried—rich or not, he had short legs—around the front of the Olds, finished opening the door for her, then helped her out. Jane is so tall; she rose and rose as she came out of the car, and stood a good two inches above him.

"Carlos Valparaíso. *Para servirle.*"

Jane brightened, as all of her charm came back at once. I wasn't sure if she understood from her college Spanish that Valparaíso was offering to serve her in any way she might need.

"I'm Jane," she said in English, poised and pleasant. Cool but nearly warm. I threw open the back seat and May tumbled out into my arms.

"Sorry," I said. "We have to find a bathroom."

As I passed him, headed toward the open door, Valparaíso scooped May out of my arms. "Welcome to Mexico," he said to her in English. "We'll get you taken care of." He carried her through the door, then passed her off to a maid who seemed to be stationed there awaiting her assignment. "*Necesita ir al baño*," he said, and the maid put May down on the floor with its square reddish tiles, and took her hand to begin leading her away. May looked back over her shoulder toward Jane and me, her eyes bulging in panic.

"You'll be all right," I said to her.

"Follow me," Valparaíso said. "I got some people I want you to meet in the pool room. You're just in time for lunch."

"We better wait for May," I said. Jane said, "I'll go with her," and strode off on her dancer's legs behind the servant and our daughter. "I'm coming, baby," she said.

Valparaíso didn't seem happy to wait; I could already tell he was in fact a very impatient man, despite the first impression he'd made on me. Then I saw him control his impatience, and drain the excess energy out of his shoulders. "Hey, she's a real beauty, *torero*," he said to me. I knew from the interview that he called me this because of my scarred cheek, which only a bull-fighter should have. Even though there was nothing glorious, nothing manly about my wound, I still thrilled at being compared to a bullfighter. And at his realizing that my wife was beautiful, just like a bullfighter's wife would be. Just like his wife was, no doubt.

Then I noticed a fighting bull's head mounted on the wall across the room. The head was jet-black, and its horns were wide and long. "Actually, I love bullfighting," I said. "I went all the time in Spain."

Valparaíso chuckled. Maybe he thought that loving bullfighting was corny. "This used to be the greatest bull ranch in Mexico," he said. "Until my family got our hands on it." Then we turned toward Jane and May as they came down the hall toward us. May broke away from Jane and ran toward me. "The bathroom was really clean," she said.

Everything was suddenly great, except for his remark about the bull ranch. I couldn't imagine what it meant, but told myself it was good to start my stay in Mexico with a mystery.

We followed Valparaíso through a room so expansive I couldn't make out its purpose. It had heavy, rustic furniture on one side, and modern leather on the other. Bulls' heads and well-made but dull paintings of Mexican landscapes hung from the long white walls, and in one corner I saw the place to hang the portrait of him that I would one day make. To my left there was a long dining room, and a table big enough to hold my senior class from high school.

Jane carried May with her left arm; Valparaíso walked between us, and sped up as we crossed the great room, so that I had to stretch my legs to keep up with him. I saw into the next room. Framed by a glass wall was the long green reach of his backyard, and the red communications tower. But in the room itself sat another big table, round and made of metal, surrounded by a people a little older looking than Valparaíso, whom I guessed to be in his late thirties. As we approached the door, he took Jane's right hand and my left, and pulled slightly ahead of us as we stepped into an enormous sunroom with a long swimming pool. Now through the glass wall I saw the green volcano, capped in thick gray clouds, and then I looked at the people. Two men stopped strumming their guitars; other men and women kept on laughing among themselves. Their table was piled with bottles and plates of food, and near them stood another round table, a small, glass-topped one where a pair of blank-eyed servants sat, thinking their own thoughts.

The people at the big table didn't look so terribly elegant, or in most cases, so terribly beautiful. Two or three good looking blondes looked up as we came into the room, and a few strong looking, and maybe even cruel looking men in their forties did so as well. The guitarists were gray headed and thick bodied, and had the look of chieftains. Nobody there was remotely as beautiful as Jane. But they were rich. I knew at once that I had never stood in front of so much money. I was the only one there who really didn't belong, and I looked with a pang at the servants' table.

Valparaíso raised Jane's and my hands in the air. "Look," he said merrily to his guests, "*más gringos.*"

If he'd called me a *burro* I wouldn't have felt more uncomfortable, but when the seated people applauded, I didn't feel like they were making fun of me. They seemed happy to see us, and

made room for us at the table. It was only after I sat that I saw Ellen, the other "*gringo.*" She sat across the table, and toasted me
wryly with a half-full shot glass.

I leaned to Jane, and comforted myself against her as I whispered, "There's Ellen. The other teacher."

The servants got up from their table and began clearing
plates, while other helpers carried in more food. Valparaíso
himself set a short glass in front of me and filled it with tequila.
"Try it," he said. "You've never tasted anything like it."

He poured Jane some as well, then everyone lifted their
glasses. "This guy looks like a bullfighter," Valparaíso said. "But
just like Ellen, he's here to teach our *indios* some English." I
looked at Ellen across the table. She was a big but shapely
woman who looked a little abashed at having her name said out
loud. I nodded toward her, and she smiled shyly, with her lips
closed. Later I understood that she was embarrassed by the little
gap between her front teeth.

"And Dan's wife, Jane," Valparaíso said. "Who looks like a
goddamn model. *Amigos, les presento* the model, the bullfighter,
and—the English teacher."

People laughed, clapped, even whistled, so I was the only one
who heard Jane gasp at the attention. She hadn't even sounded
so surprised on the day she met Doris, and my sister asked her,
"Do you sleep with Dan in Austin?"

"Careful, though," Valparaíso said. "This guy's going to want
to take your picture. Ladies, tell him to make you look like his
wife."

Again they laughed, even the women. They were rich, so why
should they care how beautiful Jane was or was not. I felt myself
flush a bright red, and my scar burned. When Valparaíso said,
"*salud*", everyone lifted their shot glasses. Jane and I looked at

each other, and I saw that she wasn't going to hold me to my promise. She didn't care if I drank or not, so I didn't know what to do. I had promised not to drink for a while. Had *a while* passed? Did being in a new world, a new life, constitute *a while*?

Jane drank while May stared at her in outright horror. My daughter had no idea of where she was, or how she'd got there, and she had no mechanism for hiding her fear. But I did. I put the glass to my mouth and sipped, then paused in sheer pleasure. I didn't know tequila could be like this, so warm and smooth and downright friendly. Valparaíso put his hand on my shoulder. "See what I told you. This shit is homemade, in my own fields. You can't buy it anywhere for any price."

"This is great tequila," I said to him, then set my barely touched glass back down. "But I'm not drinking much these days. Not right now, at least." I looked up at my new boss, who still had something boyish in his green eyes and carefully cropped blond hair. But it was the face of a hard boy, not a vulnerable one, and I braced myself for a taunt. *My tequila not good enough for you, campesino? Is the* torero *afraid of a little tequila?*

"Bravo," Valparaíso nearly whispered. "I can't drink myself. It sends me to the fucking moon." Then, louder, he said, "Daniel not only looks like Manolete, he loves bullfighting. He's a *gringo* who doesn't faint when they put in the sword. That's what he told me."

People laughed and applauded, but I had no idea what any of it meant. The woman to my right, maybe in her late forties and heavily made up now that I really looked at her, leaned toward me. "Carlos seems to like you," she said in a voice that sounded cured by tobacco. "Welcome to Mexico."

Valparaíso poured Jane another shot, then stroked May on her high curved forehead. She looked up at him with her eyes still bulging. "You bring your swimsuit?" he asked her. "Later you can swim in the pool."

I lifted my glass toward Ellen across the table. "*Viva México,*" I said, then held the glass in front of my face.

"*Viva,*" most of the crowd answered.

3.

———————

My first weeks on the job, students sometimes asked me if I spoke "*más agua*." I couldn't imagine why they were asking if I spoke "more water," and wondered if they were employing some cosmic Indian figure of speech: "White man speak more water." The majority of my students were in fact more or less pure-blooded *indios*. Mazahua Indians, as it turned out, and they were asking me not if I spoke "*más agua*," but rather "Mazahua." Once I got that through my head, I could admit to my third-graders and first-graders and fifth graders—the boys with their hair cropped right down to the skull as protection against lice, the girls modestly wearing polyester skirts over their polyester pants—that no, I didn't speak Mazahua. "Teach me a word," I said.

"*Chicwa* means rabbit," several kids would say at once. For some reason, *chicwa* was the word they wanted me to know, maybe because it was one I could pronounce to their satisfaction. One day during recess, some kids chased a rabbit in from the fields surrounding the school, and a group of older boys managed to corner the animal in the rubble of a construction site and stomp it to death. They carried the little corpse into my classroom, where I sat daydreaming about getting back to my new house and working in my newly assembled dark room. The dead rabbit snapped me out of my reverie, and I pulled my little Minolta spy out of a desk drawer, then trained it on the proud kids and their catch. It was going to be somebody's dinner, for all I knew, so I tried to hide the shock I felt at the sight of the limp animal.

It wasn't easy to get these kids to smile. They seemed to have been born with the knowledge of how hard their Mazahua lives were going to be, but when I said, "*chicwa*," they grinned. My taking their picture didn't even bother them, like it sometimes did. Not that they thought I was stealing anybody's soul. I was just offending their modesty, tempting them to think grand thoughts about themselves. Setting them up for a fall, in other words.

The contrast between their attitude to photography and mine was similar to the one between their views on religion and mine. I appreciated their dignity, already hard-won at age seven, and their faith. I just didn't share in either one.

When they asked, "Are you Catholic?" I told them that I used to be. That when was I was their age, I was indeed Catholic. I didn't tell them that I had grown out of the faith as easily and inexorably as I had the wardrobe of my childhood. That God and the Church had just fallen off me one day when I was twenty, stationed by the army in Spain, roaming through the Seville Cathedral, the biggest in the world, built with riches looted from New Spain. The all-too-earthly, all-too-human made-ness of the building did my religion in, just like that. In one of the dozens of side chapels, I looked up at poor bloody wooden Spanish Jesus, suspended there in centuries of agony, all to salve the bad conscience of the conquistadors, and said, "Poor fellow, they made you too, didn't they?"

Whenever God came up, I just changed the subject. But I had to learn to overcome their reluctance to be photographed. Valparaíso had made it clear that he wanted me to take their pictures. "Show them what they look like. Then show them pictures of kids from Houston or London or wherever. Let them see what they could look like if they washed their faces and wore new shirts." Valparaíso said this over a dinner of grilled rabbit at the hacienda, just before Jane, May and I moved out to our new house in Polotitlán. Ellen was there too; she was staying in the hacienda for a few more days. And so was the Señora Valparaíso, Angela to us, her new friends. She and Ellen had begun jogging and swimming together when we got back from work.

This seemed to be Valparaíso's plan: By bringing *gringos* to teach at his school, he would infect his students with middle-class values. We, by osmosis, would teach his students to want more. That way, after they finished *secundaria*, or eighth grade (his eventual goal for the school) they would cross the two-lane highway to his factories, and work there to make the money to buy those things that their parents had no use for. Refrigerators. Ball point pens. Sunglasses. All of which Valparaíso made in some wing or other of his factories, along with crop dusters and industrial glass.

At one staff meeting at the school, Valparaíso exhorted the faculty to teach the children "not to be satisfied with what they have. Because they don't have anything—and nobody should live like that. Not them, not you, not anybody."

And who was I to disagree? I wasn't satisfied with what I had either. Or rather, Jane wasn't, not in the long run, and so I couldn't be. And that seemed fair.

During the meeting, I sat beside Ellen as Valparaíso paced in front of us. The fifteen or so Mexican teachers listened intently. Some raised their hands to second Valparaíso's ideas. One gutsy fellow, a pencil-thin man with pinched, dry features, tried to remind *el patrón* that there was more to life than acquisition. The man's name was Gonzalo, and I sometimes interrupted his geography class to teach his students an English lesson. "Let us first teach them to love themselves, to respect themselves. They will learn to want good things when they see that they themselves are of great value. Not because they see their teachers wearing new shoes."

I flinched a bit at this. Ellen and I probably made twice as much as the other teachers. But I hadn't bought new shoes, or anything except for some dark room equipment, since we'd gotten here. So I hoped that Gonzalo's remark was not directed at me.

Ellen, on the other hand, sported a brand new sweater she had bought in some exclusive Polanco store as soon as the weather turned cool. It looked nice on her, though, and, given her touch of homeliness, and the competition she no doubt felt with Jane—we were the only *gringos* between here and Mexico City, and so we saw each other socially at least twice a week—who could blame her for wanting to look good?

After Gonzalo spoke, Valparaíso flashed us all a wide, just-one-of-the guys grin, and said, "*Hombre*, let's don't get too evangelical. We're only human here."

Everybody laughed except Gonzalo. I wondered if he would be fired for disagreeing with *el patrón*. But apparently he wasn't. When he left a couple of weeks later, everybody said it was his own decision.

"Anyway, that's one reason I brought in the *gringos*," Valparaíso said. All of the Mexican teachers looked at us, and I cringed in the sudden ray of attention. "Daniel is going to take their pictures. He's going to show them how beautiful they could be."

I thought that his not mentioning Ellen was rather pointed. But afterward she didn't seem to mind. "I grew up poor," she said as we walked away after the meeting, with fifteen minutes to kill before classes restarted. "On a miserable South Texas farm. My grandparents didn't have indoor plumbing. I think these kids should want more."

That was a little gung-ho for me, but to each her own. "Let me take your picture," I said. I took her into my classroom, pulled out my Spy, and tried to get her to smile. Which she did. Shyly, vulnerably, touchingly. Click.

When I started bringing in the black and white photos and pinning them to a bulletin board in the library, the kids seemed the opposite of embarrassed. They lined up to look, and stared at the photos as if they were icons of actual power. Their response to my simple photos of Ediberto with his crusty face, and of the three Lupitas of *grupo* 2B, each putting a hand over her mouth as she smiled, and of Javier and Bernaldo as they looked in shocked satisfaction at their dead rabbit, moved me more than anything had in a while, and made me feel good about photography again. I was just coming out of a period of doubting the value of static images. But these kids wouldn't stand for fifteen minutes at a time in front of a moving image. You can't study a moving picture, not like you can a photograph, at least, and these kids were hungry to study. Maybe not English, to be truthful. Maybe just images of themselves. But that was all right.

We moved into our new house, a big stucco building with an enormous yard dotted with *magueyes*, surrounded by a tall wide wall. It was twice the size of our Austin apartment.

"Sit down, Dan," Jane said one day when I came home from school during our long lunch break. May was outside, driving her tricycle among the cacti. Our maid—boy, did that sound strange to me—had already finished cooking the green chicken enchiladas we were about to eat, and was out shopping for tonight's dinner. "I don't know how to say this. So I'm just going to say it."

She wanted me to sit, but I stood paralyzed in front of her, my school bags dangling from my hands over the blood-red tiles of our living room. "My life is over," I thought, and felt myself turn into a rock, just so I wouldn't faint when she said the horrible words.

"I'm pregnant."

I dropped the bags and gasped when they hit.

"God," was all I could say.

"I hope it's okay. We've been through so much so I hope it's okay."

I had been so braced against searing pain that for a moment my only reaction was to feel nothing. Not even the joy, the euphoria, that started to wiggle free in the back of my brain. Then the tension lifted. I shook myself. I could move, so I took Jane in my arms. She resisted at first—she probably wanted some actual words out me—but then she relaxed against me. I cried, she cried, and we pushed our cheeks together so the tears mingled. She lifted her fingers and touched my scar, something she seldom did. We staggered together in a parody of dance and collapsed onto the couch.

I was still crying when I lifted my face away from hers and said, "Yeah, it's okay," and we both laughed.

The door banged open and May rode in on her trike. "Let's eat," she said. Even when she spoke English, her "e" sound had already become spiky like a cactus leaf or a Spanish vowel. We wouldn't tell her about the baby just yet. We would eat our green enchiladas, made by our genius of a maid. Maybe we would tell her that night.

On December 11, when Jane and May showed up at the school for the Guadalupe Day activities, Jane still wasn't showing. She was dressed in tight black pants and a turtleneck sweater, and the more vigorous men among my fellow teachers were not slow to approach us on the basketball court as we walked to my classroom. They hovered, and said hello, and asked how she found Mexico. Jane answered pleasantly, struggling charmingly with her Spanish. "*Verduras?*" she said, when she meant "*de veras?*" "Vegetable" instead of "really? no kidding?" Twenty or so kids, boys and girls, gathered around May, and ran their fingers through her thick brown hair, which had just the beginnings of an African kink. With a little work on Jane's part, the kink worked itself out as a wave.

When we had first arrived in Polotitlán, May was terrified by the students' attention, and would run from them as if she were a *chicwa*. I had to explain that the kids were really very nice, but that they had simply never seen a little girl with hair like hers. Now, just four months later, she looked baffled but tolerant.

The next day was December 12th, the feast day of the Virgin of Guadalupe. Nobody did a stroke of work on December 12th, not even in Valparaíso's factories, which were known for taking a dim view of "irrational" holidays, those that encouraged practices such as religious pilgrimages, which held the country and Industrias Polotitlán back. But not even Valparaíso could fight Guadalupe. The pope couldn't fight Guadalupe, if he ever took a mind too. So, her day was a holiday for us, and even the afternoon of the 11th was devoted to Her honor.

Many of the kids were already in costume for the pageant,

which was held on a temporary outdoor stage, set up in the middle of the basketball court. A girl actually named Virgen (who studied English with Ellen) was playing Guadalupe. A boy from my fifth-grade class, Humberto, was Juan Diego, the Indian to whom the dark-skinned Virgin appeared.

The Guadalupe story actually gave me a pang for my childhood in the church. Who wouldn't love to believe that the mother of God had once appeared to a downcast Aztec, not long after the Conquest, and told him that God loved him and his people too. Or that she had made roses grow on barren soil, and when Juan Diego wrapped them up in his cloak to take them to the haughty Spanish bishop as proof of the Virgin's favor, her image had somehow embedded itself in its cheap cloth and become the icon of icons. No, it was easy to understand how somebody could believe this, if they had to for their psychic survival. I just had to believe in something else. In Jane and me, fucked up as we were, and a little bit in art.

Still, I loved photographing the show. Little Virgen strained for a heavenly effect, and forgot to keep her eyes downcast like Guadalupe's. Humberto was shy at first, but became something of a ham by the time he presented the cloak to the bishop, played by a soft-spoken teacher, Vicente, who sometimes whispered vocabulary questions to me while I had his students working on an English exercise.

"*En inglés, cómo se dice 'borrador'? Cómo se dice 'quiero'?*"

Onstage, he was probably too soft spoken to be heard by the entire assembly, but his face did register the required amazement at the sight of the icon. "*Madre de Dios!*" he managed to shout, then gingerly lowered himself to his knees in adoration.

I shot away with my new Nikon, which picked up every blemish in Vicente's cheek as he lifted his hands toward heaven. I knelt too, and tilted the camera up so that I caught the snow-capped volcano that stood beyond the school, and used it as an out-of-focus frame for Vicente's round face, moonlike right down the craters of his pores.

When the play ended, Jane stood up from her front row seat and applauded lustily. All around her, teachers, parents and students reacted with *campesino* reserve. May looked up at her, seeming a little embarrassed by her mother's enthusiasm.

The four *gringos*; Ellen, Jane, May and me, huddled in front of the stage as the crowd dispersed to begin the holiday. Ellen and Jane were sometimes cautious toward each other. Jane had seen Ellen climbing out of Valparaíso's pool, along with Angela, Valparaíso's wife and Ellen's new best friend, and she had once noted that my colleague had a swimmer's body. Jane was even a little jealous when I showed her the pictures I sometimes took of Ellen between classes. Ellen never lost her shyness in front of the camera, and that made her pictures so appealing. And to tell the truth, she was pretty appealing in general, the way she tried to hide her teeth even while she was making jokes about them. And Ellen was impressed with Jane—she'd told me so herself—but she was sometimes a little intimidated by her. But today everybody was relaxed, either because of the sweetness of the pageant, or maybe because we were all basking a little in Jane's pregnancy. I had told Ellen our good news, but none of the Mexican teachers. I was still feeling my way with them.

We three adults laughed at the memory of the play's simple pleasures. But happily, not ironically, not in smug superiority. I was completely sincere when I pressed my hand against Jane's flat belly and said, "It's a miracle.

It got cold in the winter, Mexico or no Mexico. The volcanoes were topped with snow, and I had to scrape frost off the Olds' windshield before I left for school in the morning. Bundled in the new wool sweaters we'd all bought in a Zona Rosa market, Jane and May would come outside to say goodbye to me as I drove away, and Jane would close the big gate, wide enough to let in two cars at once, after I left. Then I taught all morning, either with Ellen or by myself, counting the minutes until lunch when I could go back home. I liked my classes. My students weren't learning anything, but I enjoyed standing in front of them and looking into their bright brown eyes. But still I hurried on the three-mile drive back home, eager to eat my maid's cooking and to lie down with Jane for a little siesta while Carmen tended to May. I'd sometimes ask Jane if we could quietly make love. She always said 'no,' that Carmen and May were just outside the door. But the question seemed to please her.

For our second baby, we wanted to do Lamaze. Our doctor for May's birth was a cranky old man who had kept me far away from the delivery room. This time I was going to be involved. Jane and I both wanted that. When we started telling the new friends we were making that Jane was pregnant, they all assumed she would be going back to the States to have the baby. To Houston, which has the greatest doctors in the world. But Jane and I said no, we wanted to have the baby here. We wanted to be together every step of the way, and we wanted to have a Mexican baby.

But it was hard to find a local doctor who knew anything about Lamaze. We looked around Toluca, the nearest city, but struck out. We didn't want to go all the way to Mexico City. Who wanted to drive an hour and a half or more in Mexican traffic with a laboring woman in the passenger seat? So when we found a willing doctor with a Polotitlán maternity clinic, Jane and I were very pleased.

In the evenings after May was asleep, Jane and I would do her breathing exercises on our bed, and then I would rub the lovely growing mound of her belly with oil, so she wouldn't get stretch marks. Then we would either make love or not. On some of our quiet nights we lay in bed, heavy wool blankets covering us against the cold, and listened to the radio. After dark we could pick up stations from San Antonio and Houston. On Sunday nights a Houston station played old radio serials, and we would have these moments in which time seemed not just suspended, but rolled back. For a short time we became an innocent couple of the early Depression, ennobled by the hard times we were sharing with all our neighbors. Jane would press her back against me and I would reach over her side and rest my hand on her belly, waiting for the night when the baby would first kick.

One night "The Jack Benny Show" started to break up, and then we lost Jack and Rochester altogether. Ignoring the roiling static, Jane rolled over and lifted herself on an elbow to look at me. Except it was dark, so I don't know what she saw. I could barely make out the outline of her face.

"Tell me again why your father ran away," she said. I guess the radio was making her think about him. It was having the same effect on me.

I wanted to drop on my back and look up at the ceiling, but didn't. I kept looking into her eyes without actually seeing them, actually seeing only the darkness between us.

"I'll never know for sure. My mother is not the most reliable source. I always imagined that he got tired of being around Doris."

That was a canned answer. I had in fact just been remembering an explanation my mother sometimes gave, that Dad had left because he was afraid he would kill himself, as his own father had. According to Mom, my father, at thirteen, was the one who found his old man, my grandfather—whom nobody ever talked about—strung up in a barn, his face wrenched and distorted and just plain horrible. And he, my father, didn't want Will or me to have to cut him down from the ceiling one day.

My mother's mind was already wandering far and wide by the time she told me this, so I couldn't be sure it was a true story. Jane and I already had my cowardly foolishness in our past, and I just didn't want to put such an image in her mind if I didn't have to.

"What if this baby is retarded?" Jane asked, apparently accepting my statement at face value, even though she'd heard it before. "Would you leave too?"

"What a thing to ask. 'This baby' is going to be a genius."

"Seriously."

I pressed against her, and pulled the blanket up over her shoulder. May was asleep in her room. Before long we'd have to find a crib that would look okay with her furniture. We'd probably drive into Michoacan, where they had all the beautiful wood.

"I'm not going anywhere," I said, then got out from under our warm blankets to turn the radio off.

II.

(Three years later)

4.

———————

My clothes lay beside the wardrobe in a neat, waist-high stack. Jane had been kind enough to fold even the jeans, though she hated for me to wear them to work. Those jeans had recently made her ask if I would ever start dressing like an adult. Now I looked at them, wondering how many I could cram into my little bag.

The wardrobe door stood open. She had already spread her clothes across its rack, filling the space so completely that I wondered where my things had ever fit.

Outside the long low house, Jane gave her horn a short beep. Through a north window I saw a framed chunk of the volcano. From this angle I could not see where the tree line, or the volcano's snow-capped head, began. Just a swatch of pines, cut off from their context.

Into the green bag that had just arrived from my brother as a Christmas present went a pair of jeans and one of the khaki slacks Jane had been so happy to see me buy, plus five days of underwear and socks. Two tee shirts and the leather jacket I bought last month in the Zona Rosa market. She honked again, leaning on the horn a little, before I zipped the bag.

I would never photograph again.

What was there to shoot? The life had been drained from every object I ever touched: The leather-backed chairs that Valparaíso gave us upon our arrival—they didn't sag; they hadn't lost their color, but the way they once anticipated human weight, that had faded. That same desire for contact, if only with the eye, had departed from the deep blue Puebla crockery, and the light gray sofa. These objects had once wanted to be seen, as had May's stiff Mexican doll, face down now on top of the television. Or kicked, in the case of Sammy's soccer ball, inert beneath the cedar dining room table.

Somehow they knew, Sammy and May, the moment I stepped out of the bedroom. May was the first to slam into me and press her wet, hot face against my new leather belt. Along with her tears came a howl. At six, she cursed God and life and maybe me as well. I wanted to drop to my knees, and press my own face against hers, but the force of her cry wouldn't let me bend. If I shared this with her, I would die. Then what good would I be, sprawled on the red tile floor?

Sammy, the dark one, the one who looked like his mother, knew something was wrong and crawled under the table to free his soccer ball with the heel of his hand.

The boy then lumbered after the ball, and broke one of Jane's rules. On a dead run, he kicked the ball. Here, inside the house, and just this once the ball actually left the floor and ricocheted off the couch and against a lamp. "*Gol. Gol. Gol,*" he laughed.

I felt sick at watching the lamp wobble, but not fall. What would happen if something broke? What an explosion there would be.

When May started gasping for breath, and I bent to one knee, Sammy asked, "*a dónde vas, Papi?*"

"Home to Texas, *mijo.*"

"To see Aunt Dodo?"

"Yes. To see Aunt Doris. Grandma. Uncle Will. Uncle Will has a baby now."

"Is Aunt Dodo still a baby?"

I had to peel May off then, stand her up and step away.

"*Mami* is making you go away, isn't she?" May shrieked and flushed dark red.

I could only nod as Carmen, our deeply embarrassed maid, stepped into the room and with her dry hands held the children as I picked up my bag and walked away. Even though I saw myself as stumbling like a drunken Mazahua through the door, in Jane's eyes I probably walked at my ease, self-absorbed, oblivious to the hour, to the fact that she had to get to work.

Jane was quiet as I dropped into her new VW Rabbit's passenger seat—a company car, given to us by *el patrón* after the Olds died—and in a slow, dreamy motion, managed to close the door. She might have said something. I felt so far from my ears, my hands, my eyes, that I couldn't be sure of what was happening. She must have been beautiful, but only her rage—her hate, even—clearly registered.

If I regained my strength before we two reached the highway, I might finally do some damage of my own. I might twist the wheel and finish the two of us in a ditch. The right word from her and I might even bruise the skin she so wished were light. On the other hand, there was a sweaty film over my eyes. I couldn't even see her; she'd think I was swatting at flies.

She pulled up to the bus stop. She looked at me and I tried to see her, but I couldn't keep myself in this moment. All I could get was the old luxury of her face. I thought of reaching out to her for one last touch, but she pushed herself back against the driver's door.

"Okay," I said, my dry throat catching at the words, "explain this to me again."

She didn't even have to clear her throat.

"I have to get to work," she said.

"No, Jane. Tell me why you're doing this."

"I'm late."

"I don't give a fuck."

"Nothing new there. You never give a fuck."

"What did I do? Tell me."

Jane opened her door and stepped out, then hurried around the front of the car, glaring at me through the windshield. She jerked my door open. I didn't look up into her face. I stared stupidly into the middle of her tall, dancer's body, lean again quickly even after the second kid. She gestured with the door, advancing it toward me as if threatening to close it on my outstretched arm. As if she were a bullfighter, flicking her small cape toward an exhausted animal, trying to coax a climactic charge. I sat there stupidly, and then got out.

After she got back in the car and screeched away, I watched as she drove on to the school where until yesterday we had taught together. I felt surrounded by perfect silence, lost in a dead zone of time.

I hadn't even told my students goodbye. Had I loved their Indian-ness enough? Taken their side against Cortez, against Valparaíso? In my heart at least, had I? Now that I was dispossessed, was I finally in their shoes? No, these were the Adidas I bought on that last trip back to Texas, the ones I jogged around the school in as the kids, my students, trooping home along the highway, called my name and imitated my running. I was, to them, a jogging *gringo*, the strangest sight on earth.

Alone among the Indians, I stood between a *milpa*, a corn field, and the road, and waited for a bus. A dust devil, one of the local constants, tossed handfuls of eroded earth behind me as the bus appeared atop a rise. I wondered if I were climbing into the wagon of my own physical death as I crowded in with the broken-hatted men and the women who tie their babies across their backs. If I die on this bus, I thought, if our driver tries to pass when he shouldn't, no one will ever know what happened to me. Sammy and May will think I disappeared.

Hours later, after the bus passed San Luis Potosí, headed north toward Laredo, the desert was filled with Joshua trees. They looked like an abandoned army, put at attention when Quetzacoatl was banished, but never told "as you were," or "at ease." Funny words from my army past. Did they really mean it when they said "at ease?" Could they really order you to be "as you were?" How far back did I want to go? All the way back to Texas?

I was thinking of my father's flight when the bus pulled up to a miserable desert stop. I was ten years old, holding books in my lap on the bus ride home from school. Through the window I saw my father's blue pickup approach the bus and pass us, headed south. We never go in that direction, I had thought. It was my last glimpse of his beak of a nose, and his hard angular head, except for the time I spent studying the black and white Brownie photos of him that I had taken, and he had left behind.

As the bus idled, letting a couple of *campesinos* come aboard and buy their tickets from the driver, I stood suddenly and scrambled off the bus, pushing past the new riders. As the bus continued to idle, I stood in front of the bus stop, a faded café with a broken door. Even in December the sun made me squint at the sand and the *maguey* cactus.

I stood beside the road, the battered, if majestically named Pan-American Highway, and the Flecha Roja made a bass rumble and started to pull away. Then stopped. Its door opened, as if the driver were going to insist that I climb back aboard and go home once and for all, but instead an Indian man in a torn sweater and frayed straw hat stepped down carrying my green bag.

"Excuse me," he said. "You forgot this."

I tried to smile, but couldn't quite.

Now the bus left with a squirt of diesel smoke and the world slowly became still. As the bus disappeared I felt the silence coming, rising from the desert and repairing itself.

I wasn't like my father at all. I wasn't going anywhere without my kids.

Across the way, two Indian children, boy and girl, rested beside the road. The girl held a stuffed iguana in her lap. The boy squatted behind a small wooden cage, made of nothing more than twigs, and in that cage stood an angry hawk. Since the *peso*'s crash, I had seen stranger and stranger objects offered for sale along this highway. Desert animals I had no name for. Dried skins of beasts I thought must exist only in those hard mountains of the Huasteca. The desiccated skins of what was left of Mexico. They'll sell their own skin next, I sometimes thought. They know nothing about self-pity.

Did people stop their cars here in the middle of nowhere to buy stuffed iguanas? That was impossible to imagine. The scene was more tableau than marketplace. It was a demonstration of how very still these children could be. But a hawk. A hawk was worth buying. My father had a beaked nose, and, even in the old family photos, cold and powerful eyes.

"How much?"

Neither child actually moved. They simply angled their eyes toward me.

"For the hawk."

The boy looked back down. I unzipped my bag as I carried it across the street.

"I don't have much money," I said as I handed the bag to the boy, and opened it for inspection.

When the boy didn't move, not even to tilt his small, brushy head, I pulled out the clothes and spread them on the desert floor, as if I too were a market vendor.

"You can have everything."

The boy stood and looked at his sister, who with the slightest of gestures, a motion no mere tourist would have understood, extended her stuffed iguana toward me.

I started to say, *no, sólo el halcón,* but stopped myself. Maybe I could use the iguana as well. I pushed the clothes into my new bag then rezipped it and handed it to the boy. He stood gracefully, and slung the bag's strap over his shoulder. Then the two walked away into the Joshua trees and the *magueyes.*

I squatted by the road and was glad it was winter, so that my hawk and I wouldn't broil in the sun.

A car appeared on a distant rise and headed toward us. I lifted my hawk cage and looked inside at my prize. The bird scarcely had room to move, but with a blink it made certain threats. It focused on the ragged indentation in my right cheek, and on the scars around it like the sun's rays in a child's drawing.

I stood awkwardly, then walked onto the road and set the cage down facing south. The approaching car was still a mile away. Its motion only became visible as I stepped off the road and back onto the desert.

I looked at both the car and hawk. Back and forth, back and forth. I had often thought, God is so much crueler in Mexico. Jane had recently told me that God had come to her in a mystic vision. She sat rocking Sammy to sleep in the same chair she had once used for breast-feeding him, and God said to her "Go ahead, have your divorce." Simply because she was so terribly unhappy.

I had never offered God a son, and never would. But a hawk? Why not?

The car—no, it was a red pickup with Texas plates, driven by a beefy Mexican—honked and swerved around the cage. The hawk didn't move. It blinked, but not in fear.

I turned the cage so that the bird now faced the traffic bound south for Mexico City. With the horrible emptiness between here and there, the drivers would be flying. The next one would kill him. I badly wanted to see the hawk die.

Then came the perfect engine of destruction. A smoking eighteen-wheeler appeared at the top of the rise, then bore down roaring, trailing its thick black smoke, shaking the earth as if it were the bull of all bulls, the bull of the cosmic *corrida*.

I dropped to one knee and stopped breathing during the truck's last fifty yards. The driver probably didn't even see the tiny cage; it didn't blow its pounding horn as it passed, didn't acknowledge that this spot in the desert existed. I thought I was screaming, but it was the truck that roared for me. The truck made me vibrate with sound, forced me to watch, to not close my eyes as the eighteen-wheeler reached the hawk. I lost sight of the cage behind the first set of wheels, then saw it bouncing in the same direction as the truck, toward Mexico City.

The cage rolled like Sammy's soccer ball, but when the trailer was past I saw it was still intact. When I stood over the bird, it blinked up at me and simply did not give a damn.

I sighed and picked up the cage and the iguana, then carried the two across the street to the café. It was dark, dirty and stuffy inside, but the exquisitely bored man behind the counter didn't seem to mind.

"I'll trade you this for three beers." I extended the iguana with one hand.

The man pointed at a sign. Cash only.

I could turn the bird loose, I thought. While the man runs for his life, pursued by this small and elegant harpy, his wrenched-out eye hanging loose from its socket, I could take all the beer I wanted.

Instead I dug a handful of *pesos* out of my pocket and set them before the man. "Bohemia." The price of beer was a cruel joke these days.

"*Vamos a la capital,*" I said to the bird. "*Tú y yo. La ciudad más grande del mundo.*"

I finished the beer, then ran outside at the pneumatic hiss of a braking bus, one pointed south toward *el D.F.* I carried the cage in one hand and the iguana with the other.

"You're bringing that thing on board?" the driver asked, nodding at the hawk.

"It's caged." The driver examined the container with his own powerful eyes, eyes used to seeing all the way across Mexico, then I climbed in and sat down. I set the stuffed iguana between my feet and held the hawk in my lap as the bus rushed toward the black-lunged, broken-hearted city.

5.

Mexican history is filled with plans. *El Plan de San Luís. El Plan de Ayala.* My own plan came to me as I got off at the bus terminal and climbed the interminable narrow steps first up and then down into the subway station. I wondered if the metro planners had consciously wanted its passengers to feel they were entering a pyramid. A band of kneeling children and seated women surrounded the subway entrance, halfheartedly peddling chiclets. My bird cage was getting heavy, and I wanted to have both hands free to carry it, so I approached an old woman who had nothing to sell, who only held out her dry palm to ask for *limosna.* I offered her the iguana, then set it in front of her. "Maybe you can sell this," I said, then backed away feeling awkward, as if I could see myself through her ancient and judging eyes. I hugged the cage against my chest. No one looked at me and my bird.

I knew one person in Mexico City's twenty million. Ellen had left Polotitlán and moved here a year before, and now she taught in an English-language school in the Zona Rosa, a school I'd sometimes imagined working in when I got tired of teaching English to mournful children. I would go to Ellen's school right now, look her up, and ask her to get me on. That was Part A of my plan. I would get a job and recuperate here in the capital, not far from Jane. I would replenish my strength then decide what to do. Would I go back for her and the kids? Just the kids? Or finally slink back to Texas?

A train was pulling out as I reached the bottom of the stairs, so I sat on an empty bench with my hawk. *Chilangos*, as the residents of Mexico City are called, have pretty much seen it all. None of them looked directly at the hawk, but they didn't sit beside me either. That was fine. The hawk shuddered when another sleek, French-made, Zona Rosa-bound train appeared. I thought the bird might give a shrill predator's cry, but no, just silence punctuated by a blink of its eyes.

Once I got off at the Insurgentes station, I rushed down Hamburgo—the streets of the Zona Rosa are named for European cities—past the VIPS restaurant and the Gemelos II Theater and onto Londres. I thought only of the school, of the job and clothes and apartment I would soon enjoy. I didn't think of Ellen, or any other woman, until I walked through the wrought-iron gates of the InstitutoBilingüe, where a handful of college-age students leaned against a scarcely trickling fountain, cradling their texts against their chests, laughing among themselves.

I wasn't afraid of anyone stealing my hawk. In the countryside, where people still understood the value of hawks, they might, but not here among the capital's would-be bilingual secretaries. So I set the bird down just outside the door to the main office, then went in. I tried to smooth my hair, and felt my face-scar pound just once, as it does whenever I fear that I am about to be judged.

"*La profesora Ellen no está*," the receptionist said, chewing her gum nervously, as if the sight of me disturbed her. And who could blame her? No doubt my hair pointed in every direction, and gleamed with grease. Possibly my red eyes bulged above deep black rings. My shirt seemed to have changed color on the road.

"Of course I can't give you her address," she answered my next question with a snap of her gum. "How do I know who you are?"

I thought about the Bar Ginebra just across the street. I'd always liked its dim lighting and high ceilings, and how it was filled with white-jacketed waiters and tall potted plants, big enough to hide behind. The receptionist asked if I wanted to leave Ellen a message. I fingered my *pesos*, tried to estimate how many I had left, and said no.

The Ginebra is always cool and dark as a cave, so I had to bend forward to read my newspapers, but at least here the hawk wasn't quite so visible. From time to time I put the paper and my tequila down to stare at the bird. In the dim light I saw how its eyes were at once deep and flat, and how little glints of light flared in its pupils. I tried to feed it the bread sticks the waiter served along with my drink, but when the bird simply stared ahead and blinked, I wondered how long it had gone without food.

The newspapers were a comfort. *Unomásuno* always soothed me, even if its deep analyses resulted in almost entirely grim reading. This paper was an orderly, cleanly designed tabloid. Stories ran from one page to the next. It must have been quite rich, in the days before the devaluations, as its reporters roamed the earth. According to *unomásuno*, the news from North Yemen was somehow very similar to the word from Washington, and similar enough to reports from the Pipino Cuevas camp, where the ex-middleweight champ was preparing his comeback.

I found something in the English-language daily—a room in

a boarding house for European and North American men. The quoted price was low, considering the address. Río Ganges, number 12. All the streets named for rivers were in the Cuauhtemóc neighborhood, across the Paseo de la Reforma from the Zona Rosa. Exactly the part of the city where I had always daydreamed about living. With Jane, May and Sammy, of course.

I ordered some beef tacos, then pulled out shreds of meat and pushed them carefully through the twig bars, but the bird wouldn't eat.

From my jacket pocket I slipped out my little Spy. I had put it in my pocket after our Christmas trip to the snowcap on Polo mountain, so inside the camera I carried undeveloped images of Sammy and May at work on a snowman. I had a clear image of what they would show. May facing me with a snowball, snow crusted on her orange knit cap. Sammy on all fours, digging into the snow. I had only shot Jane from the back as she knelt in front of our son. Her hair had pushed bushy and dark from under her own knit cap, which our maid had given her for Christmas. It was already too late to ask her to smile for the camera, though I wasn't quite sure why.

I thought about taking the hawk's picture, just to see how it would react to the flash. But I didn't want to mix his image in with Sammy's and May's, and set the camera back on the table.

I paid for my drinks and food, though I had to dig deep into my wallet to do so, then picked up the cage, not caring who saw it, and started to leave the bar feeling pleasantly dull and free of insight. I wanted to be gone before the Zona Rosa streetlights came on and the mimes and street musicians appeared.

Then a woman stopped me from behind with a hand on my shoulder. I turned too fast, and squinted to clear my vision. The half-opened door to the sidewalk rested against my back, and let in a little light. The hawk moved inside its cage.

One of Bar Ginebra's columns stood just behind the woman; it was thick enough to frame her whole body, except for the arm that just now returned to her side. I blinked and concentrated on the column, because the woman's face made me look away.

She had been damaged, probably burned; in spots her facial skin had browned and thickened. A thick scar ran across her forehead and curved down her left cheek. She's probably used to this reaction, I thought, feeling the briefest burn across my own torn cheek. She didn't seem to mind the way I had to struggle to look at her.

In a very correct Spanish spoken in a twangy, Midwestern U.S. accent, she said, "I had just worked up my nerve to go to your table. I was ready to ask if you'd join me. Or me you." The tight skin on her face didn't move when she spoke. I couldn't make a quick reply.

"I saw your Spy," she said. "Maybe you could take my picture." When I couldn't answer, she said blandly, in English. "Let's talk at least. What kind of photographer wouldn't look up when a subject like me walked into the room?"

"I don't know," I murmured, looking away to the floor, leaning back away from her, opening the door another inch. "I'm a little low..."

"I have money."

She took the cuff of my sleeve in her fingertips, at pains not to touch me. Her hair was cut short and was a mix of white, gray, and dimmed brunette. She seemed ancient, a relic of some age the archeologists haven't gotten to yet.

"Really," I said. "I've had enough."

"It's all right," she insisted, her pull constant at my sleeve.

"I've got lots of money, actually, and I didn't do anything to earn it."

A Mexican businessman came through the door. He looked away from me, and pressed his briefcase against his ribs. I felt myself aping him, squeezing my newspapers against my side, and looked down at her fingers. Her hand looked younger than her face, and she wore a wedding ring.

"I still wear it," she said. "I've seen yours too. The white indentation on your finger. You wonder how long it will last."

Her voice was pleasant enough. She was just burned, that was all. I looked at her again, and imagined her walking toward me, stepping in and out of the shadows, strolling as if on a catwalk, her face growing slightly more distinct with every step. In my imagination, I let her get close, right up into my face.

The light from the still-open door softened us both. I flinched as she reached toward me and lightly stroked my cheek.

"Let me buy your hawk a drink, then" she said.

Luckily, in the bar they kept the lights low. I thought the dark might help me sit by her comfortably, and get me through whatever might happen next. My new drink waited beside hers.

"How much Mexico is there inside you?" she asked.

I snorted, then after a swallow set my glass down too heavily. "Do you mean, am I corrupt? Or brave and enduring? Not afraid of death?"

Then I sighed and had another sip. The salt on the rim of the glass tickled above my lip, reminding me of a long-gone mustache. "Sorry," I said. "I don't have much to say right now."

I looked away from her and thought that in a minute she'd ask herself why she ever stopped me, and I would leave. To where I didn't know. The hotels were cheaper downtown.

"Please talk as best you can," she said. "I want to know why you're here. Tell the hawk if you can't tell me."

"There's nothing to tell you. My marriage is maybe ended, so I came to Mexico City. What else is there? I should go."

I pushed my drink away, but she covered my hand with hers, pinning it to the table. I didn't resist, but still felt the surprising strength of her light hand.

"Who is your favorite Mexican couple?" she asked. "Who were you and your wife pretending to be?"

When I didn't respond, she went on, "Diego and Frida? Malinche and Cortez? Maximilian and Carlota?"

I stared now into her face, patched on one side, scarred on the other.

"Juan Diego and the Virgin, I suppose," I said.

She seemed to study me, but her eyes were as dead as her flesh. Then she shook her head in a subtle, but still theatrical negation.

"I'm the Virgin," she said. "The dead Virgin."

"Your husband might be dead—"

"I will never discuss my husband with you."

I looked down at our hands, and eased mine free. In this little friction, I felt the softness of her palms, the giving flesh of her fingertips. When I closed my eyes, her hands were softer than Jane's.

"How old are you?" I asked.

She leaned back in her chair. "I'm dead, remember."

I sighed, pushed my chair back and thanked her for the drink.

She said, "You haven't asked why I'm in Mexico. Which is probably unlike you. You're probably a curious person. Do you know the *ánima en pena*? The souls of people that died suddenly? Out of grace? Who have to walk the earth forever, circling the place where they lost everything? I'm one of them."

I moaned. The perfect Mexicanness of the *ánima en pena* had always gotten to me, and I'd asked the kids at school to tell me the stories.

"Jane is my wife," I said. "She lives in a small town seventy-five miles northwest of here. With our children. My children."

She nodded. "You realize you'll never love anyone that way again, the way you love Jane. That's how Diego felt about Frida, for all his fucking around."

I relaxed when she said that, almost said "aah," out loud. That's who this woman was, a Frida Kahlo without talent. A woman stuck on pain, and incapable of transcendence. Occasional mutation was the best she could hope for.

"What happened to your face?" I asked.

"What happened to yours?"

When I didn't answer, she said, "I could solve some of your problems."

"What problems?" I said.

"Not all of them. But I do have lots of money."

I settled back into my chair. Still looking at her, I thought about Valparaíso. I didn't know what she meant by "lots." It was a word *el patrón* wouldn't bother to use.

"Well," I said, my throat tight and dry. "Why should you?"

"You look dead enough yourself to be good company. I'm surprised they let you in the bar."

I shifted in my chair, then glanced back over my shoulder to see if anyone was judging my appearance. "I know I could use a bath. But don't take this comparison too far."

"How long have you been dead?" she asked. "Since you got married? Since you were born?"

"You look much worse than I do," I said. "Let's get that straight."

"Would you walk with me?" she asked.

I closed my eyes and waited a second for some strong inner voice, or some vision, to tell me to escape.

"Maybe you're right." I opened my eyes and tried to look at her without flinching. "Maybe I'm one of those dinosaurs. You kill them one day and they die the next."

I hoped she would laugh too, in sympathy, but her face was set like flint.

I reached into my jacket pocket and took out the little camera.

"Smile," I said, framing her carelessly in the focus. I didn't really want to take her picture. I just wanted to see her blink in the flash, and she did. I wished my hawk were a macaw. Just then I wanted a loud, mocking shriek.

I was sorry I wasn't a tourist, I thought, as we walked in the middle of one of the Zona Rosa streets that are blocked to traffic. It seemed important to trivialize my life, to reduce it to a manageable point.

Laura—she announced her name while allowing me my anonymity—had convinced me I had nothing better to do than accompany her, and led us to where the street mimes had begun to perform. A big, single-file circle of spectators had formed around them. I stepped back out of the circle as the mimes began a new skit. One wore a top hat and a tuxedo. A woman was dressed in a leopard-skin leotard. The crowd laughed nervously. The mimes were known for picking someone out of the crowd and playing their skit around them, embarrassing all but the most clever or stoic victim. But I didn't watch the beginning of their performance, because I saw Laura from behind, without the distraction of her face.

She wore jeans and had put on a lined jean jacket against the January night chill. She had the figure of a young woman. Even the angle at which she stood, one knee cocked and the other straight, and the way she put her hands in her pockets for warmth, drooping her elbows at a casual angle, made her look young. I remembered her soft hand over mine.

"Sometimes they do Diego and Frida," Laura said. "And sometimes just Frida. She's finally caught up to him."

"I should go," I said after setting down the cage and pulling on my jacket against the January chill, "and find a place to stay."

Laura glanced up at me. I could look at her now and not flinch. She didn't look quite as devastated as I had first imagined. The scar hadn't taken her entire face, and I was starting to wonder how I could shoot her. How soft would I make her, how hard? In color or black and white? But I didn't want to let any curiosity develop, not even about her burns.

"Where are you going?" she asked.

"I'll try the hotels downtown."

"You can stay with me," she said. "I have a gigantic room."

"What would be the point?"

"No point. Just sleep. Shower. It's already paid for. You can bring the bird. I have some hawk food in the pantry."

"No thanks."

"You think Jane will find out you stayed with another woman. That I will spoil your chances with her."

"Fuck her," I said. "What the fuck do you know?"

"Oh, come on," she said, her voice more even than I'd heard

61

it. "Let's just put the bird up in my room for now. You can do whatever you want."

I sighed, disappointed in myself for giving in. "Just quit talking about being dead. All right?"

Laura had a suite in the María Isabel on Paseo de la Reforma. Its name had stuck with me, even though I could never afford to stay there, because it was similar to María Cristina, the name of the hotel where Jane and I and the kids spent weekends in the city. Laura's rooms were on the fifteenth floor, and from her balcony I looked out over the avenue below, which the emperor Maximilian had built for his daily carriage rides from Chapultepec Castle to the government offices downtown. The street was renamed "Reforma" after the war, which left him executed and his empress, Carlota, in a European madhouse.

Maximilian had been deceived about Mexico. He was told that the people wanted him as their king, and the public demonstrations of love that his advisors arranged upon his arrival convinced him it was so. He seemed a humane enough foreign despot, but his kingdom was a shell, an illusion, and he wound up shot between the eyes.

"Hey," I called back into the living room. "My name's Dan."

We left the hawk there and went down to the bars. I felt wonderful at first, the most relieved I'd been in weeks. We drank straight shots of tequila. Restaurants surrounded us, but I couldn't feel hungry. She got mad when I asked again about her husband. She insisted that she had died along with him, and that got to me.

"How old are you? What happened to your face? Tell me what happened to you?"

She didn't answer. People looked, but I felt I had my teeth into something I couldn't let go of.

"I died in a fire, asshole," she insisted, banging her fist on the table again, knocking over our drinks. Her voice was enraged but her face remained a taut, ridged blank. She tried to hit me but I leaned back, making her miss. She stood up to take a better shot.

"Fuck you," I said. "You're not dead."

It seems a bouncer threw us out. The rest comes in disconnected flashes. We staggered arm-in-arm down an empty street. We sat on some sidewalk, apologizing to each other. I held her in pointless tenderness, then asked her once more about her husband. I even asked if I could take her picture. She shrugged her shoulders against my arms. Somewhere we watched a *dragón*, one of the fire-eaters who performs at traffic lights, then collects tips from drivers. Laura told him in fluent Spanish to do something really spectacular.

The young man took offense. "It is spectacular by its very nature," he said. Then he spread Vaseline on his lips, filled his mouth with gasoline, held up his torch and blasted his fire toward us. I felt its warmth against my face, but its whooshing sound and the sight of his burning mouth made my face hurt. For just a second I was flat on my back again in the backyard of the Austin duplex where Jane and I once lived. There was a gun in my mouth and hole in my cheek and I wondered if I was dead.

My next two memories run together. First, we stood outside the modest María Cristina. I was telling Laura that I wanted to go inside, to check in perhaps. I believe she physically held me back. We both got angry again. I said the María Cristina was ten times the hotel the María Isabel was. Next I was leaning against the back wall of a hotel elevator, then staggering out on the fifteenth floor.

"Jesus Christ," I kept saying, now aware I was very drunk. Both of us had trouble walking. We banged against the hall walls. She laughed, but I just wanted to somehow get through her door and collapse.

I did that, on her floor. She knelt and shook me. "Don't go to sleep. Take a shower. Take my picture."

My mouth moved; I felt my jaw work. But I couldn't make the sounds come up.

It was still dark when I woke. Laura slept beside me on the carpet, her back turned toward me. Jane had slept with her back toward me for months, maybe years.

Laura had thrown a blanket over us. I eased from under it and went to the bathroom. My stomach was sour and churning and my head throbbed as I went into her bedroom, thinking I could sleep some more on her bed. But the first light of morning came through the window, and I went to close the curtain. The closet beside the window was open and filled with a man's clothes. They were her husband's, no doubt. He might be dead; he certainly hadn't stuck with her after her disaster.

There were knives in my head as I pulled out a silk suit, and then some fine vacation clothes.

"God," I murmured, and then quickly put the clothes back into the closet.

There was no point in lying on the bed, so I went back into the living room. The light now illuminated Laura's face, and softened it. But I knew about the tricks that light can play, and wasn't tempted to reach down and touch her. Instead I put my hands to my pounding temples. I stood in a kind of paralysis for a minute, looking out her window, then went back to the closet, pulled out a blue silk shirt, and held it against my chest. It looked to be my size, and so did the dark dress pants I took from another hanger. Then I simply grabbed two more handfuls of clothes, and hoped that they would somehow match.

I breathed deeply, then took the clothes into the bathroom and turned on the shower, hoping Laura wouldn't wake, hoping she wouldn't get into the stall with me. I was sure that scars covered her entire body, that if she stepped into the shower its hot water would break around her purple lumps of tissue, and bead around them when she stepped away from the stream. Her body would look like the relief globe my father bought me, not long before he left. I used to run my fingers over its tiny mountains and pray for a hurricane. As far as I was concerned, God could wash away Fuente, Texas anytime he wanted.

My normal morning hard-on grew absurdly. Stupefied, I looked down, then turned off the water. Jane hadn't seen me like this since before Sammy was born. I ought to show this to Laura, I thought as the water in my pubic hair cooled. Somebody ought to see.

After I dressed and walked back into the bedroom, Laura was awake, but still on the floor. Her voice cracked a little.

"You're wearing his clothes."

"I'll bring them back," I said, "in the next couple of days. Is he coming back? Is this a problem?"

"Well, they do look ridiculous on you."

She let her head drop back on her pillow. "Do you need money?"

I shook my head. "Maybe I'll see you," I said, "when I bring the clothes back. Take care of the bird, okay?"

"You want some breakfast?"

65

"I can't talk now. My head's about to explode."

Out in the hall I changed my mind about the bird and caught the door before it locked behind me. Laura looked away toward the wall as I walked past her to the coffee table in front of her couch to pick up the little cage. I saw its hawk shit in the morning light, and wondered what food it could possibly be processing.

I wasn't kidding about my head. This was worse than the other hangovers I'd had in the past year; it was an all-out agony I'd never felt in years of drinking. I hurt so that I forgot my dirty clothes and my jacket and camera in Laura's suite. But still I could remember the address from the ad. Number 12, Río Ganges, only a few blocks away.

Out on streets that looked dull in the morning smog, Indians slept in doorways, and sweepers with their straw brooms pushed garbage along the gutters. I found the good neighborhood bakery and bought coffee and the heaviest sweetbread they had, then in the most expensive casual clothes I'd ever worn, sat on a curb for breakfast.

6.

Mexico City moves slowly on Sunday mornings. Families hadn't yet arrived at Sullivan park, a finger of green on the edge of Colonia Cuahutemoc. The park was completely empty except for me, the bird, and the odd shopper carrying home pastries for breakfast.

I looked for a moment at the Mexican Red Cross building across the street, and dimly remembered that this was where Trotsky was taken after Stalin's agent drove a hammer into his head. In the old days, the foreigners here were Trotsky and Cortez, Tina Mondotti and Edward Weston. Since then we *gringos* have been second-rate at best: the Shah of Iran and me.

I opened the sports tabloid I had just bought, and was reminded that this was Super Sunday. Dallas vs. somebody. I laid the paper on the grass and tried to relax so completely that the pain would float up and out of my head. A heaviness came over me, pressed against my face, almost got inside, almost let me sleep. Then it lifted, leaving me weaker than before.

When I opened my eyes, my bird was looking right through me. With every blink he ratcheted up the power of his lenses, the way I would if I were trying to shoot him as he soared overhead.

At the end of the park that fronts Reforma is the Monument to the Mother. She was thick, just as my mother had become, but she looked very Indian, like that Olmec figure who is sculpted squatting, with her hands clutching her knees, teeth bared and gritted in childbirth, her baby half emerged between her legs. She looks plenty fierce. Birth here can be rough.

I was in the Polotitlán delivery room when Jane had Sammy. Had is one weak verb to describe what she actually did, what she went through.

Jane is no wimp. I have to give her that much. While she lay in that Polotitlán clinic, a place where only peasants came to give birth, she cursed me up and down, back and forth. "Cocksucker. Motherfucker. *Chinga chinga chinga* you *hijo de puta.*" But she wouldn't take any drugs. She just told me to press my hands hard against her back. "Harder, harder, be harder." When I told her that I felt something surge around the base of her spine she sat up on the table, her eyes round as apples, then dropped to her feet and started waddling to the delivery room. A nurse came in and told her to lie back down, that she would roll Jane in on the table. No way. Jane was walking. She had not been this tough when May was born. She had wanted every drug that day. Mexico had toughened her up.

Her but not me. My head swam as I followed her, and I felt loose inside. When the bastard of a doctor, who was in such a hurry, reached inside Jane with long scissors to cut her water bag, the walls of the clinic opened up, and I was in the middle of an earthquake. I fainted, that is, and when Jane screamed and Sammy emerged I was outside in the courtyard, where the burly doctor had dragged me, and I was looking up at the deep blue sky.

Boy or girl, I wondered, then heard the doctor say, "*Es hombre.*"

Now she *has* him. Now the verb will do.

While I had been sitting there, three families had come into

Sullivan Park. They were working class, here in a fairly prosperous neighborhood. Children squealed, climbed on the monkey bars, and kicked balls. Fathers read newspapers—one had picked up mine where I'd left it. Mothers sat and watched.

I pulled the money out of my pocket. Last night's binge had just about cleaned me out. Hawk cage in hand, I set off again down Río Nilo, then turned right on Ganges.

The faded-white stucco house looked tall for a two-story, so the rooms would have high-ceilings. Its second-story windows were big, the kind you unlatch and swing open. Downstairs the windows were barred. It was a big house, as wide as it was tall, but its front door seemed too narrow for the house's height. Over the roof's wall the gray tops of three small concrete rooms appeared, giving the house the impression of human baldness.

A supermarket, part of the Aurrerá chain, stood across the street. Aurrerá was the kind of American-style store I'd scorned after moving to Mexico, but now when I went there I took comfort in the ringing of its cash registers and the sight of sack boys filling white plastic bags with middle-class customers' food.

The narrow door of the house partially opened and a young woman stepped out. She had a nice figure, with deep curves at her hips. Thick black hair bounced against her shoulders as she walked toward the store. The daughter or the house girl, I thought, out for the day's shopping. She came a little closer and I saw bright rouge on her cheeks. I tried not to stare. Then I saw she was a man. I turned away when he passed, then moaned out loud.

But I picked up my hawk cage and went into Aurrerá. The pretty man was easy to spot.

He carelessly dropped a loaf of white bread into his basket, then some cheese, then a frozen hen. Delicately rocking his hips, he walked all the way across the supermarket to get two bottles of cheap wine, then looked back across his shoulder at me. He had frankly beautiful eyes, big and deep, shaped like almonds.

He left the store and trotted on tiptoe back to the house, the upper half of his body scarcely moving, one stiff arm holding the plastic bag, the other folded across his chest. He dug in his pocket and looked back again, this time making a more suspicious sweep, then opened the door only wide enough to admit his hips.

After I rang the buzzer, the door opened a few inches.

"Who?" he asked in the short Mexican version of the question. His voice was soft and careful.

That's a good question, I wanted to say. "My name is Daniel."

"I've got a knife," he said. "Why are you following me?"

"I'm answering the ad."

"With a fucking eagle in your hands? We don't need any more crazies here."

"I just want a room," I sighed, and my head throbbed.

He opened the door and motioned me in with a long butcher knife. His nails were painted a violent scarlet. As I stepped into the small foyer, he closed the door behind me. There were big offices to my right and left, and a wide, curved staircase straight ahead. A long sectioned couch, covered with a white sheet, fit under the stairwell. An abstract metal crucifix hung on the wall above the couch.

The pretty man held the knife between us, pointing its tip toward my face. He smiled, and showed me his crooked white teeth. His eyes twinkled and narrowed as if he knew all about me.

"Why don't you put the knife down?" I said.

"You put down the bird."

70

When I did, the pretty man drew himself up, adding two inches to his height in triumph, then placed the knife on a table in front of the couch.

"I have a pistol too, so don't try anything. It's hidden so that you'll never find it."

"I misunderstood the ad," I said, and picked up the cage. "I'll leave."

"Jorge!" a man called from the top of the curved staircase. "What in the hell are you doing?"

A white-haired, soft-looking man who looked to be in his late fifties hurried bare-footed down the stairs. He tucked in his shirt as he descended.

"My name is Pierre," the white-haired man said. He put out his hand to shake mine, but stopped short at the sight of the cage on the floor.

"My God," he said.

"It's okay," I said. "I was just leaving." And I was. I wasn't ready to live with Jorge, who glared at me as I backed toward the door.

"Wait," Pierre said. He hurried out a side door, then called for Jorge, who sullenly left the foyer. This gave me a chance to look around in peace. The carpet was a little worn, but there was beveled glass in the office doors on either side of the entryway, and the floors were of a dull hardwood. I walked to the door of the office to my left. A long, heavy wooden desk stood near its back wall. An old unplugged TV stood against another wall. I heard a scraping sound, as if the two men were dragging a heavy metal object.

The other office was completely empty except for a long stainless steel table. A few yellowed, but framed, photos of small churches hung from the wall above the table, along with some

71

old tin *milagros*, the kind you find in the entrance to country churches. I went in to look at the photos, and saw that they were magazine cutouts. Framed magazine cutouts. A stack of magazines stood on the floor under the table. Sure enough, Pierre had the issue of the Mexican photography magazine, *Imágen Dos*, in which I had actually published a photograph. I turned to page thirty-two and found my full-page black and white shot of a steep, crowded street on the island of Janitzio. The shadows of the high, narrow walls had fallen perfectly across the intent-looking people carrying their plastic shopping bags.

Pierre called.

"Young man," he said, in that Spanish formulation I never quite understood. Even kids in the market would call me *joven*.

Not sure whether I should show Pierre my photo, I carried the magazine into the foyer and saw that they had fetched a tall, faded-white metal birdcage. It was as big around as a barrel and taller than Jorge.

"It was for my parrot, Carlota," Pierre said. "May she rest in eternal peace."

Jorge made the sign of the cross, and echoed him. "*Que en paz descanse.*"

"The hawk and the cage. It's a sign," Pierre said. "An omen, as when the Aztec prophets saw a burning ear of corn in the sky which foretold the coming of Cortez."

Then Pierre laughed, bending forward at the waist. He was making some kind of joke. I didn't quite get it, but hearing laughter relaxed me a little.

"May I?" he said and approached the cage with soft, reassuring steps. He reached down for my hawk. I hesitated, then realized what a burden the bird had become.

"You're no parrot," Pierre said into the cage as he turned. "You would have eaten poor Carlota ten feathers at a time."

He set the small cage inside the big one, and nodded for Jorge to man its open door. Pierre fiddled with the small cage, then found the twig that held its front wall in place. He eased it free, then stepped back slowly as the wooden cage fell open.

The hawk puffed its feathers and had just bent forward when Jorge clanged the metal door closed. The bird inched forward somehow—you wouldn't say he'd taken a real step, or flown, exactly—then Jorge leaned toward the cage and emitted a loud, wordless parrot cry.

I was proud of my hawk for ignoring him.

"Now," Pierre said to me. "Let's find a home for you too."

"Oh," I said, then remembered the magazine in my hands. I had wanted to show him my photograph, and get a pat on the head. But I couldn't bring myself to say anything, so I set the magazine down.

Pierre sat on his sheet-covered couch, and I on the other side of his crumb-littered table on a metal chair Jorge had dragged in from an office.

"Tell me," Pierre said, "who you are and what you want."

"I need a room to live in. *Para vivir.*"

He eyed me up and down. Not unsympathetically, though. Curiously, I thought, with the eyes of a man hungry for knowledge. He looked at my hand, and I had to resist the impulse to hide the white indentation on my ring finger.

"Are you married?

"I suppose."

"Do you drink?"

"Not most mornings."

"Jorge," Pierre called without looking back. "Bring some

73

wine. Do you pray? For reunification? Or in gratitude for your freedom?"

I felt relief at identifying Jorge as the houseboy, but my nausea returned at the talk of prayer. Pierre looked down at his pink feet.

"I'll be honest," Pierre said. "I am a former priest, if there is such a thing. I am quite interested in prayer. So please, what do you pray for?"

"Well, I don't pray at all. My wife did all the praying for us. She says God just gave her permission to divorce me."

"Was she Mexican?" he said softly. "With Mexican women you don't have a chance."

"Mexicans," Pierre continued. He seemed to want me to read volumes into the way he grunted the word. "This is a country filled with badly aged children," he said. "They are doomed."

No matter what else he might be, Jorge was obviously Mexican, but as he poured our wine into clear glass coffee cups, he didn't seem to resent Pierre's racial theories.

I was nervous about drinking so early, and still hung over, but maybe it was for the best. Pierre lifted his cup in what seemed to be a toast.

"Heavenly father," Pierre said, "we thank you for this wine, and for the service of our son, Jorge." My arm froze halfway between us when he began his invocation, so he extended his cup and clicked it against mine, sloshing a bit of wine onto my fingers. "*Shalom*," he said. I set the cup down without drinking, while Pierre sipped once, then twice. A crust of last night's or last week's bread lay beside his cup; I expected him to take it up, tear it, and declare it the body of Christ.

"You are Catholic?" Pierre said, and I nodded. He went on, "I sense something about you. Some *tristeza*. A condition I know as well. Why don't you go home?"

His gaze and his question made me reach for the wine cup, which I held for a moment before my lips, then sipped. The wine was cheap, but I'd had worse.

"I have kids here."

Pierre set his cup down and folded his hands before him.

"But do you have hope?"

I shrugged. The faces of Sammy and May wouldn't come to me, only a vague outline of their bodies, of them asleep in their beds.

"No," he sighed. "You have no hope."

I grunted and answered, "That's not true. I'm alive."

"Alas," he said, and made a clucking sound. "What happened to your face? Were you in the war of Vietnam?"

My scar throbbed at the question.

"I was there in 1954," he said dreamily. "Captured at Dien Bien Phu. It was definitely *bien fou*. Ha! My life was spared, so I became a priest."

It was hard to talk. I felt like I was flat on my back.

"Would you like to make a confession?" he asked. "It can help, whether or not you believe."

I picked up the *Imágen Dos* then, and handed the magazine to Pierre, open, of course, to my photograph. With the magazine still in my hand, Pierre studied the image as if it were some kind of icon, something that had meaning in and of itself. I should have just blurted out that I'd taken it, but I was waiting for him to speak first. This had somehow become a test of wills, for both of us, I think. Pierre's eyes clouded over, and with one long soft finger he touched the photograph. Still we didn't talk, but now he was starting to seem simply goofy.

Then Pierre nodded, and said, "I took some days of my honeymoon on Janitzio. Here is our old hotel. How did you know this, Daniel?"

"I took the picture."

Pierre had composed himself by the time we reached the roof, which was piled knee-high with industrial debris, and I stepped carefully around chunks of concrete and spiraling, rusted metal shafts. He stood inside a triangle formed by the three small concrete rooms.

"What is all this?" I asked.

"The remains of my rooftop machine shop. This used to be where I repaired the broken hearts. Unlike our Aztec friends, who used to feed broken hearts to the sun. But when I couldn't heal myself, Daniel, I let the shop fall into disrepair." Pierre grinned at me, as if daring me to decide between laughing at him and nodding in solemn agreement.

"Do people live up here?"

"In the day these will be my monk's cells," Pierre said, patting the wall of the nearest room. "And at night, a center of culture. We'll have lectures and dances, and charge a small fee. You can teach photography, Daniel, if you're looking for work. Anders, one of the Swedes, will be your neighbor." Pierre pointed at a room. "He may teach German when he gets back from Cuba. He suffers too. He needs time in his cell."

"My neighbor?"

"Yes. Here on the penthouse. You'll have everything right here. European company. A view."

I looked through the empty door of one room. A wall had been painted white. Paint-streaked newspapers lined the floor; their words lay in an indecipherable jumble.

"A Desert Monk once said, 'Go, sit in your cell, and your cell will teach you everything.' That's what you want, isn't it? And the rent will be very reasonable."

I read the date on one of the newspapers. Its headlines and faded photographs were obscured by white paint, and I had to squint to see that the paper was fifteen years old. "Did the monks study old newspapers?"

Pierre shrugged and walked away. "Come see the bathroom. I built it for Teresa. My fiancée. My ex-fiancée, that is."

I stepped over junk to follow him inside a concrete shell. Someone had painted a few white strips across its walls, and loose boards and discarded pipes lay jumbled. "It has special features."

Pierre showed me two metal braces he'd fastened to the wall in the dark corner which would one day be the shower.

"When your wife visits you can lay this board across, *comme ça*. You two can make love in the shower. A man doesn't need anything else, as long as he can embrace his wife."

The bathroom was as cluttered as the rest of the house. Even in our best days, Jane would never have come to me in there, would never allow May and Sammy up on this roof.

"I see you are a man of good character. Good taste, *aussi*. What do you say?" Pierre laid his hand on my shoulder. "Will you stay with us?"

The smog topped us like an opaque bowl. January mornings are the worst time for pollution. A thermal inversion sits over the city and won't let the bad air escape.

The neighborhood's taller buildings, including the under-construction Pemex Tower, rose into the black cloud that we were breathing, and in the distance the Ángel de la Victoria statue still looked vaguely golden, even in the pollution.

Looking down I saw that a circle had been cleared in part of the rubble, and that a table made of welded odds and ends from his debris stood empty inside it. The table had a kind of odd perfection, symmetry grand enough to include its mismatched parts.

"I finally gave in to the Aztec spirit," Pierre said, "and built an Aztec altar. We keep sacrificing our guests to the sun, to make it appear from behind the smog." He laughed then, and peeked at me from the corner of his eye, and showed his yellow, chipped teeth. "Not to incorporate human sacrifice, to spice up the eucharist, that was my great mistake here as a priest."

"I don't believe you were ever a priest, okay? And I don't particularly want to live with Father Anybody right now."

"After dinner you can put your hands in my wounds." Pierre laughed then, and ground his teeth. I sighed, and my hangover felt like it was eroding my brain.

"I'm sorry," he said. "I've offended you. You're a good Catholic, and that's fine. In any event, until the smog does clear, the air will remain so polluted that you and your wife can make love on the roof itself and no one will see. I'll have it cleaned off in a week."

"I don't have any money," I said.

He sighed. "I didn't think you did. I'll take the bird."

You've got a deal, I started to say. But when I couldn't make myself agree, Pierre said, "As collateral only. Just like the national pawn shop."

I managed a gesture of thanks with my head, and Pierre nodded again. "*Bueno*," he finally said, and put his arms around me. His embrace pushed me back a step, and rubble crunched beneath my feet. "A period of grace."

Pierre showed me a big comfortable room on the second floor that I could use until the roof was ready. It had old solid furniture, and a firm double bed. He hoped to eventually rent this room to a couple at a double rate. Until then I could have it for the same rent I would pay on the roof. That is, if I could get my hands on some money.

Jorge seemed pleased. "Now you're an honorary son of Father Pierre," he said, "with full privileges."

I wanted to go to my room without learning what those privileges were, but Jorge followed me, so I had to close the door in his face. "He could have been a Cardinal," he whispered from the hall. "He blames me, his only son."

Because it was almost time for kick-off, I knew I could catch my brother at home. The same house I'd grown up in, which he had taken over recently, just before our mother let it fall completely apart. Some guys would be over; they would have beer and sandwiches and make bets on individual quarters, even occasional plays. I needed to call Will, and tell him that I was okay even though I hadn't shown up in Laredo when I was supposed to. I had to call collect, of course, from a pay phone in front of Aurrerá. I was surprised that it worked, more surprised that I got through on the first try. The connection was a little scratchy.

Jackie, Will's wife, said, "Yes, we'll accept," then yelled for Will. After a moment he came on. I could hear the game in the background.

"Dan, are you okay? Where the hell are you? Are you in Laredo?"

When I said, "Mexico City," he didn't reply. I couldn't even hear him breathe. I knew he was straining to accept the fact that I hadn't come home. That I had to be in some kind of trouble, here in Deepest Darkest Mexico. That he still had to worry about me, his older brother. So I said, "Tell Mom I'm okay. And I am. I just got a place to stay. It's nice."

"She's right here. You tell her."

"Daniel," my mother said, and the line crackled, "I was afraid something happened to you."

"Something did. I decided I needed to stay here." When she didn't answer—she might have been watching the game out of one eye—I went on, "Sammy and May need me. I need them."

"Well," she said. "As long as it's for them."

"Jane too. Maybe we can work something out."

"I'm sorry you feel that way, son. I really am. I clung to a mistake, and now look at me."

Which mistake, I wanted to say. Then I heard my sister Doris with her voice of a child, a voice that matched the age in her eyes, rather than her thirty-five years. "I want to talk to Daniel," she said, then forced her way on to the phone, as was her way.

"Where are you? Are you still in the army in Spain?"

"I'm in Mexico, Dodo."

"I'm not a dodo bird. Let me talk to Sammy and May. Are they doing real good?"

"They are. They say hello."

"Have you seen our daddy in Mexico?"

"Not yet, Dodo. I'll bring him home if I do."

"You'll bring him home if you do?"

"That's right."

"Is Jane a nigger, Dan?"

"Jane loves you, Doris. She loves you a whole lot."

"Goodbye, now," Dodo said. "The damn game is on." Then she hung up.

I stared at the telephone dial until the shrillness of the dial tone got my attention and I hung up. I had wanted to ask Will for a loan.

The door to the house was locked, so I used my key for the first time, and let myself in. I hoped none of the other boarders would arrive and find me unexplained among them.

In Pierre's office I plugged in the TV. It was an old black and white with a bulging screen, just like the first one we had back home. The picture began as a point of light in the center of the screen, then slowly spread. The image wasn't much, but I watched a few plays. The always grandiloquent and dramatic Mexican announcers were inspired by Deion Sanders. We are witnessing the apotheosis of a cornerback, my friends, they said.

When he was calling games, my father had never carried on quite like this. With him a tackle was always just a tackle. In his eyes there was never any reason to make things more than they were.

7.

The next day I had to struggle to get out of bed. Still naked, but modestly crouched, I looked out my window. Counting those up on the sidewalk, cars were triple-parked, and at the newspaper stand beside Aurrerá, the full range of the Mexican press, from base to brilliant, already lay spread on the sidewalk so that passersby had to step onto the street to get around them. That meant it was at least 8:30. Ellen might already be at work.

I didn't want to put on my borrowed clothes. *Ni modo*, as the Mexicans say. Nothing can be helped. For the first time in my life I pulled on colored bikini underwear, then forced myself to look into the mirror at the scarlet band across my groin. I felt perfectly ridiculous, and quickly stuck my legs into a pair of dark slacks and pulled on a sporty v-neck shirt.

Down in the kitchen I stirred myself a cup of Nescafé, then looked in on the hawk. If he resented his parrot cage, he didn't show it. His eyes were as severe as usual, but nothing more. "With my first check," I told him, "I'll get a book on the care and feeding of falcons."

"*La profesora Ellen no está.*" The receptionist looked up at me with some hostility from behind her counter.

"But it's almost ten. Isn't her class at nine?"

"Yes," she said, chewing her gum with aggravating pops. "And she's usually very punctual."

"Give me her address then. Maybe she's sick. I can check on her."

"That I cannot do. The rules are very clear."

I tapped the countertop, smiled at the receptionist, and walked out into the Instituto Bilingüe's courtyard. Maybe Ellen would eventually arrive, late *a la mexicana*. That wouldn't have been like her before. Jane and I had wondered how punctual, Teutonic Ellen could stand Mexico at all.

The classrooms that surrounded the courtyard all emptied at once, and a wave of students swept toward me. I was afraid they'd run into me, but the wave broke cleanly, then re-formed as the students wedged through the courtyard gate back into the streets of the Zona Rosa, leaving the courtyard quiet. Pigeons resettled in one corner and began to coo.

I asked a few lingering students if they knew Ellen. Finally a young woman said yes, and told me where she lived.

A radio played hushed classical music in room 305 of the tall apartment building in the Colonia Roma, just southwest of the Zona Rosa. Mexican doorbells buzz too loud, so I knocked softly. I half wished Ellen wouldn't be in. I didn't want to tell my story, but the door opened and I looked into Ellen's awkward smile.

"Well?" I said. When she put her arms around me, I responded, and to my surprise, our hug lingered. I rested my face against her shoulder and caught myself rocking against her.

"Dan, is it you?"

"Yes." I felt foolish at having answered, and realized that I had been afraid she wouldn't recognize me.

She stepped back and smiled miserably. "Where's Jane?" she asked.

When I only shrugged my answer, and tears rushed up into my eyes so that I had to look away, she groaned. "Jesus, Dan. What happened?"

I shrugged again and tried to clear my throat.

She took a deep breath, shook her head, and invited me in for breakfast. I sat on the end of her apparently expensive leather sofa, and peered into the kitchen as she added a few eggs to the omelet she'd already started. There was a brandy bottle on the coffee table, and some decanters. "Mind if I have a drink?" I called out as I poured. The apartment was bigger than I'd expected to find so near the Zona Rosa, and her glass and metal coffee table called for careful handling. Teaching at the Instituto Bilingüe would solve my money problems, if nothing else.

"Why didn't you go to work today?" I asked.

She stopped her stirring motion, which made her shake gently from her shoulders to her hips, and looked at me with one eye closed, the way she did when she had a sudden doubt.

"Did they give you my address?"

"They printed up a little map, so your disappointed students could come by for their English lesson."

"Bullshit. Anyway, you have more questions to answer than I do."

I refilled my cup. "But I can't answer them. I thought you could explain everything to me. As the outside observer."

"The last time I observed," she said, gripping the frying pan with potholders and carrying it out to a small table beside the windows, "I envied you."

I finished my second glass and carried the bottle over to the table. I ate greedily for a moment, and fresh green peppers crunched between my teeth. Then I stopped and sipped brandy. Ellen had hardly eaten.

"Something went wrong after Sammy was born. That's all I can say."

"You both wanted another baby, right? You couldn't have been sorry to have a son."

My hands slipped onto my lap as I remembered the hours after I fainted and Sammy was born. Jane kept bleeding, and our doctor had disappeared. Still light-headed, I looked for him all over the clinic, cursing him in English, shouting demands at his beleaguered nurse. "I don't know where he is," she said, and shrank away from me behind her desk. "He said he would be right back." I hurried into Jane's room, where blood pooled up on the towel beneath her. "What the fuck," she muttered, her voice weak but angry. "Am I going to die?"

I finally had to drive to the house of a doctor who worked at our school, and ask him to tend to Jane. He yelled at me for not taking Jane to Toluca, or Mexico City, or Texas to have the baby. Only idiots and Indians had their babies in these clinics.

He was normally a bitterly funny man, but then he was genuinely angry. "What were you trying to do? Be as one with the Mexican people? I never took you for a hippy, *pendejo*."

"We're so stupid, Dan," Jane agreed with him as the doctor and I took turns changing the bloody towels beneath her. Her sweat-drenched hair was stuck tight to her skull, and fear lay clearly exposed in her eyes. "You'll take good care of the kids if I die? You'll finally grow up?"

Ellen's hand reached mine from across the table, and I realized I was staring out her window toward another apartment building. I withdrew my hand and sipped a little brandy.

"Did I ever thank you," I asked Ellen, "for taking care of May the day Sammy was born?"

"I'm sure you did. Why?"

"I'm just trying to pay my debts."

"I don't know what you mean. But tell me what happened. You both seemed fine when I left."

"I know we fucked up, having Sammy born in that clinic. We should have at least gone to Toluca. But it was her idea too."

"Go on."

I shrugged. "Afterward, she just started pushing harder and harder, and one day she finally pushed me out."

Ellen leaned back away from me, and seemed to have forgotten her eggs. Her eyes were so intensely blue that they hurt me, and made me glance at the pale wood floor.

She cleared her throat delicately. "Is there another man?"

"Not that I know of. Not since Austin."

Almost whispering, Ellen asked, "Another woman?"

I had to laugh. "Yeah, my mother and my retarded sister. Why do you ask about another man? Do you know something?"

Ellen said no, at first pensively, then tossing her head a bit as if to send the idea flying. But at least her stare softened, and became a simple gaze. She leaned back in her chair and stared out her floor-to-ceiling window. If the air weren't so dirty she would have had a nice view of a small park and a not-too-busy street lined with colonial-style houses and sleek apartment buildings. If they could ever dig Mexico City out from under its own shit, it would look just fine.

"So, why did you leave?" I asked. "One day you were just gone."

"It's a pathetic story," she answered. "Maybe I'll tell you sometime."

"Speaking of pathetic stories. You've heard, I suppose, about how I fainted when Sammy was born? How Jane almost died?"

Ellen touched my hand. "You're being too hard on yourself," she said. "I'm pretty sure Jane doesn't see it that way."

I shrugged. "You know anything about hawks?"

She smiled. "Only buzzards."

"*Buitres*," I said. I loved that Spanish word. It made vultures sound so distinguished. Bwee-treys. Without even closing my eyes I pictured a trio of the carrion kites gliding eerily backwards over the nearly empty landscape Ellen and I had both grown up in.

"Anyway," I said. "I just wanted to talk."

"Fine," she said. "Let me have some of that brandy."

"That's the spirit." I pulled the bottle top off so quickly you'd think the drink was for me. And, in fact, I splashed a little more Fundador into my glass.

She didn't put the drink to her mouth. Instead she rested it just below her nose and seemed to meditate over the brandy's burning bouquet.

"Remember our first day in Mexico?" she asked.

I grunted in surprise. "Sure."

"When I first saw Carlos's hacienda, I thought, by God, I'm finally somewhere."

Ellen cleared her throat, and I looked away from the window and back toward her bookcases. "I grew up poor, Dan. What about you?"

"What?" I grunted. "I'm not following you."

"If I hadn't gotten a scholarship, I would have never even gone to college."

"You've lost me."

"I'm just thinking about how funny life is."

I set the decanter down with a thud.

"What about a job?" I said. "Is there any work at your school?

Ellen shrugged one big shoulder. "I'll ask." She hesitated, then said, "Did you tell Carlos you were leaving?"

"Valparaíso? Yeah. I was over at the factory anyway, so I went by his office." I didn't tell her how I'd hoped he would wave some kind of rich man's magic wand and do something for me.

"I've got a boyfriend," she said, brightening. "He's a photographer too. He works for the A.P. He was all over Central America, shooting the wars. He wants to meet you. He wants to talk about photography."

"Sure," I said, though the idea made me grind with self-loathing. I had called myself an artist. I was too good for journalism. I stood up and said, "I'll see you soon."

"Dan," she said, "leave something, will you? I'm not going to believe you were here."

"I would have to pull a hair out of my head to leave something that was mine."

"What?"

"Never mind."

It's a few miles' walk from the Zona Rosa to el centro. The stretch along Reforma immediately north of the Zona Rosa is lined with airline offices from all over the world. Mexico is friendly with everyone. Aeroflot, Air France, Aviateca, Lufthansa, Korean Air. Anywhere I wanted to go, these offices could send me.

I had meant to borrow some money, but couldn't quite ask. Ellen had acted so weird.

Cars crept by in Reforma's daylong rush hour. People on the sidewalks moved with more energy than the cars. This is a business district, so I was one of the few people not dressed for work. The motion in Mexico City makes more sense than the seething bustle of New York. It has a subterranean cohesion, a sense of people tramping the same buried highway.

El centro is a different world from the Zona Rosa. You see no tourists, despite Bellas Artes, El Museo de la Ciudad de México, the National Palace and the Metropolitan Cathedral. This last rests beside the ruins of the Templo Mayor, which the archaeologists are now digging up, painted serpent heads and all. The palace, the cathedral and the other monumental buildings around the *zócalo* were built with the stones of the old temples themselves. They are that drenched in human blood.

I always have the feeling that a living organism had been dismembered on this spot by Cortez, the violent father, then patched back together before it quite died. Mexico City was saved by a magic just powerful enough to keep up a heartbeat, but not strong enough to heal.

Like the work the doctor did when Sammy was born and Jane lay bleeding.

I always did this in el centro. I brooded and grew grandiose. Mexico's history is Mexico's history. It isn't mine. I was a tourist here, an obscure guest in History Land.

To calm myself I began framing everything around me as photographs, and snapping them with blinks of my eyes.

There are plenty of dwarves downtown. I shot a three-foot businessman dressed in pinstriped suit and tie. In a street blocked to traffic, a trio of dwarf musicians played a guitar, a trumpet, and a bass. They sang a romantic ballad, and passersby dropped coins into an upturned, full-sized hat. I snapped them again and again in a series of blinks, then went on to a tropical band composed of eight blind musicians blaring away on the next corner. They sounded awful, but people still filled their buckets with coins.

Everywhere people moved with the same sense of hidden compulsion I'd seen since leaving the Zona Rosa. I wanted to emulate that as I walked, and tried to direct myself to places I knew. El Salón Familiar, my favorite Mexican bar. The American Bookstore, where I'd bought my books on Cortez and Moctezuma. But they didn't have anything on falconry, and I only had money for a newspaper, not a book, not a draft beer.

So I gave myself over to the human current and crossed the zócalo in front of the great cathedral. I walked through the massed vendors with their balloons and caged pigeons and umbrella hats and their t-shirts of Zapata, the Virgin of Guadalupe, and Ché. In the market atmosphere of the zócalo, I now heard the shouts of the vendors, and read the slogans on their shirts. It is better to die on your feet than live on your knees, Zapata. The Virgin herself said nothing. On t-shirt after t-shirt, she just looked down at her feet, down at us poor abandoned children of Eve. Pray for us now, O clement, O loving, O sweet Virgin Mary, that we may be made worthy of the promises of Christ. But those words weren't off a t-shirt. They were mine, remembered somehow from a childhood of funeral rosaries.

I turned onto a street that was under construction and stopped short at the sight of massed people tramping past its barricades, bound for the zócalo. They all looked the same: all five-foot-four, all stocky, all round-faced, all dark-haired. All women had braided hair, all men wore battered hats. I was pained to imagine my former students growing up to become the same person. To become part of the same larger person, rather than individuals. It seemed a failure on my part, even if I had loved some of them for who they were. Roque, who scratched his head when confronted with an English problem; Lourdes, who teased me for my ignorance of Mazahua.

If the crowd had carried placards protesting this injustice or that, I would have been all right, I would have sympathized and imagined myself raising a fist in solidarity. But they were simply walking toward the great square, and only incidentally toward me. But I was afraid they would eat me. A writer has said that the Mexicans of el centro had eaten the conquistadors with their eyes, and I felt their appetite and ducked away to find myself in the navel of the world, but without the modest sum the Mexican government charged for admission.

That is, I was at the edge of the Great Temple. I couldn't get in, but I could look down from street level to the temple's base, to the steps which led to Huitzilopochtli's altar, where humans once had their hearts torn out thousands at a time, so the sun would keep coming up in the morning.

I thought of Laura as I stared at the temple, and wondered how she had been damaged. I imagined her face on fire, her running through the hotel room, not sure if she should jump off her balcony or into the shower. How had she put the fire out? Her husband must have burned her, I thought. That's why she won't talk about him.

But afterwards, why had she wanted to live? I often looked at people and wondered how they stayed alive. My mother, especially, after my father left and she had nothing but her angry boys, retarded daughter, and bitter little town. That's why she kept Doris, I decided. Her sisters all pushed her to commit my sister, but my mother refused. Doris, the perpetual four-year old, had kept my mother alive. Four is a good age, after all. May was an intense pleasure that whole year. Jane made her a pair of cardboard wings to wear in her preschool class' yearly Day of the Child parade, and I took her picture as she skipped along the streets of Polotitlán in her best imitation of a butterfly.

"Roses!" a tiny pocked vendor shouted up toward my face. "Buy your love a dozen roses. Tepeyac roses. Miracle roses. Holy red roses."

His flowers seemed perfectly ordinary, but what rose, what flower, isn't some kind of miracle? I wanted a dozen or two, but, *ni modo*. I turned the pockets of my fine Italian pants inside out, exposing my poverty and shrugging with what I hoped was true Mexican fatalism.

The dwarf whistled in either approval or ridicule, then lumbered away toward the center of the zócalo, chanting a sales pitch concerning his roses' tender thorns.

The salsa music blaring through the narrow front door of the house stopped me. I'd hoped to let myself in quietly, maybe find some food in the refrigerator and slip up to bed without any questions or introductions. But I eased through the door and into the middle of a party.

The foyer seemed huge and crackling with energy until my eyes adjusted to the dark. The 'party' was just six men dancing to a portable tape player. I lingered in the threshold, with the door against my back, and watched Pierre, Jorge, and four men I didn't know dance with half turns and little steps across the small space. Jorge saw me right away, and I couldn't help but look at his feminine hips. He smiled dreamily, then glanced away. Pierre was the most practiced dancer. He dipped low when he half-turned, and I could just hear the clicking sound he made with his tongue. Pierre nodded a salute, then danced over to the table, picked up a bottle of wine and a clear glass coffee cup, and danced over to me. I stepped in and let the door click closed.

"Have something to drink, Daniel. Refresh yourself. Dance."

"I don't think I can catch up," I said. "I'm pretty tired."

"The night is quite long," Pierre said. "There's some chicken in the kitchen. Bernard was experimenting."

He nodded toward one of the men. Bernard was the wildest of the dancers. Ignoring the tropical rhythm, he simply raced around the foyer like a maniac. "*Il est un chef formidable.* You do speak French, no? Bernard is a chef at Maxim's de Mexique. He practices his receipts here on us. Go, enjoy your chicken."

I took the wine and walked into the curving hallway that led to the kitchen. Pierre hadn't asked for money, and a chef from Maxim's cooked here for us. Life wasn't all bad.

I loaded my plate with the remains of a chicken in some kind of sauce. I glanced at the bird, afraid Pierre had cooked the hawk. I'm something of an *ignorante* about food. I couldn't even say chicken in French. But I had used "there's a chicken in the kitchen" as an English pronunciation drill, back in Polotitlán.

The music came toward me as I devoured my meal standing over the sink. Carrying the tape player, Pierre led the group dancing single-file through the hallway and into the kitchen.

"We're going up on the roof," he said, eyes half-closed. "Come." He shuffled out the kitchen door and started up the stairway to the roof.

Jorge pinched my cheek as he passed. "Come on," he said. "All the sons of Pierre dance, whether we're any good at it or not." I felt the sharp point of his nails and the others all laughed. Each one carried a bottle of wine. Bernard guzzled from his. The caboose, an Asian man who let his hair grow long on one side then combed it over his bald pate, watched the others' feet and imitated them as he advanced.

"Hey, buddy," he said to me. "Monsieur Pierre first class."

The food had revived me. Feeling a sudden pride in my resilience, I found a half bottle of wine and carried a chicken bone into the dining room, which was half-filled with stacks of old newspapers. The hawk's cage stood on top of a battered formal table.

The hawk and I peered at each other, though I couldn't prove I registered with the bird, who blinked with his normal discipline. If I had been born Aztec 500 years earlier, I might have taken his feathers to make a hood. I might have been an eagle warrior. Hawk, eagle. Close enough for the likes of me.

I put the chicken bone on top of the shit-splattered newspaper in the bottom of the cage. I looked at the hawk while my hand was in the cage, but he paid me no mind, not even when I let my hand linger.

Pierre set the tape player on top of his rooftop altar, then turned the music down. He stood still, but the others didn't quite stop dancing. They each found a clearing in the rubble and shuffled in place, half turning back and forth, to a quiet *cumbia*. They were all self-absorbed, even Jorge didn't seem to notice me up here, but Pierre said "*Mes amis,* this is Daniel, our newest, and therefore most welcome companion. He has suffered too, my friends, abandonment by love. Mexican injustice. Usurpation. Daniel is a fantastic photographer as well. He will probably want you to pose for some artistic compositions."

They scarcely seemed to have heard, but when Pierre turned the music back up they began dancing wildly, climbing up on the rubble, drinking from their bottles, as if that outburst were my welcome. A tall skinny blond man with a ragged beard banged his fist on Pierre's metal altar.

Pierre said to me, "The two blondes are our Swedes. Los

vikingos. Anders and Goran. They will be your neighbors on the roof. Anders, the tall, skinny one, was living with a *mexicana.* A journalist for *unomásuno.* Communist shit. He even had a child with her. The man is a professor of linguistics at a distinguished university, so I said to him, 'man, where is your insight? Stick with your own kind.' The Mexicans resent all of us. We are all occupiers to them.

"And Goran, the psychologist with the deep black bags under his eyes, he looks too much like a turtle for the women here. He has no success. Bernard's wife wouldn't accompany him when Maxim's sent him from France. I believe she's whoring around Paris now. Richard the Chinaman—well, we are still trying to understand his particular dialect."

I was almost afraid to talk, now that I had spent my last *peso,* as if the sound of my voice would remind Pierre of my debt. But the rooftop party had taken a certain shape, and asking me for rent, or for money for the chicken, lay outside the evening's frame.

Pierre put his arm around me, and pressed me to his side. "It's all working, Daniel," he said. "Ever since I began with these altars, our lives have had meaning. God remembers."

Anders, the tall, skinny Swede, smashed a wine bottle over the metal altar, then jumped away from the flying glass. Everyone laughed, except Jorge, who pushed him away and began brushing the shards off the tabletop. I expected Pierre to be angry at this desecration, but he seemed above the antics of his renters. The *cumbia* throbbed right through him, and he danced against my side, his white hair brushing my face.

"Everything is permitted us," he said, "as long as we remember how to ask for it. Even happiness. We've forgotten how to make our offerings."

"I was an altar boy," I said. "But that was a long time ago."

Pierre laughed. "I knew that, Daniel, the minute you walked through my door. The Holy Spirit led you, and informed me."

"I don't know about that," I said. "I was just answering an ad."

Jorge ran past us, and half-hid rather theatrically beyond one of the block-shaped rooms. There was another outburst from my housemates, and Pierre grunted and gritted his teeth. "These Vikings are a great scandal," he said. Then, to me, he added, "An elder among the desert fathers saw a certain one laughing, and said to him: In the presence of the Lord of heaven and earth we must answer for our whole life; yet you can laugh." There was a pinpoint of anger in his eyes that I had hoped sixty-year-olds wouldn't feel.

"You have to laugh," I said. "Don't you?"

Pierre did laugh then, as theatrically as Jorge had concealed himself. He bent at the waist and looked up at me. "You're teachable. How fine. Listen, here's one for you, photographer. 'The monk should be all eye, like the cherubim or seraphim.'"

"I'm not exactly a monk, Pierre. Right now I'm more of an English teacher than a photographer."

Pierre turned his face away in apparent disappointment with me, so I wandered away, stepping over twisted metal, past the monk's cell Pierre was planning for me, to the roof's low wall. To my left I saw Jorge pouting in the dark.

He stepped toward me, into the dim light cast by the street lamps. His mascara was streaked; his eyes were wet and sad. He took my right bicep in his hand, and his long, purple nails pinched into my arm.

I eased free. "Why so sad, Jorge? This is a party, isn't it?"

"For you it is. I am the one everyone torments. I am the sacrificial lamb."

"For God's sake, Jorge," I said. "Don't talk such crap."

He stepped toward me so quickly I was afraid he would throw his arms around me. But Jorge came to a precise halt just a foot from my face and said,

"Take my picture."

"I'm retired from photography," I answered. "And I lost my camera."

"I've posed artistically before. Someday I'll show you my portfolio."

I blinked then, and tried to imagine the way Diane Arbus would have shot him; or rather, how I would get him if I were playing at Arbus. I'd have his face almost pressed against my lens and find the pock marks beneath his face powder. Something as derivative as that.

"I think I'm going to bed, Jorge. It's been a long day."

"Daniel," Jorge said, and threw himself against my chest. I stepped back at the impact and heard little bits of concrete crunch beneath my feet, and felt his wet cheek against mine. "Everyone here is so cruel."

As I pulled out of his arms, the Swedes' laughter echoed off the unfinished rooms. Anders shouted something about a 300 *peso puta*, and Goran answered that such bargains no longer existed.

"If you use anyone else as a model, you'll be sorry," Jorge said. "No one can pose like me."

The Swedes and the French chef and the tongue-tied Asian left noisily, looking for that budget whore, still arguing among themselves about her existence.

Pierre shook his head sadly at their uproar, and lit a cigarette. "Aren't you going with them?" he asked.

"No," I answered. "That's too wild a crowd for me."

Pierre stared at his cigarette, then lost interest and threw it onto the rubble.

"What about the kingdom of God? Are you interested in that crowd?" Pierre asked. "Wherever two or more are gathered in his name, he is there. Don't you want to enter?"

"So you and I, we could be in the kingdom of God right now?"

"So they say."

"No, thanks," I said. "I'm tired of being a *gringo* in the kingdom of God."

Now Pierre didn't have a word to say. He studied me as if waiting for the story of my life.

"Do I look dead to you?" I asked. I wasn't trying to be funny. I really wanted to know.

I slept in the next day, and after I dressed myself in some more of Laura's husband's clothes, scarcely bothering to match colors, then eased wearily down the staircase, I found Pierre, Jorge, and my housemates sitting on the sectional couch, taking coffee. Except for Pierre, they ignored me. The Swedes, in particular, seemed to be continuing a free floating argument, one that had begun the night before, or maybe years ago in a Stockholm bar.

"Take a seat," Pierre said. "Now Bernard is practicing his pastries."

I had hoped to find Pierre busy clearing off the roof so that I could move up there to my cell, and maybe offer some of those English or photography classes he had talked about. I hoped Pierre was serious about having his cultural center. "Daniel,"

Pierre said, looking at me from under a cocked white eyebrow. "Please join in our debate. I say it is the man who suffers most, but others here disagree. What do you think?"

There was a cry of *merde!* from the kitchen. "Bernard is furious," Jorge said, to me rather than to the others. "He says the restaurant doesn't appreciate him. He's thinking about going back to Paris."

"Not until he's fed us some cookies," Anders said, wagging a finger in the air in what was maybe a self-conscious parody of professorial style. Louis had told me that he taught in a private university, and I tried to picture him in a college classroom, teaching his doubtless well-off students.

"What do you say, Daniel?" Pierre insisted.

I shrugged as I poured myself coffee. "I'm not exactly sure what you're talking about. But I'm pretty happy myself." And I was. It was a great relief, this borrowed life. None of it was mine: clothes, house, coffee, pastries, so I didn't have to take any of it very seriously. Of course, the things that I did consider mine had somehow slipped through my fingers.

I wished I had someone to share this insight with, but instead I was looking into the raw, unkempt faces of my housemates. Bald Asian Richard, with the longest comb-over lock I'd ever seen. Baggy-eyed Goran and spiky-bearded Anders. Heavily rouged Jorge. Pierre I didn't dismiss in the same way, maybe because I couldn't label him as easily as the others. These were people I didn't want to speak intimately with. Then I thought of Laura, and surprised myself by wishing I was having breakfast with her.

The two Swedes snickered at my response. Anders grunted, "American optimism."

Goran spoke. "Who could be more optimistic than you, with your minimum wage whores?"

Anders looked at me. His beard bristled and his eyes were vivid, but I didn't feel that he meant me any harm. He said, "Americans always talk about their happy childhoods. About the pleasures of chasing baseballs through fields of cowshit. This is very hard for the Swede to swallow. Since our Viking days, we've had trouble amusing ourselves."

Pierre tapped on his clear-glass coffee cup with a spoon. "It is the man who suffers most," he said in a raised, dramatic—priestly?—voice, which did the trick, because everybody looked at him.

"For example, my wife is perfectly content with our situation. I go to visit her. She kisses my cheek. She asks how my roof is progressing. Then she and my daughter open a bag of clothes from the dry cleaner and get dressed. Jesus Christ, their clothes come back looking so new. They both kiss me and leave. She's made my dinner, but I don't eat until it's cold. I'm just not hungry. I'm awake when they come in, two, three o'clock. 'We went out to eat,' my wife says. 'My God, I'm in pain,' I tell her. She says, 'Pierre, go to sleep.' And Teresa, my fiancée, is even more heartless."

"I thought she was your ex-fiancée," Anders said.

Bernard carried a tray of turnovers out of the kitchen. His jaw was set angrily, and he set the tray down carelessly in front of us. "It's hot," he said, then looked away as if he didn't care whether we burned our mouths or not.

Richard gasped as he bit into a pastry, then opened his mouth wide and shook his head to let the heat escape. "Ai yi yi," he said slowly, as if reading a translation of his pain.

"I guess I'll wait," I said, then leaned back against the couch.

Richard had a drink of milk, then looked at me teary-eyed and started to speak rapidly. What he said, though, escaped me. I caught a word of Spanish, and a few of English, but the meaning he was after escaped me.

"*Calma*," Anders said, and laughed as he put his hand on Richard's shoulder to slow him down. "*Cálmate*. That's better. The subject of love has you speaking in tongues, my friend."

Then Anders said to me, "As a linguist, I find Richard an interesting case. He's half-Chinese, half-Japanese, and he was conceived on a ship escaping Shanghai after the Japanese invaded China. His Japanese father fucked his Chinese mother—or was it his Chinese father and Japanese mother—on a bloody boat, and then Richard was born in Canada. Richard is a bloody Canadian. I know what you're thinking—yes, English is his first language."

Richard didn't respond to anything Anders had said, but now he did talk a little slower. "The woman suffer too bad," he said.

"Who cares," Anders said. "For a woman, suffering is her job."

"That's quite absurd," Goran the turtle-eyed mumbled over his coffee cup. "Nothing more than a willful misreading of the truth." I nodded a silent approval of the Swedes' English vocabulary, and wondered in how many languages they argued.

"The truth," Anders snorted.

"Women do not suffer," Bernard called out from the kitchen. "It isn't in their nature."

"Please," Richard said. "Allow my point. I remember my one Czech girl. Prague, man, 1968."

Richard looked at me as he talked; my silence was making me a target for the opinions of others. He began talking about his late '60s travels in Eastern Europe. In Prague, sometime before the Soviet invasion, he apparently met a Czech woman who became the love of his life. But for some reason, either personal or political, he had to give her up. Richard grew more excited as he got into the dramatic parts, and then I couldn't follow him.

"What the bloody fuck are you saying?" Anders roared, "in your bloody Canadian accent?"

"She is too sad when I leave, damn Viking," Richard said, making himself clear by sheer force of will. "She down on floor and weep like you never see. Woman too happy to see you go. You too ice blood, fucker."

Anders turned to me and grinned. "Ask Richard what he does for a living."

I shrugged, and Richard looked away, running his hand through his now loosened lock.

"He's an English teacher. In some fucking private school on Río Tiber." Anders' face turned red, and he started to laugh. "That's some profession you two share."

Pierre tapped again at his cup, but Anders couldn't stop laughing.

"Please, *vikingo*," Pierre said. "We haven't heard from Daniel. Let him speak. Who suffers more, the man or the woman?"

"I don't know, Pierre. We all suffer the same, I guess." I said this as the others turned away in disgust from my refusal to take a stand. And they were right. I had my answer. I didn't think Jane was suffering much at all, but I felt like I'd been struck by a bolt of lightning that refused to leave my body.

Bernard changed the subject from me to him when, lightly dusted in flour, he came back out of the kitchen carrying another tray of pastries. He bawled as he approached the table, and let his sweets tumble to the floor. Then, the palms of both hands over his eyes, he staggered back against the wall, sobbing. I heard the words "God" and "life" in French, but had no idea what meaning he gave them.

Everyone but me gathered around Bernard and tried to console him. Pierre wanted to stroke his quite short hair, but Bernard flinched petulantly. Everybody spoke French, even Richard muttered something. Then Jorge tried to embrace Bernard, who pushed him away and told him to go fuck himself, *maricón.* Jorge stepped back, but didn't leave, and the others kept tending to Bernard. These men suddenly seemed quite tribal in the quickness of their reaction, and in the foreignness, the secrecy, of their speech. Forgotten, I sat still as for the first time both Jane and Laura came into my mind. I felt how incomplete Jane was, in spite of her beauty, and realized that she had expected me to provide some missing part. Laura, though, was a finished piece of work. Her disaster—fire, explosion, car wreck—had turned her into a sculpture. There in my brain she was an icon. This idea of Laura comforted me, and I tried to let her crowd Jane and my housemates out.

8.

The day passed slowly, with me just wandering around the city. After night fell I made myself wait a few more hours, then went back to the María Isabel. When Laura opened her fifteenth-floor door and stared expressionless into my face, I tried to dismiss my disappointment. Maybe I hoped she had already taken off her fright mask for the night. But she was the same scarred woman I'd last seen stretched out on her suite's floor. Dressed in a terrycloth robe, arms crossed below her breasts, she somehow made me understand that she was pleased at my trouble with words.

"Men don't usually look at me this long."

I resisted the temptation to glance away to the bland, art-lined hall.

She put out her pale hand to touch the collar of the shirt she'd given me. "Who do you imagine when you see me?" Then she reached out with both hands and closed the shirt's next-to-the-top button. I felt something alive in the tips of her light, precise fingers.

"Do you see your beautiful wife? She is beautiful, I assume. That's why you're here. You wanted Beautiful. That's quite a willful imagination you've got."

"I just came for my camera."

"Ah. You do want to take my picture. Let me fix my face."

I couldn't tell if she was joking. She stepped out of the doorway and walked back toward the bedroom, leaving the door open. I stepped through cautiously, afraid of how much I wanted to talk to her. The front room wasn't as empty as I remembered. Three piles of books were stacked neatly on the floor. In one corner stood a violin case, in another leaned a cello.

"I can't find your camera," Laura called from her bedroom. "Maybe you took it."

Below Laura's balcony, Reforma was quiet. Mexico City is not an all-night town like New York or Madrid. The stray car, a Mexican-built Volkswagen or Ford, circled the Ángel monument and disappeared silently, with no fire-breathing *dragón* to amuse its driver at red lights.

Laura had hidden herself somewhere in her suite; maybe she had gone back to bed. It was too cold to sleep on her balcony, but I could stretch out on her floor again, and try to start Mexico City over.

Jane would be asleep now, alone or with May, who sometimes woke in the night. Jane and I had learned from the experience of our oldest, and had taught Sammy to sleep by himself, but May had trouble still. I wondered if Jane had begun sleeping on her back after two years of rolling up on her side, away from me.

In sleep I had been bolder about holding onto her. Just a month ago I had woken before she did, my arm across her upturned ribs, and felt both grateful and chagrined that we still managed a little togetherness in our sleep. And maybe six months ago, after a difficult weekend trip, I woke one night on top of her, inside her already and grinding clumsily in my sleep. I had just a moment to begin a slow rhythm before she woke. In the slight moonlight I saw her look startled, then annoyed. I felt a great relief when she slid her hand down my spine to the small of my back and pressed me against her.

Neither of us came, and there was an awkwardness when I went soft. It seemed the last connection between us was retreating into my body, and as my cock shrank, the distance between us grew, even though our bodies were still flattened against each other. "Sorry," I said. "I was asleep."

Jane said, "I'm sorry, too."

Then May came into the room and climbed in between us, finding and creating her spot.

"Who do you miss the most?" Laura asked from behind me, and her voice was softer now. "Beautiful or your kids?"

"I can't answer that," I said, expecting somehow to feel a woman's hands on my shoulders. "And I won't talk about my wife until you talk about your husband."

"You can't compare the two." Laura's voice came toward me as she stepped out onto the balcony. She went past me to the rail, so I again saw her as young and human from behind. She had dressed for the street, warm and smart in her red sweater. "You'll see her again. Sleep with her, I suppose. You might even win your ring back."

"Maybe," I said, wishing she would turn around so I could look her in the face. "I wish I didn't want to. She threw me out and we have two kids. A baby boy. How bad could I be, that she would rather raise our baby alone."

"She might not be alone."

"Who knows? I don't know anything."

"Maybe she wanted someone a little more alive than you."

I shrugged, and looked out over the street. Memories wanted to come, but I held them off by looking at the dark hotels across Reforma.

"Why do you say that I look dead?" I finally asked. I hadn't realized how much that statement provoked me until I tried to say the words myself. I had to practically tear *dead* off my tongue.

"I don't know," she said. "It's just an impression."

That wasn't much help, and the question burned inside me.

"Maybe that's what Jane thought," I said. "That she was married to a dead man."

"Do you know why your marriage ended? What did she say?"

I cleared my throat. I wanted to describe Sammy's birth again, and talk about how, looking back, it felt like Jane had walked away from me forever when she refused the offer of a gurney and waddled into the delivery room. Jane and I had never talked about the birth. But she wouldn't let me touch her for months.

"Okay," Laura said with false cheer. "Then how did you two begin?"

"Oh," I said, feeling startled, as if I hadn't remembered that time in years. "We met in Austin, in a college fencing class."

"Nice. Go on."

I remembered the first time I saw Jane, but wanted to keep the moment to myself, to just go on remembering that image. She took fencing as a dance requirement. I had just seen "The Three Musketeers" the night before registration, and thought sword fighting looked like fun.

"Well?" Laura asked.

Still looking across the street, I cleared my throat. "I was in the army before college, stationed in Spain. I had these affairs with married women. It was quite a shock when they came after me. I never had a date in high school. They must have thought I was indifferent. Aloof. Right! But when Jane and I got our fencing equipment on, I went after her. I called her out. Before long she invited me to one of her dance classes."

I stopped talking then and remembered that day when I walked into the nearly dark theater where she and this smug little prick of a dancer seemed to spend hours caressing each other, spinning apart only occasionally, then coming together like two neighboring rivers that had torn through their banks to get at each other.

I had sat there quietly, both moaning to myself and laughing at my misery, trying to master it, when the music ended and she and the gorgeous dancer finished. I was hoping the magic would go out of their bodies when they walked off stage. Out of his, at least. But she was still electric and glowed like a dark torch. He did too, the asshole. He didn't acknowledge my presence, even after Jane walked up to me and wiped the sweat off my forehead.

I couldn't imagine what Laura would think of my story. I imagined it sounding quite candy-assed, and of course her face was a blank. "Go on," Laura said. "How did you get her? You sound pretty dorky so far."

"She liked it when I started photographing her."

"Let me guess. Naked, except for the fencing helmet."

This was irritating; she had us nailed.

"Not right away," I lied. The first time I had Jane in my apartment, I didn't even know how I intended to shoot her. I had asked her to pose, that was all. We stared at each other a moment, and while I fumbled with my tripod she slipped off her summer dress, then sat on my model's stool. All she had to do was shrug her shoulder and the dress came off. When she saw that I couldn't make myself look into my lens, she got down off the stool and picked up my fencing helmet out of the clutter on my floor. When she put it on, she laughed, and I could work.

Laura said, "Let me try a different approach, Dan. Who is Jane?"

I cleared my throat at the question, and Laura handed me a shot glass of tequila. I had to clear my throat before I could drink, and again after so I could talk.

"Let me tell you about her grandfather," I said.

"Let's hear it."

"He was a black boxer back in the twenties. Henry Brown. He was too scary to have a catchy nickname. He was almost middleweight champ, but wasn't exactly accepted by the family. And after the wedding, neither was Jane's grandmother, who was herself quite a beauty."

"Is Jane black?"

"One fourth. Just the fighting grandfather."

"She sounds more exotic than I had imagined."

"She says that's why I married her, because of her interesting story."

"As opposed to your own boring tale, petty and whitebread as it must be."

"Something like that."

"She's right, isn't she? Isn't that why you married her?"

I answered, "She also said that I married her because we were exactly the same height. So, I had lots of reasons.

"Anyway, I remember the first night we went dancing, after we'd been fencing a couple of weeks. We went to the first Antone's, when it was still down on Sixth Street, and John Lee Hooker was playing. I had never danced with a real dancer before. When she moved in these very precise but natural motions, and her whole body looked loose and completely under control. It felt like the crowd opened up around her. That they disappeared, really. But she called me in close to her, with her eyes, I guess. I think John Lee was getting to her, and she was getting to me."

Then I felt I'd said something too personal, and stopped talking, only remembered the clothes she wore that night, and the way her jeans made even her slender hips look curved and luscious, and the arrowhead-shaped gold tip that gleamed at the end of her thin red belt. To tell the truth, she was the most desirable woman by a long shot who had ever made herself available to me, but I kept looking at her belt. It was almost too much to look into her face, at her hair cut short and expensive but somehow looking wild. I wasn't wearing any kind of belt at all. I was a G. I. Bill guy who had to buy photography equipment, so for me every item of clothing had to have a practical purpose. I didn't really need a belt.

I felt John Lee's eyes on me as I approached her and put my hands on her hips in a slow, tentative motion, then left them there. John Lee started moaning then growling.

When he slowed down his shuffle and Jane and I danced pressed against each other, her hands bird-light on the back of my neck, she whispered a stupid question: had I ever killed anyone in the army? Even enthralled, I had to laugh. *I held down the Spanish front,* I murmured through John Lee's moaning. *Not much shooting there.*

She pulled her face away from me and smiled, as if it were quite all right that I had never killed a communist, but that it would have been quite all right if I had. Then she said, *Are you really a photographer? A serious photographer?*

Maybe one day, I said.

I looked at her, imagining I was setting her up for a shot. I wasn't afraid. *Right now I just take pictures.*

I blinked Jane away and looked at Laura.

"To make a long story short," I said. "She made me feel like John Lee Hooker was jealous of me."

"Of course. Why shouldn't he be?" she said.

Then I remembered Jane coming into my hospital room, after I had shot myself. I didn't want to think about this, but still I turned away from Laura and gave in to it.

I had been much too conscious that day back in Austin, my head still throbbing with the pure sound of the gunshot inside my mouth. I lay in the hospital bed with the TV on, the sound down below the level of the roaring between my ears, and didn't feel sorry for myself. I was still at the level of raw pain, and wasn't thinking about Jane or my fantastic, irresponsible stupidity. About May, that is. It was just me and the extra hole in my face.

Then Jane stepped suddenly and lightly into the room. She almost floated in on her dancer's feet. In one motion she had reached my bed, but still her image seemed to hang in the air behind her, so even when she was pushing up on the bed beside me, I could see her behind herself, as if her own shadow were watching us. I stiffened when she first rubbed against my side, and looked away from both Janes when she threw her arm across my chest and ran her hand up near my cheek. When her fingertips got so close to the stitches I flinched in anticipation of even more pain, she groaned ferociously and promised she would never hurt me again. I didn't say any of this to Laura. I didn't want her asking why I cared so much who Jane fucked that I would put a pistol in my own mouth and pull the trigger. I didn't want her asking why I hadn't shot Jane instead, or the other dancer, why I never even considered pointing the pistol at anyone but myself. Those were questions that people might ask, but I couldn't answer them.

Laura and I were quiet, which was strange because I didn't

think she was all that interested in my story. All I'd said was that Jane was a good dancer. I expected Laura to make a joke, and that would have been okay. But she didn't. She just finished her drink and poured another.

"Your turn," I said.

Laura looked away from me, and I felt awkward but wanted to touch her. Instead I held my glass.

"Turn around," I murmured. "I want to see you."

"Sure," she said as she turned, and her scars made me swallow. Then they somehow softened, retreated back into her face.

Her voice was calm, as was the impression her body gave. She seemed to have unloaded the bitterness I had heard in the hall. Maybe it was something that she gave in to only alone in the middle of the night. The idea that she had suffered so much more than I had suddenly touched me.

Laura stepped up to me, and absently rubbed her arms against the chill. She was so close I could easily have stroked her leg, but I slipped my hands under the backs of my legs and told myself I was just keeping warm. And that just because she was stepping toward me did not mean she wanted something.

"I see him sometimes. No, that's not right. I carry him inside me, and sometimes I can get him out to look at him and talk, but sometimes not."

She sounded no worse than wistful, and I wondered if this was how she joked.

"Him who? Your husband?"

She pulled up a chair and sat facing me so that our knees touched. Then she lounged back as if she were suddenly warmer. I shuddered, and freed my hands to rub myself. Then I put my hands on her knees, and ran them up her thighs toward her own hands. I wanted to hold them. That was how I could feel most normal with her, but she flinched as if I had reached for her belt buckle.

"Does Beautiful fuck other men?" she said. "Did she fuck John Lee Hooker?" She pushed her chair back and angled away from me.

I jerked back. "Asshole," I said, though *you ugly fucking cunt* were the actual words in my mind. And I wanted to hit her, but instead turned the blow in on myself, balling up the pain inside my chest. Then I turned away from her, moving toward the door.

I heard her running on the carpet behind me. I wanted to beat her to the door without breaking into a run, but she grabbed me from behind, balling her husband's shirt in her fist. I could've pulled away easily enough, but didn't.

"I'm sorry," she said, still behind me. Her voice was clenched in some kind of anxiety, but I pulled out of her hand and grabbed the door handle without looking back at her. "I shouldn't have said that."

"Please," she went on. Then again, "please," and when I turned to look at her, she asked, "Will you take my picture?"

I'm not so sharp with women. They know when and how to say just the thing that will confuse me. I could scarcely manage a "what?" before Laura went on.

"I'll pay you good money."

"I don't take pictures anymore," I said. "Just keep the camera."

As I walked the few blocks to Pierre's I imagined that Jane lay waiting in my temporary bed. I imagined she would want me like she did long ago, when we used to thrash all over my darkroom floor. That was the only stretch of morning, noon and

113

night fucking in my life, and I felt it was changing me. It did change me. But what about her? That question had never occurred to me. I had wanted to change to catch up to her; she was pretty much perfect. Physically, at least.

Laura caught me just a block from Pierre's. I was crossing an empty street named for an Asian river when I heard her slapping footsteps and turned. She ran toward me, arms crossed in front of her chest against the increased cold. She looked like she wore an invisible strait jacket. Then she entered the puddle of light made by a street lamp and I saw her face. Her scars repelled me. Her little tufts of gray hair repelled me.

She panted when she stopped in front of me. With a short gasp for breath she handed me a folded traveler's check. "Take this," she strained to say. "Let me pay you in advance. For the picture."

I backed off, hands at my side, and looked away from Laura.

"Just take it," she said. "I have too much, really." I forced myself to look at her, and now that she had stopped gasping she wasn't so bad. She suddenly looked very ordinary, in fact, as if she might put on glasses to read in bed when she got back to her room.

"Not right now," I said. "Let's just call it a night."

"Stop," she said as I turned, and reached out to grab my arm. "I know Jane. I know who she is."

She put the folded check into my shirt pocket.

9.

I waited for Ellen outside El Instituto Bilingüe the next day. She stopped short at the sight of me. I hadn't slept well, and probably didn't look so good. Or much like myself in the cream-colored, European cut slacks, and yellow polo shirt I'd pulled on. Ellen looked frazzled herself and oblivious to the cigarette burning between her fingers.

I usually liked the Zona Rosa at 10 A.M., how the chairs are upside down on the outdoor tables, and men who will later be waiters hose down the patios, squirting water through the table legs, and pigeons fly up with their throaty cooing when the stream splashes near them. Most of Mexico City never seems fresh or clean.

Ellen dropped her cigarette, then kicked it down the street with a swipe of her foot.

"Dan, are you okay?"

"No," I said. "Not really. What about you?"

She nodded abruptly, as if reliving an unpleasant memory. "I had a fight with Eric. My photographer friend."

I cut her off. "Listen, I have to talk to you about something."

She looked at me warily, wearily, then shrugged her shoulders.

"I have to go to class, Dan. I missed yesterday, remember?"

"It's about Jane," I said, then clenched my fists and raised them shoulder high.

She winced as if she knew what was coming.

"I heard this story from a very strange woman. I don't know what to believe."

Ellen let her books dangle at her side. "Go ahead, Dan. I'll just have to be late."

But then I couldn't talk. I could not say the words. "Maybe later," I gasped. "When we have more time."

"Say it now, Dan."

Pigeons had settled under a sidewalk table behind me. They gurgled and pecked at crumbs. I wished the hawk were with me. He would tear the pigeons to bits.

"She, Laura, is an American who married into a rich Mexican family. The Fonsecas. Have you heard of them? Now her husband is dead and she is pretty fucked up herself. But she said that they had parties, these stupid decadent parties. One time everyone came dressed as babies, in diapers and sucking cognac out of baby bottles. She knows Valparaíso, Ellen. She's seen him in a fucking diaper."

"A diaper."

"You don't believe me."

"No," she said. "I actually do."

We both looked across the street to the wrought-iron fence in front of her school. Students streamed in, carrying their books and laughing, in spite of the black January air. American pop music burst out of the café beside us. The waiters wanted the music in the background as they cleaned their stations. They seemed very brave to me. Armed with just a little bad music they could confront the day.

I said, "This Laura told me she had met Jane. At a party with Valparaíso. She said it was a year and a half ago. Sammy was what, a year old? That isn't possible."

Ellen squeezed her books and clenched her gapped teeth. But she didn't close her eyes.

"Come to my place this afternoon," she said. "We have to talk."

She stepped around me then, and I stood petrified. She stopped to look back at me and said, "I'll see if there are any jobs."

After Ellen disappeared through the gate, I pulled Laura's check out of my wallet. Five hundred dollars. I had never made that much for a shoot. In the Zona Rosa I was surrounded by banks, but couldn't force myself through their doors to cash the check. Pierre would be pleased. He would think I had taken a vow of poverty, that I was renouncing the world.

I stopped at the corner across from Pierre's house to read the headlines on the newspapers. My hands shook a little—almost vibrated—probably because I hadn't slept. I wanted to buy a fresh-squeezed orange juice from the thick woman dressed in black. She ran the juice stand beside the newspaper rack, and she squeezed her oranges with an implacability that I appreciated. I would simply have to cash Laura's check so that I could buy some juice. Then I heard a crashing sound from Pierre's roof, and looked up to see dust, not quite thick enough to form a cloud, rise above the parapet.

I let myself into the quiet house, then heard another crash from the roof, followed by the annoyed voice of Pierre, shouting instructions. I tried to ignore the sound, and went into the dining room where the hawk glared at me from inside his cage. He blinked several times as I approached him. The chicken bone looked untouched, so I reached in to remove it, thinking now he'll get me. But no, he didn't look down from his perch. I thought about moving the cage into the foyer, where he wouldn't seem so hidden away. But there he would be more subject to the strange games of my housemates. If I paid my rent I could put him in my room with me.

I went up on the roof, where three young Indian men were tossing the chunks of metal and broken concrete into a chute which funneled it onto Pierre's back patio. The young men were dusted with white powder, and Pierre, who stood off to one side, occasionally pointed out a particular rusted drill or rotten plank he wanted tossed immediately. Pierre was so intent on supervising their labors that he was surprised when I tapped on his shoulder.

"I'll have your rent money this afternoon," I said, and showed him the check.

"Ah," he said, scarcely glancing at me. One of the young workers cursed as he dropped a large block of concrete. It was too heavy for one man, and awkwardly shaped for two to grab.

"Keep working," Pierre told them absently. He looked at me then. He smiled but his eyes were weary and red. "You have to hurry. I've promised Daniel his cell." Then he laughed. "I've gone from priest to pharaoh. A fine promotion."

I tried to picture Pierre in a priest's cassock, and was surprised that I could somehow substitute the face and manner of some of the fathers of my boyhood for the man in front of me.

"Pierre," I said. "I'd like to talk to you about something. I've got a problem."

"Confessions, five cents," he laughed, and embarrassed me. But still I would have pressed on and confessed Jane's sins to him. But he said, "Later. Confessions are for the night. Now we have our physical labor."

He bent and picked up a bumpy ball of concrete, then put it

in my hand. "Come," he said. "Do your part. Help clear our roof."

I was glad to have a small task, and turned in the direction where the lean dark workers were rolling concrete blocks and a section of pipe. Jorge sat on the roof with his back against the parapet. He wore his eyeliner, but not the rouge. His cheeks looked dull, and lightly powdered with the white dust.

"Has Pierre put you to work?" I asked, and tossed the concrete over his head and heard it rattle against the metal chute. Then I picked up a bigger chunk and heaved it over.

Jorge looked at me as if he wanted to say something, but couldn't. He opened his mouth and stuck out his tongue to reveal a moist chunk of concrete. He looked sad but smug as he reeled the white plug back into his mouth. He gagged a little as he closed his mouth.

"There was a desert father who carried a stone in his mouth for three years," Pierre said, "until he learned to be quiet."

When I got to my room and turned down the soft bed's covers, I was glad Pierre hadn't wanted to talk. Now sleep was the thing. It came almost immediately. For a second I pictured the hawk, and was afraid I would dream about him. Or about Jane and Valparaíso. Laura, for that matter. But I just passed out.

When I woke I looked up at the room's high ceiling, at the soft, late afternoon light gathered above me. Then I felt a weight in the bed beside me, and saw Jorge lying asleep on top of the sheets. His back was toward me, and when I looked over his shoulder I saw that he held a pistol in his hands.

"Don't be angry at me, Daniel," he said when I woke him. He rolled off the bed and seemed embarrassed, as if he had hoped I wouldn't notice him. "I wasn't going to do anything."

"Where did you get that gun?" I asked.

"It's Father Pierre's. He brought it from Vietnam. From *Dien Bien Fou*, as he calls it."

"Does it work?"

"I don't know yet. Ask me after I've killed myself."

"Let me see it," I said.

"Father Pierre would kill me."

I snatched the pistol out of his hands. It was an old French 9 mm. Its handle, thick enough to hold a clip of a bullets, felt slightly uncomfortable. If I had used this back in Austin, my head would've exploded.

"Someday maybe I'll borrow it," I said as I handed the pistol back to him.

"We'll see," Jorge answered. "I charge a high price for the use of my father's weapons."

"How high?"

Jorge stepped toward me and cradled the pistol against his chest.

"I want you, Daniel. I want to hold you against me."

He got too close to me and in sheer frayed terror I threw a punch, a nameless, artless blow somewhere between a hook and a jab, and cracked him on the jaw. I hit all bone, and his face scarcely gave. Still, he bounced straight down on his ass, then looked up at me in shock.

"Jesus Christ," I said.

"Pray to Jesus," he said, and scrambled to his feet. "You're a fucking queer yourself." He lifted the gun into my face and squeezed the trigger before I could remember if it felt loaded or not.

10.

_____

A cigarette clinging to her bottom lip, Ellen answered her door. She coughed nervously, and behind her the empty apartment was full of smoke, as if she'd let the city's pollution inside.

"Well?" I said, but she looked away when I walked through the door.

I started chattering before I reached her too expensive couch. "I'm losing my mind," I said. "I just hit a guy in the face, with my fist, just because he came on to me."

"Calm down," Ellen said. "I know you're really upset."

"I don't think I believe that Laura woman," I said. "I think she just likes fucking with me."

"Want a drink?" Ellen asked, and when I didn't answer she poured me an inch of Fundador.

"Okay," she said, standing over me and lifting her own brandy, but not all the way to her mouth. "I've got something to tell you. I meant to do this the other day."

I laughed nervously and lowered my face over the drink. On my way to Ellen's apartment, I had thought about not drinking, for a while at least. But never mind that. The brandy burned in my throat, then throughout me. The Virgin of Guadalupe appeared behind my closed eyes, wavering a little, almost flickering. Pierre might have told me that she was the only woman I could trust.

"I had an affair with Valparaíso," Ellen said. "It lasted about a

121

year, and when it was over I took the money he'd given me and came here."

I opened my eyes. "Say that again."

I added a third to the total volume in the glass and began drinking it down. The top of my head felt light, as if it might float to a better place.

"What do you mean you had an affair with Valparaíso? How could l have not known that? Did Jane?"

She breathed out hard through her rounded lips, and leaned back on the couch. "Think about it."

"I can't. Tell me what happened."

"Are you sure you want to hear this?"

I felt myself smile, and hoped I didn't look too macabre. I hoped that I looked dead but charming, like one of the sugar skulls they sell for the Day of the Dead. Before she said a word, I remembered that Valparaíso had sent his wife packing just a few months after we arrived. I hadn't connected that to Ellen, or Jane. I hadn't given it much thought.

"The first part is the worst. I swam in his pool with Angela. You knew that we hung out? I suppose you were surprised. A small-town Texas girl buddy-buddy with Carlos Valparaíso's wife."

"A little."

"He never swims. I think he almost drowned one night when he was drunk. But he would come down to the pool to say hello. We'd be diving and swimming laps. One day he pulled one of those metal lawn chairs up to the edge of the pool, and sat there talking with Angela. I was at the far end, by the fake ruins, ready to dive in, and I heard the scraping of the metal on the tile floor while I was in the air, and I felt his eyes on me. It was like that obnoxious sound was his eyes digging into me, and I knew he'd been looking all along and I'm not even good looking.

"I didn't swim my lap, I just sank to the bottom of the pool and looked toward them, underwater. There were Angela's legs, just beautiful. I looked down at my own.

"When I came up for air our eyes met, and then he left. I don't know what they'd been talking about, but Angela avoided me, there in her own pool. I felt changed, Dan, from one woman into another, like I'd gotten more powerful, but the power didn't seem to have anything to do with me. The next night his chauffeur knocked at my door. He bought me this absurdly expensive swimsuit and said 'Don Carlos hoped I would please and honor him by wearing it in his pool the next day.'

"I sat up all night, Dan. Putting the fucking thing on, looking at my body in it, taking it off. I spent the night in front of the mirror, freezing cold, imagining Angela's face when she saw me. I felt delirious the next day at school. I wore the swimsuit under my clothes. By the end of the day I was getting used to it, maybe out of exhaustion. I started thinking, why not me?

"The houseboy led me to the pool. Carlos was actually in the water himself, treading water and grinning, while Angela sat in that same chair. It was right where he had left it. Carlos laughed and spoke English to me, which you know Angela has trouble understanding. 'Come on in,' he kept saying and laughing. I looked away from both of them as I pulled off my clothes. I tried not to shake and just kept thinking, why not, why not, this is how it's done.

"Angela stood when our eyes met, and I had the goosebumps. She glared at me and scared me even more. She jerked the chair over the pool's edge and let it drop. Unbelievable. I mean, nothing like this had ever happened to me, and I knew, or had thought I knew, that it never would.

"Carlos came right up to me underwater. For somebody who never swam he looked so natural, like some sort of eel. 'She'll be all right,' he said, even though he must've already known he was about to send her away. 'She'll be just fine.' The chair had landed on its side at the bottom of the pool. He stood it up, then sat down in it. I went underwater to look at him. His hair floated up away from his forehead. Then he grabbed my wrist."

I set the empty glass down. "Are you saying that because you fucked Valparaíso that Jane is too? How do you know? Is it really that cut and dried?"

"You asked why I left Polo? Why I came to Mexico City?"

I thought 'oh,' but didn't say anything. The more fucked up life gets, the simpler it is.

"I know how my story sounds. But I found out just like that, in one day, that my life was built of thin air. And that I was happy to throw it away."

I felt numb, incapable of reaching out to my brandy. She climbed in my hospital bed, I wanted to say. After I tried to kill myself. She wasn't lying when she said she was sorry. I know that she wasn't lying. Or when she said I could trust her, now that she saw how much I cared.

I wasn't crying, but my throat felt cold and constricted. I could only force out a groan, or rather the groan forced its own way out, as if it were a snake I'd been carrying in my belly. Then one word followed, "how how how." I couldn't think of a second one.

Ellen leaned forward and with just her fingertips pushed the brandy snifter closer to me. I reached for it, my hand stopped halfway through, then I forced it down onto the cool glass.

"You can break it if you want," Ellen said. "If that would help any."

That sounded like a good idea, like an action a living, breathing man might take. But I had never intentionally broken an object in my adult life. I looked at the snifter as if I'd never seen one before, and felt too weak to lift it. I tried again, I wanted a drink, but only managed to knock the glass over and spill expensive brandy across the table and onto the rug.

"No problem," Ellen said. "Go ahead and break it."

After a moment I could breathe normally. Then I said, "I guess I really am as stupid as I look."

"You just think about other things," Ellen said.

"We're married," I said. "We have kids."

She laid her fingers against my scarred cheek. That was so humiliating. I had never said a word to her about the pistol in my mouth, and I grabbed her hand and pulled it away.

"Do you hear me?" I said. "She's my wife. I'm not just some asshole."

"We're all assholes, Dan. It doesn't matter who you're married to."

That made me laugh. My voice sounded far away and hysterical, and I felt like I was performing for someone, maybe even myself.

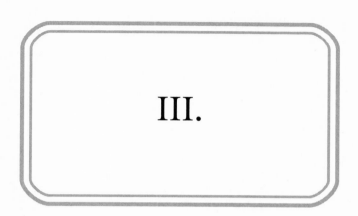

III.

11.

It was late when I came in from drinking.

The house on Río Ganges was dark, but the dim street light illuminated Pierre, smoking. He was slumped on the couch with his bare feet up on the tile table. A cigarette glowed near his mouth, and he didn't seem to notice me standing in the open door.

I was tempted to slip upstairs to bed without a word. I didn't want to discuss the sayings of the desert fathers, or his progress in clearing the roof.

Pierre didn't move or speak. Maybe he had fallen asleep with the cigarette in his hand. In catechism the nuns had told us that the souls of the baptized glowed even in hell, so that they could be hated that much more by their heathen neighbors. Pierre's essential whiteness had that effect here in the near dark. I wobbled a little as I looked at him, and the aftertaste of Mexican brandy came back into my mouth.

A dim light popped on beside the couch, and its glow fell across Pierre's round head. If I took the dirty shade off the lamp so that the light hit his face like a slab of glass, that might not be such a bad shot. Then I saw the parrot cage. Pierre had moved it just behind the table, an easy arm's reach. Inside, the hawk gripped its perch, and the light scarcely reflected off its irises.

"Aren't you coming in?" Pierre said.

"*No puedes dormir?*" I asked as I eased in, letting the door close with a sharp click.

Pierre regarded his cigarette. "Dreams torment me, Daniel. Please, take a seat. Pour yourself some wine."

I could make Pierre out more clearly now. His hair was uncombed, and rose in a few soft curls. He leaned forward, and the light slipped off his face so that his forehead was in shadow. He picked up the wine bottle and, with its neck slanted and pointed at my face, gestured toward me. When I shook my head no, he sat back so that his face was completely lit.

"Teresa, my fiancée, came by today," he sighed. "She wanted to know if I would ever be ready to marry again. I told her, I've already suffered two divorces, one from the church, the other from a woman like herself. I told her that I have had enough."

"Isn't it funny," I said, "that men who claim they've had enough generally have had very little at all."

As Pierre pondered my attempt at desert wisdom, I walked past him to stand in front of the hawk. I leaned the standing lamp toward the cage until the bird looked trapped in light. His rhythmic blinks cut through the shine. For the first time I saw the dark mustache-mark across the mean curl of his beak. A dead mouse lay disdained on the cage's floor.

"I made a mouse offering," Pierre shrugged. "But our bird is fasting. He is clearing his head, no doubt. Preparing for action."

The lamp slipped out of my hand and the lamplight shuddered on the wall beneath the curved stair. I pictured Jane then, reading to Sammy and May, tucking them in so artfully that they felt no need to ask about me. Then she went into our bedroom where the short, thin, blond man rested on our bed, his knees drawn up as he thumbed through one of my books.

100,000 *peso* notes bulged from his pockets, and he set the book down when Jane came into the room.

"There is something on your mind," Pierre said. He held up a glass of wine, already poured.

I took the wine, sipped mindlessly, then winced at the vivid memory of the brandy. "I don't feel like talking," I said.

Pierre stretched lazily on his couch. "Shall we turn the hawk loose? Just to see what he would do?"

I grunted in disapproval. I knew what he would do. He would fly straight into my face and plunge his talons into my cheeks and eyes. Pierre and the hawk would see my naked skull.

"Maybe tomorrow," I said.

"I wish you would talk," Pierre said. "You can't keep everything to yourself."

"That reminds me," I said. I had cashed Laura's check at a bar, and gotten a lousy rate of exchange. But still I had plenty of money for rent, and I handed Pierre a wad of bills.

"This isn't necessary," he said. "Are you sure you have enough?"

"Now the hawk is mine again," I answered. "I'm going to leave him out here, for tonight anyway, but he's mine."

Pierre dropped the bills among the bread crusts on his table.

"A very strange woman came by this afternoon," he said. "She brought you something. You're a brave man, Daniel, to wish to look her in the face. Perhaps that will count for something at the end."

Jane, I thought. Then, Laura.

"Jorge," Pierre called in a voice so loud and booming that it made me flinch. His voice was only a little softer as he called him again. "Bring Daniel his gift."

I winced at the sound of Jorge's name.

"I can get it tomorrow, Pierre. Don't wake him up."

"Nonsense." He bellowed the name again, and I heard feet shuffle through the dark.

"You took long enough," Pierre said as Jorge entered our little circle of light, carrying a leather camera bag.

"I'm sorry," Jorge murmured. "Please pardon me."

The contrition in his voice was so surprising that I looked up from the camera bag as he extended it toward me. Was his jaw really swollen where I'd hit him, or was it just the light?

After I took the bag I could feel the camera inside. I thanked Jorge and tried to see his face, but he turned and quietly left.

"This camera is just what you need," Pierre said. "I am eager to see your work."

I started up the stairs, then stopped and turned back toward Pierre. "That old pistol," I said. "Is it yours?"

Pierre nodded, and seemed to contemplate the question.

"*Oui*," he finally said. "It's a souvenir of my Vietnam adventure."

"Does it work?"

"*Je crois*. Why do you ask?"

"Sometimes I get tired of shooting cameras," I answered.

Upstairs I opened the bag at once, and dumped the camera out onto my bed. The camera's metal body—it was a Rollei, not my little Spy—was hard and cool, and its weight, even without lenses, was both surprising and familiar. Laura had chosen well. The camera was an old twin-lens, the kind that presents you with an inverted image that you have to mentally reverse, imagining the final image. I aimed it at a book lying on the floor. That moment before focusing was always a bit dramatic. If I hadn't done it in a while, the process was like a recovery from blindness. The blur, then the clarity. The chaos, then the detail. I twisted the f-stop, coaxing the book cover into focus until I had the book lying flat in the middle of the finder. The book was about the meeting of Cortez and Moctezuma, but its contents didn't matter. Nor did the fact that the title appeared to be written backwards. It was simply an image. I twisted the lens off, then carefully stored all the pieces. There wasn't a note inside the case, which seemed unnecessarily cryptic on Laura's part. But I was too pleased with the camera to be annoyed.

Everything about Jane and Valparaíso came to me again in bed, and just when I felt myself ready to writhe beneath the sheets, thinking about the two of them, she on top of him, he grinding her down into a mattress, I got up and went downstairs for some wine. Pierre lay on the couch with his eyes closed; an unlit cigarette hung from his mouth as if in parody of French tobacco cool. The lamp beside him still burned and my hawk blinked at me, wide awake.

Pierre was always telling me to relax, this was my home. But that was nothing to feel sublimely peaceful about. Almost a third of the wine was left. That seemed about the right measure, so I carried it up to my room, then pulled the one chair up to the window and sipped. The brandy taste was gone now, and I could drink again. I looked regretfully at the bed. I had wanted to sleep.

Jane and Valparaíso kept pressing in on me. Drinking wasn't keeping them out, not at all, so I tried to think of other things. I pictured Laura's face, a bullfight, an unnamed Astros pitcher, Barton Springs, May, Sammy. But these images were dead for me. I couldn't make them move. Then Doris. I could always count on Doris, my moon-faced older/baby sister. I put her on a swing, and remembered her praying to herself, or to God, I guess, back when I was still in high school.

"Thank you God for the pretty way I swing," she had said to the air. But when I made the swing start to move, I lost Doris, and got my father instead. I wanted to force him out of my head almost as violently as I did Jane, but something about his image made me stop just as I was beginning the effort.

He had a calmer look on his hard face than I usually remembered. There was even a trace of a smile in his eyes, if not on his lips. He came closer to me, he got bigger. His face was white and purified. He stretched out his hands in a vaguely religious gesture, and then he dangled from the roof of a barn, a rope around his scrawny neck. At first his back was toward me, then he spun slowly and I saw his popping eyes, his bleached face, his long black tongue. Or was that his father? Had my father loaned me his eyes, to let me see what he had seen? To tell me why he'd run away?

Or was I just drunk?

I opened a film pocket in the camera bag, and Laura's note was there. *I've moved back to my house,* it read. *Come take my picture.* She included the address. I recognized it as the Lomas de Chapultepec area, where Jane and I had once gone to a party in Valparaíso's city house. Nobody wore costumes, much less diapers. Maybe Laura and Ellen were both lying.

Downstairs I looked for more wine. My eyes were well enough adjusted to the dark so that I moved easily through the foyer, and I had that in-the-dark feeling of weightlessness. The wine was all gone, so I grabbed Pierre's cigarettes, lighter and fluid.

I swung my window open and lit a cigarette. It was cool outside. I had too easily equated the stillness of the house with warmth. I'm no smoker, so after taking a couple of shallow drags, I tossed the cigarette out the window, then looked out and up to where the pollution caught the city's lights and reflected them back down. With the right filter and artificial light, I could probably reproduce that sick softness, somehow wrap it around Laura's face. But no, a stark white backdrop would be best, so that face of hers would lift right off the paper. I would take her fucking picture, all right, and show it to her, so that she would want to kill herself.

To get rid of this feeling, this wishing that various people were dead, I was going to fill my mouth with lighter fluid and try the dragon thing. To blow fire out the window, light up Río Ganges, burn up my unhappiness. But there was more to fire breathing than flame and lighter fluid. As a safety precaution, the *dragones* smear Vaseline on their lips, even inside their mouths.

I went into the bathroom and, to my partial dismay, found a family-sized jar of petroleum jelly. I carried it into my room, smeared it all over my mouth, then took in what seemed a reasonable amount of lighter fluid, flicked on the lighter, and spat fire out the window. I heard it whoosh in front of my face, and had to concentrate on not falling backwards out of my chair. The fire ran in both directions, away from and towards my lips, but consumed itself before it reached me.

When it was over, I realized I'd closed my eyes the whole time, and that I'd only had an inner vision of the fire, followed by a vision of the Virgin of Guadalupe. Not a real vision. I'd just seen her in my mind's eye, like I had been doing all night. I was shaking. Did she have Jane's face, or Laura's or Doris'? I couldn't be sure. The scar inside my mouth tingled. The dead skin felt like it was coming back to life.

I have to catch the bus to Polo soon, I thought. I'll pick up my tripod and lights, and get the darkroom ready. I'll fuck Jane on the darkroom floor. I'll remind her how she likes it.

This time I used more fluid and forced myself to watch as the comet came out of my mouth, and to listen to my own bitter bellow. I didn't care how many fucking Swedes I might wake up.

The Virgin of Guadalupe did actually appear then, inside my eyes, wearing her own Indian face. I saw her brown skin, her hands folded in prayer, and her downward-cast, modest eyes. She didn't look powerful enough to help me.

"Pray for us, O holy mother of God," I said toward nothing, not even pretending that I was speaking to the image. "Poor banished children of Eve, moaning and weeping in this valley of tears." I dropped the lighter on the floor.

"This enough moaning and weeping for you, Holy Mother?" I asked. Then I closed and locked the windows. The feeling hadn't gone away. The fire had all been on the outside, and hadn't burned near enough to my heart.

Someone tapped at my door just as I was turning down the sheets. I stopped and looked back over my shoulder, but didn't respond. The tap again, a little louder. I went through the motion of asking who it was, and Jorge cracked the door.

"Daniel," he whispered. "Let me come in. I heard you cry."

"No. I'm going to bed. It must be 4 A.M."

"Yes, it must be."

He opened the door a little wider.

"I have to talk," he said.

I sighed, regretted that I didn't have a chair, then sat at the head of my bed and drew my knees up in front of my chest.

Jorge took my silence as a yes and hurried to the bed's opposite end. He sat delicately, on one leg and buttock, as if to assure me that he wouldn't stay long. Then he unfolded his leg and pushed up onto the bed, leaning forward and supporting himself with his hands.

"I want you, Daniel," he said, looking straight into my eyes. "You're all I can think about."

I nodded stupidly. "Even after I hit you?" I said.

"That doesn't matter. Everyone likes to see me bleed."

"I shouldn't have done that. I don't even know why I did."

"I know why," he answered. "It's because you want me too, and you're afraid."

Jorge moved toward me on his hands. I put my bare foot out to stop him, and he took it. My sole tingled between his surprisingly rough palms. With an easy tug, I pulled my foot free.

"Women can't make you happy," he murmured. "If you give me strength, then I can give it back to you."

"Don't come any closer," I said, and was relieved that he stopped and sank back on his haunches. He did reach out to my foot again, and stroked its sole, making me want to laugh.

"There is nothing to be afraid of," he said.

"Oh yes there is."

"You smell like gasoline," he said, and rose up into my face. When I caught him by the shoulders he tried to push through my hands, but couldn't. I held him poised just a foot over my mouth, and saw how he had washed off his makeup. I saw his clogged pores, his glinting, pleading eyes, and his dry-lipped mouth. "I can get you the gun," he whispered. "I'll kill her myself. Who do you want to kill?"

When I saw the bruise I remembered hitting him, and in my memory I hit him harder than before. I hit him so hard my hand sank into his jawbone, pushed deeper and deeper all the way to the wrist.

"Do you want your gun or not, motherfucker?" he said, but somehow made it sound like an endearment.

I felt drunk again. Every object in my room shifted.

"Yes," I said. "I do."

But Jorge's lips against mine and his 4 A.M. stubble ground against my face made my entire body throb with displeasure. When he pushed in his tongue I gagged and pulled away.

Jorge gasped, "You taste like a PEMEX pump."

"Jesus Christ," I said. "Please help me. I just need some help."

"Grow up, *gringo*. Down here it's eat or be eaten."

"Why don't you leave me alone, and just fuck yourself? I've really got enough problems."

"Do you? Do you want me to shoot you, so you can quit suffering?"

"Now you're talking."

"You're such a loser. It's macho to fuck queers here. You know that. You lived out in the *campo* with all the horny cowboys. Where all the women keep their legs crossed and the boys grease their assholes. Look, you've even got the Vaseline ready. You were just waiting for me to show up. I'll take all the risk. I'm dying for you to fuck me, *cabrón*."

He dropped onto his back and stared at me. He wouldn't be any more naked when he took off his clothes. Is this how I look to women, I asked myself, when I'm desperate for a piece? This must be the bottom, I thought. If I do this, then the worst will be over. And I'll have the gun.

The room shifted again, and I felt myself move toward him. Oh my God, I thought.

But when he reached up toward me I stopped and leaned

back away. "I'll make you a deal," I said. "In exchange for the pistol, I'll take your picture."

Jorge sat up so quickly that I lifted my hands to defend myself. But he stopped just short of my hands, narrowed his eyes in a purely willful desire, showed me his teeth, then licked his lips with the longest tongue I had ever seen.

"I can just use my mouth," he said, then fluttered his tongue toward me. "All mouths are the same, *pendejo*. All orgasms are the same. Don't be such a fool."

"Really, Jorge. I want to use my new camera. Right now."

He swung his legs around and started to push himself off the bed. Then he stopped and looked back at me over his shoulder. "Let me fix my face," he said.

"Don't forget the bullets," I called as he stepped out the door.

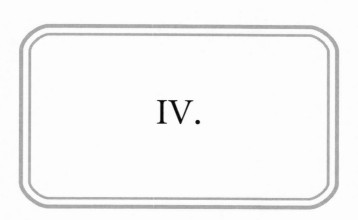

IV.

12.

In the front room of her house, the chairs were all of heavy wood, covered with well-worn leather. Beyond, the dining room was almost completely filled by a thick, heavy-legged table, and dark, high-backed chairs. This was a young couple's house, but they had furnished it as if they were minor feudal nobility.

Twentieth Century art hung on the walls. A Tamayo and a Dr. Atl. Maybe her husband had been struggling to modernize, to lighten up. But he'd married the wrong *gringa* for that.

Squeezing the leather strap slung over my shoulder, so that the comfortably small camera, unburdened by protruding lenses, didn't jostle too hard against my side, I thought that the vast Dr. Atl landscape felt unused, as if Laura's husband had closed his eyes whenever he approached it.

I called her name, but she didn't answer. I picked up her note off the lamp table, reread its invitation to come and find her, then dropped it and walked through the dining room into the big, gloomy kitchen, where I called her again and kept walking. One room led straight to another, as the house was built around its interior courtyard, and so I kept moving forward, into the library where I could just make out the shapes of the books, and where a puddle of moonlight lay across a glass-topped wooden desk.

"Answer me, Laura, or I'll just set down your fucking camera and leave. I'm not that thrilled to have it."

"Quit whining." Her voice came through the door. "I've already paid you to use it."

I opened the next door, and there she lay on a couch, her face propped up on the palm of her hand, a cigarette burning in her mouth. In the fireplace, a fire which barely warmed the room illuminated her face with a sliding, shifting light, showing her scar-less neck, the blue robe she wore, and the curve of her upturned hip. There was a coffee table in front of her couch, and on it sat a couple of half-empty bottles, one brandy, one tequila, and two glasses, each holding a sip of alcohol.

"I missed you," she said. I heard how she softened her words, and thought that with one more drink she would slur them.

"Did you hear me?" she asked. Her head still propped on one hand, she reached out for one of the glasses. "I've been thinking about you."

"Can we turn the lights on?"

"Maybe later, if you absolutely need them to work."

I sighed, and took the camera strap off my shoulder, then set down the small black box. I hadn't resisted photography very hard after all.

"The fireplace light might do all right," I said. "I'll put on another log."

"I have the perfect face, don't you think," she said, and with her elbow pushed her long body forward along the couch so that she halfway sat up. "I can drink all I want, and still have my picture taken. I simply never look drunk."

"Your face might not change, but you do talk more shit after a couple of bottles."

"Have a drink then, so you can enjoy the gab." She lifted one glass and gestured toward the other.

"No thanks. I'd feel like I was drinking after your husband. After what's-his-name."

She stretched out on the couch again, and put her hands together behind her head. "*Maja*," she giggled.

Then she untied the strap around her waist, and with both hands slowly opened the robe just wide enough so that I could see everything. From the neck down, her body was perfect; it looked lazy and soft. Her small breasts sank slightly into her chest, but otherwise didn't move. Her belly dipped toward her hips. With the motion of the weakening fire, shadow and light shifted across her white flesh. She crossed one knee over the other, so that just the top line of her dark hair showed, and itself seemed a thick shadow.

"*Maja desnuda*," she giggled again.

When I looked down at the camera on the coffee table, and felt the room cooling as the fire settled back down into its wood, she cleared her throat and said flatly, as if she had disengaged herself from her voice, "Did you try to kill yourself?"

"Okay," I said. "I will take that drink." I looked back up at her, trying to control my vision of her by narrowing my eyes. I could pop up the camera top and look at her image reversed, I thought. Or throw the camera into the fire. Then she closed her robe, carefully tying its belt, and sat up.

"You look cold," she said. "You're shaking."

"I'll put on another log," I answered.

I was glad to have a reason to turn and do something. I knelt in front of the fire, pulled a split log out of the small pile of wood beside it, then tossed the log in. The fire made a small but satisfying whoosh at the added fuel.

"This is the first fireplace I've seen in Mexico, outside of Valparaíso's hacienda," I said.

"It was my husband's first concession. I presumed there would be hundreds more."

"What about you?" I asked. "Have you ever tried—"

"Sure. I put my head in an oven but accidentally turned on the flame."

"I'm going to leave," I said. "Just keep the camera. I don't feel so good."

"Oh, come sit here beside me. Have a drink."

I stood, clearing my throat again and again, but my sounds were muffled by the hiss and pop of the fire.

"All right," she said. "Go if you want. But I don't know who else you're going to talk to. Who else can tell you what you want to know?"

I shook my head and felt it clear, as if I'd come up out of water. "Pour me that drink," I said.

"Let me show you the house," Laura said. "I haven't given the tour in a long time."

I stood beside her, ready to follow. She closed her robe tighter, so that just a little of her chest appeared in the v. Then she looked around the room.

She said. "This was my sitting room, where I'd read and practice music. I play the violin and the cello. I'm a little better with the cello. Do you play an instrument?"

That made me laugh nervously. "Afraid not. Tell me about your husband."

"I wrote letters at this desk, and sat here to read the ones from home. Chicago, Dan. I'm going to try and anticipate your penetrating questions. Tell me how well I do. There are letters from my father here in one of the drawers. I didn't bother to do this, but they could be divided into the ones pleading with me to come home, those cursing me for marrying a fascist Latin industrialist, and the last few, where he begged forgiveness and understanding."

I didn't know if she was expecting me to ask to read the letters, or if she wanted me to sit on the various pieces of furniture, but we stood as if waiting for something.

"You're getting carried away, Laura," I finally said. "I just wanted to hear about your marriage. To compare it to mine, I suppose."

"What for? All unhappy marriages are unique, right? But never mind, I'll give it a try. Yes, we did fuck in here from time to time. It seemed to turn him on when I read. Especially when I read my old comic books. I always liked the boy's comics. Spiderman. The X-Men. The Fantastic Four. For a while back in the '60s I was Sue Storm, the Invisible Girl. They couldn't have been more explicit about women back then, could they? You couldn't see her. You couldn't even touch her when she had her force field up. I have always wondered what her husband was like in bed. Presumably Mr. Fantastic's cock could change shapes just like the rest of his body. Stretch, expand, tie itself in knots. He wouldn't even have to be in the same room to fuck. He could just stretch his dick out to the bedroom or kitchen from the couch, where he would sit watching the news. At that point such a tiny portion of himself—just six or eight inches out of hundreds—would be inside the Invisible Girl that he would scarcely feel anything. It's kind of sad."

I said, "You're going to make me cry."

She nodded, her face blank as usual. "Before Frida and Diego, they were my favorite couple."

I shrugged, resigned to being misunderstood. I had loved the

147

Fantastic Four myself and was always at the drugstore with my dime or twelve cents the exact day a new issue arrived. But that was a distant, if clear memory, and for the first time I thought of Laura as a case of arrested development. She might be an ancient-looking child.

"Okay," I said. "Just tell me about Valparaíso's party."

"About Jane and El Señor Fantástico? Guillermo and I went to parties at Valparaíso's, and sometimes Valparaíso came here. Guillermo was Mr. Formal, so here we'd wear evening clothes, which I've hated ever since I was a kid. Put me in an evening gown and I'll still wish I were Sue Storm. But Carlos only threw costume parties. One night Guillermo and I came as bullfighters. We had real swords under our *muletas*. You probably don't like the bulls. It's probably a little bloody for you. But that night I was suitable for framing. I felt as stiff and safe as a statue in my tight black spangled suit. I only carried the little *muleta*. The big cape was too heavy for me. For Guillermo himself, actually. But every time I waved my little red cloth at a man, he simply had to bend over, hold up his fingers over his head like dear little horns, and come charging toward me. Some cheated, of course, and ran into me. "You're gored.' they said. *Cogida*. It also means fucked, as in sexually. *Estás cogida*, they said. You're either gored or fucked."

I love bullfighting too, I wanted to say. I even prefer the great torero Manolo Martínez to Diego Rivera. But I was trying both to picture the party and blot out my picture of it: the musical trios that strolled among the guests dressed in their costumes: togas and habits and loincloths and Superman suits, the men in their death-masks, men dressed as dancing skeletons, charging at Laura. Before Laura said anything more I saw Jane, dressed as the Jane of the movies and books I used to love. As love-slave of the Ape-man. Jane's smile and slitted eyes looked smug, as if she were finally in her rightful place.

Laura said, "Jane came as some sort of French hooker. She wore a beret, tilted across her forehead. She carried a trench coat slung over her shoulder, and she wore all black, from her boots to her chin. I thought she was supposed to be a poet or artist until I saw the way she walked. The way she moved her hips and looked into men's eyes as if she might fuck them until there was nothing left. 'That's it,' Guillermo said to me. 'She's a whore. A French prostitute.' We were actually all impressed. We seldom got a quadroon at one of our parties.

"She showed her character through the way she stood, the way she walked, the way we had to look at her. Not so much through her costume. She must have had to throw something together. I tried to talk to her, just for a second. But she stayed in character. She blew smoke in my face and told me not to work her corner. I said to her, 'It's too late. I already have.'"

I looked away from Laura. In my mind, the trio was replaced by a brassy mariachi. They blared in the middle of the party, and the bass lead singer roared above the hubbub. There was so much noise inside my head that I had to sit down. I remembered the last costume party Jane and I went to. It was Halloween in Austin, and we decided to go at the last minute. I went as a boxer and Jane painted on my bruises and scars. In three minutes, and with virtually no props, she had turned herself into a French whore. Whatever that meant. Could she really have repeated that convincing but humble performance here on her grand stage? That night it had been so hard to drink with my gloves on, but when I took them off the effect was ruined, I was just a derelict in his underwear, so I put them back on, clutching at my beer bottles between two huge useless hands.

"Sorry," Laura said, sounding very far away. "I should have lied. I should have told you she came as the Virgin."

"That's all right," I murmured. "What about him?"

"Valparaíso? He was the Ayatollah, if I remember right."

"It doesn't matter," I said. I leaned back in my chair and opened my eyes. I saw Laura at the far end of the room with the light from the fireplace jumping behind her. With her face she looked like a prizewinner at a costume ball. I could see her in a suit of lights. And I could see a bull crash into the Mexican party in my mind; I could see him stab and gore the costumed guests. He lifted them and tossed them and streaked both of his horns with blood, while thick ropes of slobber hung from his massive bottom lip.

Laura handed me a drink. I looked up when I felt the cool glass in my hand, and for just a moment saw her as scarred, but still as beatific as Guadalupe. Eyes cast toward the floor. Cherubim at her feet. The Virgin come to the rescue.

"Flame on," Laura said. "This is not the best tequila."

She reached out and touched my gnarled cheek. "Poor baby," she said. "It's throbbing."

Then she put her hand beneath my chin and with the slightest pressure made me rise toward her. I thought she wanted to kiss me, and I thought, all right I'll do it. But I was still relieved when she turned slightly and presented me with her profile. Our bodies came together lightly and only when we began a lethargic dance did I hear the faint hum of music from the next room, of an unintelligible but harmonizing trio.

"When we're out together dancing cheek to cheek," Laura sang in my ear in a soft and pleasing voice. This wasn't a Los Panchos tune; she was hearing her own music.

I murmured. "I like the bulls. One Sunday we'll have to go see Manolo Martínez."

"You know," she said, looking up at me. "We might be the perfect couple. I'm not sure, but maybe." Her skin seemed to harden against my face, and I relaxed my hold on her. I realized I had my right knee snugged between her legs, and pulled it back.

"Why? Because we both have physical scars? Are you really that literal?"

"Why not?" she said lightly, leaning back, maybe hoping to force me to look at her. "We've both been turned inside out. We wear our inner lives like costumes."

I groaned and leaned away. I looked at her, that was the least I could do, but I could only fumble for words. The radio trio warbled in the other room.

She narrowed her eyes. Just as I began trying to guess what that gesture might mean she slipped her right hand under my balls. She held them gently, trying not to scare me, I suppose, then slid her open hand and long fingers up over my crotch, which gathered itself anxiously at her touch.

"Do you believe everything I told you?" she said. "Do you trust me?"

I had to laugh a little. "No, not really."

This was true. If not for her description of Jane I would assume, or pretend that I assumed, that she was lying about everything. But that alone wouldn't hold me back. I have always appreciated acting just as much as dance.

"We need more drinks," she said. "You do believe that, I suppose."

Tequila would have been the safer choice, but I wanted to get all of this over with. So as she stepped back and began to turn away I grabbed her forearm and pulled her toward me. As her face rose up into mine she closed her eyes. Maybe she didn't want to see my fear. If she hadn't done so, if she hadn't shielded me against her flat eyes, I might have run. But when I pressed my face against her and opened my mouth I heard my groan as if it came from another room, from the radio, maybe. It overwhelmed Los Panchos. Her tongue, too, seemed to come from far away; I felt it unfurl toward me, and when it fluttered cold and hard against mine I started to gag, but when she reached deep enough, I felt something like life stir inside her. Like the memory of life, at least.

So I picked her up and carried her as if she were my bride, and was relieved that she felt light in my arms. But then I had to ask, "Where's your bedroom?"

"Jesus Christ," she said, and wiggled loose. When she didn't seem to find my confusion charming, I was afraid she might reconsider, but she reached back for my hand and led me into the next room. There she turned on the overhead tracking light, revealing her heavy massive four-poster bed. She untied her robe and let it hang open.

I reached toward the wall to turn off the light, but she grabbed my hand.

"No," she said. "And you're not putting a sack over my head either."

Okay, I thought, and began undoing my clothes as she yanked back the covers. With her back to me she shrugged off her robe and let herself up on the bed. Her breasts rocked as she lay down and stretched out, opening her body, and she looked away from me, then back into my face as I slipped up beside her. I poised over her, and started to lie across her when she pushed at me, lowering me onto my back. Then she rolled up on my chest. My cock hardened when her thigh brushed against it, and I told myself to relax, that everything would be fine.

Her body felt cool and soft against my fingers and when she pressed against me I ran my fingers along her spine and up onto the mound of her ass while she bit at my neck and my ear. She rubbed her hair against me. I still didn't feel ready, and was relieved that my cock grew and pushed against her.

But Laura rolled us again so that I was on top, my torso slanted upward above her. She slapped me lightly in the face. "Look at me," she said. But I already was, I really was. She slapped me again and my face tingled and she said, "Look, goddamn you. Look." Then I pinned her arm and pushed down on her. She freed her arms and wrapped them around my neck, and her legs around the backs of my thighs.

I did close my eyes then, and closed they would stay. I didn't want to see the erotic images we made, didn't want to remember and play with them later. I tried to lose myself in my own darkness when her hand moved to guide me to the lips of her cunt. But I felt the lights of the room against my eyelids.

I was already going soft as I began grinding against her, struggling with her dryness. With the willfulness of whole business. Inside my mind I scrambled for an image, for something to guide me. For a moment I got Jane, biting at her lower lip, pouting the way that I used to like, but I had to blink her away. Then came Jorge, sitting on the edge of my bed, creeping toward me on all fours, eyes like almonds. My last try brought me the Virgin of Guadalupe. As a bonus I also got Juan Diego, kneeling at her feet which were shielded by cherubs. "My dearest child," the Virgin said to him. "Am I not the Mother of you all?"

I had already slowed, and my cock had started its rewinding

back up into my groin. I stopped struggling and Laura loosened her arms, then I peeled myself away.

We both breathed heavily as we looked up at the ceiling, then Laura got up, turned off the light, and said, "This is the point where I'm supposed to console you."

I wanted to joke, but couldn't say anything. My mind was mercifully free of images, but of words, too.

"So," she said, and I could hear her hands slap against the sides of her thighs, "here goes."

She climbed back on the bed, then pulled the sheets up over us.

I wanted to stammer out some excuse. It's been too long. It hasn't been long enough. Never with the lights on. Last night a man wanted me to fuck him. At least I'm not crying, I told myself.

"Guillermo is dead," Laura said.

Maybe that was supposed to relax me, to ease my fear that he would burst in with a pistol.

"I had figured that much."

"He was very good to me for awhile. For years. It's partly my fault that he died."

"What do you mean?"

"I don't know if I can tell you this."

"Try." Teach me how to talk, I thought.

She breathed deeply.

"Long story short. I eventually had an affair, after I realized that he was out there getting his fill. But it was with his brother, and they fought."

"What do you mean, they fought?"

"They fought with guns."

"I shot myself," I said up toward the dark ceiling. "My wife was fucking another man, and I put a gun in my own mouth. Not his. Not hers."

We both lay as if paralyzed beneath the sheet, but then she started to move. To shake, actually. She was trying to keep from laughing. I felt mortified when she let out the first cackle. I could tell she was fighting it, I could feel how she was trying to clench her teeth together, but that only made her response more embarrassing. "Go ahead and laugh," I said. "Enjoy yourself."

Then she howled. If she'd rolled away from me, and wanted to enjoy her laugh all by herself, that would've been it. I would've been up, dressed, headed either for Texas or Jane. But Laura turned toward me, and dropped her shaking, laughing head onto my chest.

"I'm sorry," she gasped. I remembered the weight of the small pistol in my hand, and saw it rising up in my hand toward my mouth. Saw, not remembered, because by that point in my suicide, I had already closed my eyes. Just as it was about to go back into my mouth I sat up, turned on the bedside light, grabbed the blanket and threw it all the way off the bed. Laura's laughter became less convulsive but her body still shook, vibrated, almost. I eased out from under her, sat up, then looked down at her live, trembling, happy flesh. "Get this," I said. "I'm going to eat you with my eyes."

She squealed, and tears squirted out from her eyes, which didn't look dead, maybe just because of the liquid she was pumping out. Then she jerked violently, almost in spasm, took my arm and pulled me toward her.

I barked something that was almost a laugh of my own when my cock crept back out of my scrotum, then hardened against her fingers. I started to breathe when she guided me inside. She had finally stopped laughing.

"*Cógeme,*" she said. "*Cógeme como un toro.*"

That's me, I thought. A regular bull. I'll have you in the infirmary for weeks.

13.

Her music woke me.

I hadn't heard a live cello in years. The sound was dim, but like the breathing of an enormous bird. As Laura's playing gained and lost in intensity, the bird seemed to fly toward me, then away.

Then I heard a softer sound; Laura was either humming or singing very softly.

I was sorry to hear her voice. The cello alone was fine.

I got up, pulled my pants on, then grabbed the camera in her study and carried it toward the music. This was the reverse of last night's entry. Now the house was full of soft morning light, and floating motes. The tile floors felt pleasantly cool against my bare feet, and the music, now that I could hear clearly, was fluid and relaxed. Laura had stopped singing.

When the cello sounded like it was in the next room, I unsnapped the cover to the Rolleiflex and let it hang forward.

She didn't look up as I swung the door open and stepped in. I stopped at the sight of her; in the morning light I could see more of her real face than I'd expected. Relaxed and leaning toward her cello's neck, she was not entirely ruined. Pale human flesh showed between her patches of scar, which weren't quite as thick as I'd sensed them in our habitual near darkness. Then I realized I'd been hoping to see Jane, and looked away.

Laura must not have been any happier to see me, rather than

Guillermo, in her study, and for an awkward moment we looked down at the red tiles. Finally I looked at Laura, to confirm that something of her own face really was left, and when I saw that she had flushed a light pink, I said, "Play something." For a moment she ignored me, then she pressed the instrument against her body and lifted her bow like a straight razor to its neck.

I flipped up the camera's lid and felt the old satisfaction at hearing it click into place. Looking into the viewing screen, I saw Laura, but backwards, in twin-lens perspective. Then I could calm down, seeing her—not Jane—backwards and framed in glass. Laura started the music again. Through the lens I saw her scarcely move her fingers against the cello's neck, and then draw her bow across its body. It seemed to be the same mournful melody as before, but now she played a little slower. If she had lingered over her notes any longer the sound would have irritated.

Laura handled the cello with perfect calibration, like an expert mother. Then, during the strokes when she applied the bow with more pressure, and seemed to sink deeper inside herself, the cello seemed to be her perfectly tuned man, her missing Platonic double.

"Just keep playing," I said as I snapped my first image. Shut up, I told myself. Let her lose herself.

According to my lens, she drew her bow back and forth, tilting it up and down, all with her left hand. The cheek that she turned toward me seemed to be her left. Mentally reversing her image engrossed me so that her cheek's disfiguration was simply irrelevant. The morning light was plenty for 1/15, but I hadn't needed a steady hand in so long that the calm in my wrists, forearms, and fingers surprised me. Her motion might blur her arm a little, but that was okay.

After snapping the first shot and advancing the film, I said, "You sound fantastic. Your music is waking me up."

I asked Laura what she was playing. She didn't answer, didn't seem to concentrate harder, didn't acknowledge I was in the room. She opened her eyes just as I looked up from the camera, and a light actually glinted deep down in her pupils, as if some barrier inside her had given way and she were rising back to the surface of her self. My hands wanted to shake. Don't get any closer, I said to myself.

I tried to chatter as I shot, and thought that I should save some film for when Laura was through, as most of these shots would blur, now that I trembled. But then I realized that only her arm and bow would be out of focus. I was under enough control so that I could capture the rest of her perfectly still body and instrument, which would be in contrast to her arm's motion. I felt a moment of guilt as I hit the fourth shot, and then quickly the fifth, as if I had lost some restraint that I'd promised God or Jane or myself that I would keep. I breathed out and blew the feeling away, and my hands steadied.

I shot until I had to change film. Then I shot more, until she sighed and leaned one cheek against her cello's neck.

When Laura opened her eyes, she murmured, "I haven't played in a long time."

"You could have fooled me," I said. "You sounded great."

She nodded. "I never feel like you're telling me the truth. Not about anything important, at least. What are you hiding?" Then she stood and leaned her cello against the wall, and rested its bow on the small stand beside her chair.

"Maybe I know what you mean," I said. "And maybe I don't."

I put the camera down beside her bow. This brought me near her, and I could have reached out to her. But she stepped away, and crossed her arms over her breasts so that each hand rested on the opposite shoulder. Then Laura dropped her hands as if in exasperation.

"Let's go to the bullfights Sunday," she said. "I still have season tickets."

Her eyes had filmed over, but a dull light appeared behind her tears, like the reflection of a moon. I didn't know why she was ready to cry, but I didn't appreciate it.

"I thought I could trust you," I said. "I thought you were really dead."

Even though she said that she seldom used it, Laura's darkroom was fully equipped. I only had to fill the three trays with their chemicals and begin. Each developing photograph lingered at a point where Laura's face was indistinct, and I had that familiar feeling of minor miracle when the white paper came to life. I saw Laura and her cello, at first ghostly, then transparent, then simply there. As I pulled the first print out to dry, the first image that I'd printed in months, I completed my cycle of response. This was a technological product, a photograph, and I took my craftsman's pride. As one photo after another developed, I began imagining the ways that I could touch Laura up, airbrush away the scars. Maybe I could figure out what she'd looked like before the fire. Before Guillermo burned her. Maybe the negative and the chemicals could tell me.

But I wouldn't have to bother. When I sat down on a leather-covered stool beside the sink, and yawned with the pleasure of stopping, I saw the photos that were already pinned to the darkroom wall. Some were of a youngish, European-looking Mexican man, and others of a young *gringa*. Still others of the two together, arm-in-arm, and a few in which the *gringa* stood between two men, her arms around the shoulders of both, their arms crossed behind her so that their hands peeped out around her hips.

I forced myself to rise slowly from the stool, to walk just as slowly toward the wall, and then not to study Laura's picture, her portrait from before the fire, until I had unpinned a black and white and held it in my hands under the light. Her dark hair was pulled back tight above her ears, and her high forehead was creased a little. But it wasn't a crease, it wasn't a worry line, it was the same two-inch scar that appeared in my just-snapped photo. I recognized the slightly puggish nose, but also the patch of thickened skin that curved from her nose under her left eye. The eyes themselves were the biggest change. The only change, maybe. They were deep and intelligent and ironic.

I re-pinned the photo, then stepped back. The casual conglomeration of images made the wall look like one of those Mexican altars where the dead are kept alive "in the partial heaven of memory," as one of the *unomásuno* writers said the other day. I stepped forward to concentrate on individual photos, but found my eyes bouncing away from the pictures of him, Guillermo, and his cruel smile, his lean rich Mexican smile.

I only looked at the pictures of Laura alone.

Here she inclined her face forward, so that the shot was mostly forehead and eyes. The forehead scar was in my face. Where was the white smooth face she must have brought to Mexico?

In a stack of black and whites I found Laura standing between two men again. The taller, more intense looking one was the husband from so many other photos; the other man, yes, the brother, resembled him strongly. The brother had the same deep-set eyes as Guillermo, but the brother's were more open, less arrogant. And his jaw didn't jut out for the camera as Guillermo's did.

The three were on the beach, in bathing suits, with Laura in the middle in a dark one-piece. She had an arm around each man, each man had an arm around her. Both of them let their free hands droop in front of their genitals, as if to protect their *huevos* from the Acapulco sun.

Then there was a picture of twenty or so rich bastards burning and cooling themselves around a swimming pool, at Guillermo's Acapulco home, no doubt.

Valparaíso stood in the pool at one corner of the photo. His torso was beaded with water, and he held up a glass toward a servant, a dazed looking Indian boy, just down from the mountains, no doubt, who was bent over to pour from a pitcher. I almost howled at the sight of the woman beside Valparaíso, but then saw that it was his ex-wife, Angela, smiling warily beside him in the water. When I couldn't find Jane I wadded the photograph into a ball.

I carried my finished prints back into the house and found Laura in the kitchen. The fruit and vegetable-filled shopping bags lined along the floor showed that she'd gone to the market.

She looked up from the cutting board where she was chopping carrots and green onions.

"I thought your husband burned you." I said.

She stopped cutting for a second, but kept the tip of her knife against the vegetables and cutting board. Laura's hand tightened around the knife handle. She looked up at me, but her eyes had gone flat again, and I couldn't read her face.

"I assumed that he burned you, I mean," I said.

"You assumed no one would marry a freak like me."

Laura looked down at her cutting board and cleared her

throat. Then she pushed a few thick slices of carrot across the board. Orange and green slivers clung to the knife, which was sticky with vegetable juices.

"Tell me what happened," I said.

She tapped at the board with the long, wide blade; her knuckles whitened around the handle.

"Do you love me?" Laura asked.

She looked up after she spoke. I wondered if my eyes appeared dead to her. But they couldn't have. I could feel how my burst red veins had swollen them. I wondered if she fixed on my own scarred cheek, and wanted to touch it. I felt my own thickness, my own gnarling, and flinched.

I closed my eyes and heard that long-ago crash, that once-in-a-lifetime explosion in my mouth. It was both inside my mouth and roaring around my head all at once. Hot air rushed across the torn fringe of my cheek.

When I opened my eyes I was surprised to see Laura in front of me, clutching her knife but forgetting her knife.

"Love?" I said, fingers pressed against my cheek. "Love you?"

"I'll only tell you if you love me."

"I'm sorry," I said. I blinked several times as if my eyelids were lips, as if their damp lashes might produce the appropriate words.

"I love Jane," I said.

14.

Chapultepec Park is farther from Lomas de Chapultepec than its name implies. I had imagined that I was ready to walk for days, to empty myself by crossing the urban desert. But by the time I'd crossed the final street named for a mountain range, *los alpes, los andes, los himalayas,* made my way through the last of the fine old houses, mostly in the Spanish style, and trudged up Reforma to the park entrance, I was ready to take off my shoes and rub my feet. If I had, though, one of the folk medicine vendors under the arch commemorating *los niños héroes* would have tried to sell me an herbal blister cure.

One bright-eyed, very Indian-looking fellow was literally selling snake oil to a circle of onlookers, but the crowd seemed more interested in seeing him put a live snake into his shirt, and then watching the creature's bulge writhe around his body, than in buying his remedies. In the distance I heard the pan flute and drums of Andean folk music, and closed my eyes to listen.

Then I opened them, as women kept cramming in under my eyelids. Jane and Laura, of course. Jorge? How to count Jorge? Next the Virgin of Guadalupe, with a scar zigzagging down from one eye like a permanent teardrop.

A family to my left had a badminton game going. To my right a few boys played a crude game of soccer. They surrounded the ball and kicked it all at the same time, like my former students did when they destroyed the rabbit. Their angry words bit into the Andean flutes in a chorus of hard feelings. One day Sammy might kick a soccer ball on this same patch of grass. If Jane stayed in Mexico. If she stayed with Valparaíso. Not that Carlos Valparaíso would spend much time with the big families here in the park.

May had loved coming to the Chapultepec Zoo ever since the baby panda was born here a few years ago, apparently the first panda born outside of China. May used to sing the kid's song the little bear's birth inspired—*osito panda, aún no anda*—as part of her daily kid routine.

My feet still hurt, but I left my bench and walked ahead, into the thick woods of the park. High above me and to my left I saw Chapultepec Castle, where Maximilian and Carlota once lived, but soon the path had me surrounded by tall, thick-trunked trees whose branches began far above my head and blocked my view of the castle. The trees had been nearly this tall when Maximilian and Carlota arrived from Austria. Since he was an amateur botanist, he had probably once studied the tree right in front of me, when he should have been busy saving his own life.

One thing I can't remember is the names of trees. Pines, yes, palms, yes, Joshuas, yes, and the live oaks and mesquites that I grew up with. But not much else. I used to think that if I'd been raised by a father, he would have taught me the names of trees. I would understand the world better if he had just taught me a little about the farm he'd grown up on. As I pushed on further into the woods, following the paved path but still feeling somehow lost, I didn't bother to read the signs that indicated the trees' names. What was the point? What good had botany finally done Maximilian?

Despite the 20,000,000 people that live here, Mexico City makes you think of the dead. The dead had first claim. What if the rich didn't have to die? I thought. What if death were like Vietnam, or any war, and if you had enough money you didn't have to go? Then we not-rich really would have something to complain about.

I wished that I knew for certain that my father was dead. I wished that Sammy and May and I were in some safe after-life. Just the three of us. I couldn't include Jane. I had to make myself let go of her, first of all in my mind.

I ignored the dull pain in my feet and pushed on to the zoo. Only five months ago, I had come here with Sammy and May. While Jane shopped in the Polanco, they ran ahead of me looking for the baby panda. But they became distracted by the monkey cages, and stopped to lean in toward the baboons and rhesus monkeys. In the Chapultepec Zoo you can practically shake hands with the animals, they're so close.

May was angry with the boys who threw lit cigarettes to the orangutans, then modeled smoking for them. The apes would actually imitate the boys, holding the filtered end against their dangling lips, letting the smoke curl in front of their oblong faces.

"How do the monkeys breath this pollution air?" May asked.

I told her and Sammy about Moctezuma's zoo, which had dazzled and frightened Cortez and his men. They had never seen these new world animals, and the jaguars' nocturnal roaring and screaming had kept the conquistadors awake at night.

Sammy seemed to ponder this image, but at age two he was probably thinking about the balloon he wanted me to buy, or the fruit-flavored *raspa* he wanted to crunch with his teeth, or the children beside us who jumped and scratched their ribs in imitation of the apes.

The months that had passed since then seemed like a very

long time. Jane and I had actually made love that night in the
María Cristina, after the children had gone to sleep. I told Jane
about our day in the zoo, how Sammy and May had complained
every step of the way up the steep hill to Maximilian's castle, but
then were excited to find themselves looking down on the green
world of the park. I didn't mention to Jane that I had pointed
out to Sammy and May the spot from which the *niños héroes*
had jumped off the castle walls, back when it was a military prep
school and the kids chose to die, literally wrapped in the Mexican flag, rather than surrender to the *gringo* invaders of 1845.

I knew then that our marriage was sometimes touchy, but not
that it was just about over. I knew that I wanted her to guide me
inside her and then dig her fingers into my own thick hair. She
didn't hold on as tightly as she used to, but we came at the same
time and then she rested calmly beneath me for a few minutes.

That wasn't even the last time we made love. Just six weeks
ago, after she first said she thought I should leave, we went at
each other with the perfect freedom of strangers. The next day
as we drove to work our unmentioned lovemaking seemed odd,
but not hopeless.

But now I realized that while I had been with Sammy and
May in the zoo, she had probably met Valparaíso. I had babysat
for their afternoon together. I was the second man she fucked
that day.

I wanted to go into the aviary and look at the predator birds,
to compare them to my hawk, but I couldn't see much through
my tears, so after I lingered a moment at the bird world's entrance, I finally walked away.

Not far from Pierre's, on a restaurant-lined street beside
Sullivan Park, I stopped to eat. The sidewalk cafes of the Zona

Rosa, with its empty hubbub, hadn't tempted me. It was across Reforma in Cuautehmoc that the little *taqueriás* with the sizzling grease and the big, top-shaped *trompos* of meat made me both frantic with appetite but craving one certain taste—the same *caldo tlalpeño* Laura had been making when I left.

In one three-table den of tacos and stews, they did their cooking at the door, almost in the street itself, and you had to walk past the oily grill and smoking cauldrons to sit and order. I did this, and felt nervous until the bowl of *caldo tlalpeño* and the bread basket arrived at my metal folding table, which bore the red crown of the Corona beer logo. It was a big bowl, and the steam and the heat of the *caldo* reminded me of how uncomfortable the evening's chill had become. I wanted to eat slowly, but couldn't, despite the fact that even hot, the *caldo* tasted of the grease that would coat it an inch thick if I let the soup grow cold. I dipped in the *bolillos*, and scooped up the strong broth with my spoon, and got down to the chicken and rice and green squash almost before I was fully conscious of eating. I forced myself to stop awhile, and let myself imagine Laura, eating alone.

When the *caldo* was gone, I was still hungry. Happily, when I let myself into Pierre's house, he and the Swedes and Richard were sitting down to a meal. Wine bottles were everywhere, and only Pierre seemed to notice that I'd returned. He stood and motioned me in.

"Eat," Pierre said, gesturing imprecisely. "Bernard is cooking tonight."

Jorge came out of the kitchen with more wine. The bottles still in his hands, he took a little jump toward me and kissed me on the cheek. "What a bad brother you were last night," Jorge said, almost in my face. "We were all worried when you didn't come in."

"What's for dinner?" I said, my face still tingling.

Anders saw me then, and waved a *bolillo* in greeting. "This is living," he said in his thick Swedish accent.

"Yah," I answered, in my best Scandinavian, then turned and pushed the swinging door open and followed the dark, curving hallway to the kitchen, where Bernard had plates and saucepans and pots spread all over the stove and the fish-shaped table. Once again I smelled *caldo tlalpeño*.

"Is this a French soup?" I asked as I spooned a little of the broth into a bowl.

Bernard mumbled "no" toward his feet, making me wonder if he had driven his wife away by never looking her in the eye. Bernard went on in a French accent far thicker than Anders' Swedish. "Someday in Paris I will have a Mexican cuisine. Now I experiment."

The broth was so tasty that I wanted to dip a coffee cup into the pot for more. I did fill my bowl without much grace, then plopped in a big white slice of chicken breast, so that the hot broth dripped onto my fingers. I began eating right there, knowing this had to be better than Laura's soup, far better than anything Jane or Valparaíso's cook ever prepared. As I lifted the bowl up near my chin and spooned in the food, I tried to tell Bernard in French that he was a genius.

Bernard shrugged, and pushed a slice of tomato around the cutting board with his finger.

"Go in the dining room to eat," he said. "You act as if you were the servant here, and not the guest."

"I don't want to sit with them," I said as I refilled my bowl. "I don't want to talk."

169

"Get out of my kitchen," he said.

"What's bothering you?" I asked. "Is it your wife? You get a letter that you didn't want?"

He pushed the tomato slice off the board and onto the stainless steel table.

"You are very coarse," he said. "When the pot is empty you will wear it over your head."

Carrying my bowl with both hands, I walked into the dim hall. I would spill the soup. I would fall. Jorge would open the door against my face.

But none of these things happened, and at the table the others left me alone. But halfway through my bowl, I got squeamish. The chicken was perfectly tender, and it did taste like chicken. But what doesn't? What if we were eating the hawk?

I got up from the foyer table and went into the cluttered dining room, where my bird rested atop the perch inside Pierre's parrot cage. Hawk shit crusted over the cage's bottom, which Jorge hadn't bothered to line, despite the piles of years-old papers that choked the room. But he or Pierre had put in a small dish of water. I tapped at the cage's bars, and the hawk blinked right at me. I could sense movement inside its body, though he didn't stir.

I wished that Sammy and May were here to admire the hawk. We could study falconry together, and the hawk would be a very practical means of defense. Stand back or he'll pluck out your eyes!

Then my breath caught as I realized who had hurt Laura, as the face of the man who had scarred her appeared before me. But no, not the face, because I didn't know what her father looked like.

In my mind he looked just like my dad, like my old man who looked like a hawk.

I wanted to go to Laura right away and hear the story, to learn another way that a father could ruin a child. Then I could spare Sammy and May that one bit of suffering, at least. No one would rend their flesh. Not me, anyway. But I didn't want to tell Laura I loved her. I didn't want to pay the price of her story.

Pierre came in behind me on soft feet. When I heard him breathe I stepped guiltily away from the cage.

"I've been reading," Pierre said.

He stood beside me, his wild soft hair the color of marshmallow puffed out around his head, the light in his green eyes dancing like a candle's flame. He held out his open paperback, *Le Bestaire du Christ*, into which he had jammed a long finger. He tapped the book as if pushing a button that would produce an esoteric knowledge.

"Why would Christ need a bestiary?" I asked.

"Listen," he said, pushing his finger again.

He started to read in French, then caught himself. He groaned with the shifting of gears, cleared his throat, and began: "The noble bird was already what it has been always, the protector of the royal person." He looked up, one white eyebrow cocked, awaiting my response.

"I'm lost, Pierre."

Now he grunted in disgust. "This noble bird, Daniel. Our hawk was the protector of the Pharaoh."

He pushed the book in front of me and indicated the drawing of a falcon wearing a pharaonic headgear.

"He looks like the pope," I said.

Pierre snorted and read, "The divine falcon is shown here in the act of the fecundization of the thought of the pharaoh. The nature divine thus is infused into him and animates his intelligence."

Ah. Pierre's intelligence had been animated.

He handed me the book, but I could only make the cognates and the occasional simple clause in French, so I had to give it back. "You read," I said.

Pierre nodded and drew himself together as if ready to expound. "In spite of the falcon's violent habits, the relation which *les egyptiennes* found between it and the heart of God and of humanity connected it with the symbolism of love."

I shrugged, lost in his or the bestiary's syntax. Acknowledging my difficulty, Pierre sighed, then read, "'The Tuscan poet Francisco da Barberino described love as having the feet of the falcon!'"

"I guess I understand that, Pierre. We're all torn to pieces by love, right?"

"There's more and more," he said, looking now away from the book and toward the rigid, unblinking hawk.

"'The early Christians in Egypt made the falcon the symbol *du Christ*. The falcon was not only the emblem of the human soul, but also that of resurrection, like the eagle.'" I started to speak, but Pierre hushed me with a raised hand. "'At the beginning of the 16th century, the *Fraternité des Chevaliers du divin Paraclet...*'" Pierre closed his eyes and tapped his knuckles against his forehead, "the Brothers of the Knights of the Holy Paraclete, '...invoked the Holy Spirit behind the symbol of the falcon, to implore lui for the gifts of knowledge, intelligence, and strength.'

"That's us, Daniel. At last I know why God sent you and this bird to our house. To our little brotherhood. These are exactly the gifts we need. Knowledge, intelligence and strength."

Pierre set the book on the table in front of me, and pointed to a drawing of the *Fraternité*'s symbol—the holy spirit in the form of a hawk, rather than a dove. Its wings were impressively spread and spiky, and a halo circled its raptor's head.

"This will be our symbol, Daniel. At my machine shop right now my workers are creating just such a bird from abandoned metal. Just such an image as this. I'll hang the paraclete above our door."

Jorge had come into the room. He had painted his face with unusual verve. When I looked at him he spread his arms like wings, cocking them at the elbows and turning his head in profile. "*El amor divino*," Jorge sang out, then he flapped his arms and opened his painted lips and shrieked, and somehow managed to leer at me.

I squinted at the sight of Jorge in pretend flight, arms waving, white teeth almost hidden beneath his scarlet lips, egg-shaped eyes closed and bulging beneath their darkened lids. He rose to his tiptoes as if trying to leave Pierre's floor.

The dining room door banged open and Anders and Goran and Richard came through. Anders studied Jorge just a second, then joined in. But Anders was more rooster than hawk; he put his fists into his armpits, bent his knees, and pecked at the surly Goran. Richard pulled his one long lock straight up above his head and squealed like a species of flying pig.

Pierre and I looked at each other. His eyes were bright, but moist with sadness. Behind Pierre the hawk sat quietly on his perch, blinking only once. For a second I saw myself and the bird as Pierre must have, the day I walked into his house. For Pierre the cage and hawk hanging at my side must have looked like a kind of torch, and that I had appeared to bear a captured spark of heaven. I knew how wrong Pierre had been, that neither the hawk nor I were angels, but I still wanted to join in.

"Divine love," I said to Pierre and nodded toward our housemates as the shrieking and bird play continued. "The Divine Parakeet."

Pierre gulped, as if swallowing his first attempt at speech, then said, "According to Tertullian, the cattle and the wild beast each pray in their way. A bird which lifts itself toward the sky makes the shape of a cross as a man does when he prays and extends his arms."

The hawk blinked, seemed gathered for flight, then tightened its talons about its perch. We would be judged any day now.

15.

In my room I found a letter from my brother. Will had written to express his irritated concern for me, and for Sammy and May. "Mom is going crazy," he wrote, and I had no idea if he was speaking literally or not.

I went outside and crossed Río Ganges to use the pay phone to call him. Maybe I sounded a little crazy when I told Will that everything was all right—that I was fine, and that I was going to Polotitlán to check on Sammy and May tomorrow—because Will answered, "You don't sound all right. I don't care what you say."

There are things happening here that you could never understand, I wanted to tell him. You've never left home. You've never explored the world or yourself. Don't try and start now.

If something really were seriously wrong with me I would have said those things, but I understood how they would sound to Will. Will had never set foot outside of South Texas, but if I let myself carry on he might buy a plane ticket for Mexico City to come and rescue me, no matter how much the idea of this many Mexicans concentrated in one place might terrify him. No, I had to be crafty. I had to talk about his business, about sports, about his family, but not about the hawk or Laura or Pierre.

But he didn't take the bait. The line crackled with static for a second after I asked my questions, then he said, "Mom is very

175

worried, Dan. And I'm worried about her. She's got you and Dad confused in her mind. She says Dad ran off to Mexico to marry a Mexican and raise a Mexican family. That he did all this to spite her, or to punish her for some terrible thing she did but she can't remember what it was. And now he's dying, down there in Mexico."

"How is that confusing him with me? I'm not dying."

"Would you just come home?" Will said. "I can't handle this by myself. I have so far, but now I'm stuck and Mom is stuck. Everybody is stuck and something has to give."

"*Bien*," I said, then flinched when I realized I'd spoken an accidental word of Spanish. "I'm going to get Sammy and May. I'm going to pick them up and bring them home with me."

"Well," Will drawled. "That would be great."

"We'll be in Fuente in a week," I said. "Ten days at the most."

Just as I was ready to hang up, Doris barged onto the phone. "Are you there, Dan? Are you busy?" I could picture her perfectly, her soft, jiggling belly, her pie-shaped face blushed red with the excitement of talking to me.

"Is Jane mad at me? I didn't mean to call her that bad name."

"No, Dodo. She's forgotten all about it."

"That's good. Are you with Daddy in Mexico? Are you going to bring him home with you?"

"No, Doris. I'm not with Daddy. I don't think he's here."

"Momma says he is. She says you're living in the same house."

"Momma's confused."

"I wish you would bring him home. I'd like to hear my damn song again. Do you remember my song? They don't play it anymore."

More than once I've hummed a few bars of "The Old Lamplighter" to Doris over the phone, but today I just didn't have it in me, and was relieved when Will took the phone back. I heard Doris griping in the background.

"So you're coming, Will. I can count on you."

I was thinking about my mother having collapsed my father and me into the same person, and couldn't answer right away. My whole identity was based on not being my father. On being his exact opposite.

"I have to go," I murmured. "I have things to do."

Then I hung up.

Cars were parked up on the sidewalk, and I had to step around them to get to the newsstand and buy an *unomásuno* and the *Esto* sports paper. The dirty air of the city pressed down on the two- and three-story buildings surrounding me, but this was a moment of clarity. This was the right plan, to rescue my children, and go back home. Pierre could keep the hawk and his brotherhood, whatever he meant by that word.

16.

"Going somewhere?" Laura asked, nodding toward the bag in my left hand.

"Home," I said. "My mother is sick."

"Ah. The flight to mother."

We stood facing each other through her front door. I shifted the bag to my right hand, then turned and looked away from her, out over her fence to the tiled roofs of the neighboring houses. I thought, she never expected to see me again.

"Well. Can I come in?"

She blinked, and I saw that her right eyelid was scarred.

"What do you want? Money?"

"I've got your pictures."

Laura finally stepped back out of the doorway, but the house's darkness didn't soften her. It just obscured her body, made the whiteness of her face even bolder. Then she stepped forward again, just as I'd started to come in.

"I was just getting ready to leave, too. Why should I put off a trip for you?"

"Where are you going?" I asked.

"You're going to see Jane, aren't you?"

"She's on the way, more or less. I'm going to see my kids. To get them. To take them back to Texas."

She nodded impassively, and I felt uncomfortable in front of her.

"I saw her last night," she said evenly, "walking around the neighborhood with Valparaíso."

I tried to keep my face as blank as hers. I didn't believe her, but still I felt my teeth clench.

"Without the kids, though. He's probably not so interested in them."

"You want me to go away," I said. "All right. I'll leave you alone." I reached into my jacket pocket and pulled out an envelope full of the photos from the other day. "Take them."

She smiled, as if at a private joke. "I was just kidding. Jesus." Then she took the envelope and opened it right there.

I don't know any photographer who can simply walk away while a subject takes their first look at his work. I did manage not to step toward her as she pulled out the first image: Laura at the cello, eyes half-opened, face softened just a little, cello neck right in front of her face. I knew which picture it was without looking, because I put that picture in last, so she would see it first.

Still, I had no idea how she would react. I certainly couldn't read her face as she studied her image.

"So? What do you think?"

"Come with me," she said, slipping the photo back into the envelope. "My trip won't take long."

"I do this once a week," Laura said as the metro train pulled away from the Insurgentes station and silently entered its tunnel, headed north. We were lucky; the early afternoon train wasn't yet half-full. "Every Friday."

The train's motion made us rock from side to side, but we weren't perfectly in synch. When the train took a curve, we bumped against each other. The car was brightly lit, but the tun-

179

nel walls rushed by in darkness. The train slowed as we pulled into Niños Héroes. A few people got on and off, and Laura and I sat quietly together, my travel bag at our feet. It felt a little awkward to be so physically close to her, but I let myself lean against her anyway. When the train eased forward again, she relaxed.

"I don't get it," I finally said. "Why would a dead woman hang around the site of a miracle?"

She shrugged. "I like watching other people pray."

I felt the pleasing curves of her body thud rhythmically against my side and remembered us naked, pushing against each other. But now the screen that she had let down that night, and left down the next day, was back in place.

"I have to know, " I said to her. "Did you really see Jane at those parties. Or did you make that up?"'

Laura leaned away from me, closed her eyes, and rested her head against the greasy window.

"Okay, then," I said. "Tell me about your father. What did he do to you?"

"My father is a born-rich liberal. Every movie star who voted for Jerry Brown has done his dope."

"I don't care about that. What did he do to you?"

"It's not what you think," she said.

The old basilica is cracked and leans to one side, a victim of four passing centuries and soft, sinking land. This is the church that was built where the Virgin appeared to the Indian Juan Diego and left her image on the flimsy cloak Diego was wearing.

This is the most political miracle I know of, and I was sorry that I couldn't claim it as my own, since my own background is closer to Cortez than to Juan Diego. You could say that the Virgin appeared to protect people like Juan Diego and my students from people like me. I used to think that, at least. Now the idea that someone might need protection from me was mildly amusing. And maybe I was finally becoming more Mexican. My *mujer* had indeed become my Malinche. She had sold me out to a foreign power.

We turned from the old basilica to the new one, built in the fifties. It sits in the middle of a huge square, flanked on all sides by a run-down section of the city. In Juan Diego's day, Tepeyac was a separate town, some twenty miles from el centro.

The wide plaza was dotted with penitents or miracle seekers slowly crossing its width on their knees. Here and there thin trails of blood marked their progress. I tried to follow a man in a broken straw hat. Surely he hadn't come to ask for anything less than the life of a child or wife. A routine case of bad crops probably wouldn't make him tear the knees of his cheap pants. I imagined him crawling up the steps, and, still on his knees, taking off his hat before entering the temple. But he moved too slowly for me to concentrate on him, and I looked away. I had learned on earlier visits to churches and shrines that I didn't pity the crawlers the way I had expected. This was how they claimed Mexico for themselves, and it worked. I was willing to believe that God existed, but for them, not me.

"Doesn't it embarrass you?" I asked Laura, who stood quietly beside me. "I feel like I'm crashing a confession."

"It does," she said. "Quite a bit. Will you do it with me?"

"What?" By way of answer, Laura nodded toward one of the penitents.

"Crawl? Crawl on my knees?"

"I've been here a hundred times, and the last fifty I've wanted to try it," she said.

I looked away from her and around the plaza. The man I'd been following had advanced maybe fifty feet. An old woman in a black shawl already had her hands raised as she inched along a good hundred yards from the basilica. A youngish husband and wife crawled together, their baby in the father's arms.

"What would I ask for?" I said, looking again at her. I realized how idiotic this sounded. I could ask for my children back. For my wife back. For my mother's sanity back. For Laura's flesh to grow back. For the hawk to find some clean air and food.

She groaned. "I'm sorry now that I brought you. I want to do this, and I'd rather you didn't watch."

"You want me to take your picture?"

"I deserve every stupid comment you could make. But not today. Please. Go get a beer. I'll be finished in a little while."

"Finished with what?"

Laura looked toward the church, then dropped onto her knees. She inched away, first on her right knee, then her left. I took one step, caught and lifted her. I expected a fight, but she went limp in my arms like a non-violent protester. She seemed to have blotted me out altogether, so I let her back down and looked on feeling invisible, as if I had somehow become one of those ghosts, the *ánimas en pena*. I snatched up my bag and backed away from her. She'd covered ten feet.

Fucking exhibitionist, I wanted to hiss, but my irrelevance to everything around me was so humiliating that I couldn't talk.

None of the little shops and bars around the plaza looked very inviting. I could go back to the metro and begin my trip out to Polotitlán, but I wasn't ready for that. When Laura stood and brushed off her knees I took a few quick steps toward her, then stopped when she knelt again and resumed her crawl. I wished it were December 12th, the Virgin's feast day, when this nearly-empty plaza would be so filled with pilgrims that my feet might not even touch the ground. That would be better than this feeling naked, this going public with my emptiness. I walked past Laura without a word or backward glance, and hurried into the church.

The walls of the new basilica's entrance are covered with *milagros*, small paintings on tin showing how Guadalupe came into the *milagro*-maker's life and healed someone. One will say, for example, in misspelled Spanish, *On June 12, 1934, I prayed to the Virgin to save the life of my son, who was gravely ill. This she did, and I offer this* milagro *in thanks for all her blessings.* A primitive drawing of a boy in bed, his mother kneeling in prayer at his side and the Virgin hovering over the pair, will illustrate the text.

There were thousands of these offerings. I walked past a great cluster of them, occasionally stopping to look and read. Mercy seekers, men and women alike, came crawling in one after another. A few walked in like me, and all the pleas, directed toward small shrines with statues of the Virgin and Christ, were so loud that the basilica's entrance took on the sharp edge of bedlam.

The loudest of the women just said the same word over and over. *Socorro socorro socorro.* She made me want to put my hands over my ears. Instead I tried to concentrate on the quiet ones, the ones who simply knelt and lifted their hands toward the statues, scarcely moving their lips as they prayed.

Behind me, all of the *milagros* described a prayer that had been granted. Not one said, nice try, Mother of us all, or, we understand that you couldn't help, Queen of Heaven. We hope our daughter who was killed by a stomachache is happy with you in paradise. Still I couldn't imagine making my own request. What exact miracle would I ask for?

Then Laura crawled through the entrance and stopped. She rose slowly, first to one knee; then she stood stiffly, and smoothed her slightly torn jeans at her bleeding knees. I almost ran to her.

"I can't stand it here," I said. "I'm afraid of dropping dead."

"You're already dead. It's already happened."

"Don't start that again."

"I want to live, Dan."

She bent and ran her fingers across her knees, then smudged a little blood.

I wanted to protest, to say that just because you have crawled past me in this race you've set up doesn't mean that I'm dead, but I still felt my humiliation.

I said. "Help me, okay?"

She stared at me. "No one has ever said that to me."

Then a black-dressed, stubby woman stopped beside us as she walked out of the basilica's sanctuary, where Juan Diego's cloak hung for public veneration. The nearly toothless woman lay her fingertips against Laura's cheek. Laura didn't jump or make a sound. The woman was muttering something I couldn't make out—it wasn't Spanish—and Laura rested her hand on top of the woman's. I couldn't tell who was praying for whom.

Juan Diego's cloak, covered by thick glass, hangs some twenty feet above the ground. As a practical matter, the crowds that would form beneath the cloth might get so thick that they would be dangerous. The basilica's solution was to put a conveyor belt under the image. If you want a close look at the Virgin you have to step on the belt and let it carry you on a thirty-foot trip.

The absurdity of this mechanized pilgrimage took the edge off my nervousness. After a moment of watching people slide by under the cloak, I joined the line and boarded the belt. I had to look up and look fast, but there she was, the Mother of the

Americas, a prayerful, dark-faced Indian girl, beautiful, simple, meek. Then she was gone.

I stood behind the crowd for a moment, looking both up at the cloak, and at the backs of the worshippers' heads. The conveyor ride hadn't exactly been transcendent, but somehow I felt less humiliated. I got back on for another ride, zipped beneath Guadalupe, then immediately reentered the line. Again and again. If the line hadn't taken so long, I would have felt drunk or motion sick.

On one ride, the women in front of me knelt on the belt, and threw up their hands as we passed beneath. I rode stiffly again, but the next time under I followed their example.

As I passed beneath the angels at Guadalupe's feet I dropped to my knees and threw up my hands. The next time I knelt again, and wanted to cry out. I clenched my teeth to remain silent, but my legs shook as the belt deposited me on the smooth marble floor. I kept my feet and wobbled back into the line. Then I dropped on the rubber belt and I told myself, ask, ask before you faint, but a howl was the best I could do. It was a dog's howl, and I felt its dirty hair in my mouth. Juan Diego never howled, I was sure of that, and I felt bad about being a *gringo* among the Virgin's children. I'd seen enough fucked up foreigners here, drunk or stoned and roaring as if they owned the place.

Mexicans stepped around me as I knelt and shuddered on the floor. Then Laura stepped in front of me so that her polished leather boots were right under my face.

Gasping, I looked up at her from her torn knee to her face. I was afraid that if I reached out to her I would fall on my face, on her boots. So I just inched my hand forward, slipped it up on her boot. I looked up at her face, and behind her Mexicans stepped off the conveyor belt and eased their way around us. Her face was blank, leaving me free to imagine her disgust.

"Say something," I said.

She hovered over me silently, then bent at the knees. I thought she would try to lift me, but instead she wrapped her arms around me, gathered me against her. Through her clothes I felt her real flesh, and she bled onto me through the rip in her jeans. Her real body and blood against me felt like the unspoken answer to an unspoken prayer, like she was the one who would gather me under her wings. Then she dropped to her knees beside me.

We shifted against each other, trying for an honest embrace, but I was aware of myself groveling on the Mexicans' floor, offending their sense of decorum.

"Your father hurt you?" she asked. "Is that what happened to you?"

I pulled away, repulsed. "My father? Are you talking about yourself?"

She pressed harder against me, and wouldn't pull back so that I could see her face. I relaxed against her. "Am I right?" I moaned. "Did your father burn your face?"

"Do you love me? Tell me that you love me."

I pried her arms apart and rolled away, grateful that the pilgrims ignored us both.

I rose slowly and unsteadily, and pressed the palm of my hand against my forehead.

"Stay with me," Laura said. "Just for a while."

"I can't," I said. "I have to get my kids."

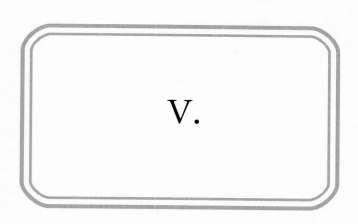

V.

17.

For all its 7200-foot altitude, Mexico City lies in a valley that you have to climb a winding highway to escape. No doubt to the displeasure of the Mazahuas on board my bus, who wore sweaters even in the heat and kept windows closed so that *el aire* wouldn't infect them with the toothaches or even paralysis that it carries, I got a window seat and slid the glass open. I looked out to the pine forest and then back down to the city, hidden for a time and then suddenly there, smoking in its pollution.

At the top of the rise lies Toluca, the highest city in Mexico, the city nearest Polo. I did partially close my window then against the greater altitude's chill. Night came before we reached Toluca, and to our left and high above us the permanent snowcap of the city's volcano, El Nevado de Toluca, shone in the dark like a giant study in contrast.

Our driver wasn't one of the real maniacs, but we still went faster than I wanted. I knew that after we left Toluca and its volcano, I'd start thinking about the agony I was headed into. The Virgin's dimly lit image glowed above the driver. She hadn't taught me what to say to Jane. She hadn't even told me what I wanted to say.

We passed a bus with *Sólo Dios Sabe Mi Destino* painted in cursive script on its bumper. Only God knows my—and here's a Spanish ambiguity—destination or destiny. The lights of

Toluca spread to receive us. The giant bronze mounted Zapata zipped past.

I was sitting on the wrong side of the aisle to see Polo's lights, which slant up the side of the mountain's base. Just as well. I was prepared to ride right past our mountain, to stay on the bus until the cleaning woman swept me off at the last stop in Guanajuato or Celaya. But when the driver stopped and called "Polotitlán," I grabbed my bag and got off.

The other Polo passengers carried their bundles quickly toward the row of cabs waiting to ferry travelers from the bus stop up into the village. The cabs, big blue Fords, shuttle back and forth from the crossroads up through Polo to its main square, which rests above the village like a partial roof on one of the mountain's few level spaces. But I wanted to travel alone, and waited. The black and brilliantly starred night was enormous. Polo mountain itself wore a rare snowcap, and I wished it would tip it for me, and welcome me home.

A cabdriver finished stuffing bundles into his trunk and slammed it closed. He wore a cowboy hat with a little tassel in back.

"*Vienes*?" he asked me, and his breath steamed in the cold. "There's room for one more."

"No, *gracias*," I said, and shuddered. No strength in numbers for me, I thought. Luckily, a car pulled up almost right away. It was nine o'clock, my driver informed me after I got in his car; I was lucky to get a ride at this hour, in this cold.

The asphalt pavement turned to brick as we entered Polo proper, and the jarring of the cab's tires made me sit up straight. This wide, ascending street, handsome during the day with its rows of shops, was quiet and dark. Even El Herradero, the best restaurant in town, site of Polo's only disco, gathering place for

Valparaíso's engineers, the place where I'd had my last restaurant meal with Jane, was closed. The donkeys were off the street. The dogs were gone. I was arriving in secret.

Past El Herradero the driver turned onto the level space and parked beside the plaza. I paid him and got out. The streetlights around the plaza stayed lit all night. Between them and the snowcap and the stars, even this moonless night now seemed unnaturally bright. The cold that stung my face and hands felt like the product of light. My Mexican adventure had wound up set on a frosty mountain.

Our house was two blocks away, off one of the side streets that ran onto the plaza. A thin-ribbed dog trotted out of an alley ahead of me, and together we passed a *pulquería*, a place that keeps its urinal on a wall right beside the bar, and where Mazahua men can afford to drink all day and all night. Almost every night a Mazahua passes out in a pool of his own vomit within fifty feet of the bar. They look like they fell from the sky and vomited on impact. The streets here off the plaza were paved with big, uneven stones, and I wondered how many of these men had fallen to their deaths on their collapse from pulque grace.

Tonight there were two such men. Their *gabanes* were twisted uncomfortably around them, and they did in fact look dead. The bony dog stopped to sniff and lick their puddles, then he wandered ahead, nose low to the ground. Should I straighten their *gabanes* to cover them? It was cold enough to freeze a man to death.

I laid down my bag, then rolled one man to free the back flap of his *gabán*. Luckily, he was light, and the *gabán* was a long one, so I could pull it almost down to his knees. The second man, though, was stockier, and wore one of those ridiculous short garments which, if he stood, would only reach his waist. I had to wrestle with his limp body to pull the whole thing off over his head, then spread its entire length over him. Now I'm a Mexican wrestler, I thought. Maybe I should approach Jane wearing a wrestler's mask. I could be the Blue Gringo. I got a little of the second man's vomit on my sleeve, and I wiped it off onto the wide-antlered deer that was stitched into his *gabán*.

The skinny dog was in front of our gate, sniffing and weakly digging. I glanced through a crack in the gate and saw that all the lights were off. May and Sammy would both be asleep by now; Jane could be too, or Valparaíso might be in there with her.

I shooed the jackal-dog away from the gate; then, just as I had done other times after forgetting my gate key, I piled up some loose paving stones, climbed them, and vaulted myself over with both hands to land with a clumsy thud seven feet below.

I approached the house through the scattered *magueyes* that filled the yard. A neighbor had once shown me how to scrape the pulque from them. Sammy's soccer ball was lodged under one; I kicked it free, then picked the ball up, so it could serve as a peace offering or a weapon.

The house was perfectly quiet. I paced in front of the door, squeezing the ball and trying to control my breathing, the churning in my stomach. What would I say to her, to him. I'm back, get out. Not you, him. Yes, you, Carlos Valparaíso. Yes, you, *patrón* motherfucker.

I looked up at the snowcap and the stars, promised Guadalupe I would make her a *milagro* if she would only tell me what to say.

But my bang at the door went unanswered; my call of Jane's name bounced off the door and through the *magueyes* and out into the street where the jackal-dog might have heard.

I found the spare house key hidden under the same rock where we always kept it and let myself in.

The furniture was there; the dishes and the brandy, too. But the children's clothes were gone, even their bilingual books, their toothbrushes. Only a few disorders were left behind. A few of Jane's dresses, pants and blouses from our days in Austin, still hung in the closet.

My things, besides the odd shirt or pair of pants lying on the closet floor, were all stored in my darkroom, a cinder-block room just outside the house. The light inside it worked, and showed me that my pictures of Jane and Sammy and May were still on the walls, and that my cameras sat forgotten in a wooden box.

The ladder I'd once used to bring down Sammy's soccer ball from the roof rested flat against the side of the house. I took some brandy and my old Nikon, then climbed it. This is the coldest I've ever felt here, I thought. It must be fifteen degrees. I drank from the bottle, looked down off the mountain to the Valparaíso hacienda's lights, and tried to feel the burn of the brandy. The camera lay beside me. I shook violently, then calmed when I drank.

I lay on my back and picked up my camera. I looked into its viewfinder and my hands shaking in the cold made the stars wobble. It looked like an earthquake in heaven, as if the walls of the temple were once again rent, and the saints now rose from the dead and walked from star to star.

I had once asked my father what lay beyond the universe. If it has an edge, then what's on the other side? We had talked one long night in Austin when Jane didn't come home. I addressed my question to the empty Texas sky and felt his answer—*nada,* my son—as a physical poke into my brain. Then I went out to buy my little .25.

Now I asked him again. Father, what's on the other side? This time he didn't poke me. Instead he showed what he had seen. The barn door open, the shafts of light, the motes of hay, the old man hanging perfectly still from the ceiling, drastically bent at the neck. Did my father see his father's face? I hoped not. I hoped he only saw his back, and that my father was not brave or perverse enough to walk around for a glimpse of the distorted face. I hoped it was only my imagination, fed by the horror films of my boyhood, that turned the body and presented its bloated face for my inspection.

My hands stopped shaking. I stopped shivering. The cold no longer tore at me. I was beyond cold now.

I set the camera down and took note of my own calm. I wonder if they'll find me up here, I thought. No one will think to look on the roof. Not until they see birds circling down to eat me….Sammy and May must not see me like that. Not partially eaten by the *buitres*. That's what my father was saying.

All right, I said, and struggled to sit up. I felt spastic and weak, and sure enough was almost dead. I crawled to the ladder, then slid clumsily down.

18.

Jane hadn't taken our blankets to the hacienda, of course, and I piled them on top of me after I lay down on our couch.

I was thinking about Valparaíso more than Jane or the kids. After we'd been in Mexico two months, he invited Jane and me to a party at his house in Mexico City. Jane was nervous when I told her. "What am I going to wear?" she asked. I answered, "Let's go shopping." For once I had some money in my pocket, and never felt more jaunty. We drove down to a Polanco dress shop, where I hoped that my gasp at the first price tag I saw went unnoticed.

But as I watched Jane slip in and out of the various dresses, I started to feel fine. She did, too, and actually became more beautiful as the afternoon passed. When the saleswoman complimented the match between a fabric whose color I couldn't name and Jane's flesh, I thought moving to Mexico was the best thing we had ever done. Six months before I had been driving a delivery truck and working part-time in a camera store, and we had lurched from one payday to the next.

"What do you think?" Jane asked as she slipped on one tight, short dress after another. I felt speechless at the sight of her, but managed to grunt some kind of approval every time. When we agreed on the most starkly black one, my sense that all was well and getting better was confirmed.

Jane left the dress for alterations, and two weeks later, the afternoon of the party, we went together to pick it up. And to pay, which I did with a more or less sincere smile.

She hung the dress in the closet of our hotel room without modeling it for me. I was disappointed until she lay down beside me, and we napped with our legs entangled.

That night, when Jane and I stepped through the massive front door of Valparaíso's city house, he greeted us, and reflexively narrowed his eyes with desire at the way her dark flesh glowed in the light of the torch he'd planted by the doorway. I winced, but his stare softened almost immediately, and he put his hand on my shoulder as he led us toward the music and mezcal. When he whispered to me "what a beautiful wife you have," it was in the tone of a frank and uncomplicated admirer.

Jane was quiet the first hour of the party, and trailed a step behind Valparaíso and me. I was a little giddy with his asking who I thought would win the Super Bowl, and if the tropical band playing in the courtyard was loud enough. I let Valparaíso pull me away from Jane, and introduce me to Mexican movie actresses I'd never heard of, dangerously beautiful idiots. One looked at my scarred cheek and asked if I was a *gringo* bullfighter. Valparaíso answered "No, he was a gold medal javelin catcher in the Olympics," which wasn't exactly a compliment. But our laughing together at the actress' grave acknowledgement of this interesting fact gave the *patrón* and me something in common.

After her second mezcal, Jane stood taller, and laughed gratifyingly hard when I started making fun of the rich peoples' clothes. That night I said what the hell, and had my first drinks since the shooting. On the patio we danced inside a grove of burning torches, and she did her dance thing, in which she was absolutely more graceful and practiced than me, but still made me feel like I knew how to dance a rumba, a step she taught me as she went along. She danced just once with Valparaíso; his blond hair contrasted powerfully with her dark. "She's something," he said when he brought her back to me. "Where she'd learn to dance like that?"

"I taught her," I said, and we all three laughed.

Back in the hotel at 4 A.M., Jane and I made love with her dress still on. I just pushed it above her waist. "I saw how those women were looking at you," she whispered as she rocked beneath me, and bit my shoulder and neck.

A few months later, Valparaíso grilled for us at the hacienda. While he stood over the kitchen fire, brushing marinade onto the rabbits, Jane, who was showing with Sammy by then, Ellen, and Angela, *la señora* Valparaíso, went to look at some room Angela was redecorating. Valparaíso downed tequilas as he cooked. It was the first time I'd seen him drink. He looked older than he had at the party, and nearly as thin as my father, who in my imagination, at least, had become nearly emaciated.

He was drinking faster than I could keep up. But soon I'd had too much tequila myself and started babbling about the bulls. How I went to the Plaza Mexico every Sunday I could. How breeding fighting bulls was an exalted calling, a kind of priesthood. How bull breeders were keeping an ancient and otherwise extinct breed of animal alive. They were in the business of arresting time, just like a photographer, only more concretely so. Working with living animals, they recaptured lost, mythological time.

Valparaíso laughed. "It's a way of making a little money," he said. Then he casually added, "Oh, it gives a little prestige, *qué me vale madre*. I don't give a fuck about prestige. Do you?"

I avoided that ridiculous question by pointing at the biggest of all the bull heads on the wall behind him. The plaque said it had been voted the greatest bull of the '66 season in Mexico City.

"Your family already owned the ranch by then, right? What was it like to see an animal like that come into the ring and know it would never have been born without you?"

"Tiburón?" Valparaíso answered, looking up at the *toro's* stuffed head. "That bull was an accident, and our lucky break. We're industrialists, Daniel. We like our baseball, but we didn't give a good goddamn about bulls." His speech did suddenly slur, and he drifted word by word into Spanish. "You know, a fighting bull is bred more carefully than a thoroughbred horse, *verdad*? But we mixed that blood like we were Indian bartenders, like we had no idea how to make a martini. If it had hooves and a cock, we bred it to our cows. My father was crazy, really. Those animals were a huge investment, but it was like he wanted to turn them into mongrels. We wanted to sell, but the ranch was this close to becoming a laughingstock. Our animals were getting booed and spat on. Then this Tiburon did bring the past back to life, just like you said. He tore up the ring in Mexico City. He knocked over horses. He charged in a straight line as long as the bastard *torero* could hold up his little red rag, then he died as if struck by lightning. I did like that animal, I have to admit.

"The next day some poor *inocente* wants to buy our bulls. 'You take him,' my father said to me. We canceled a few fights we had scheduled, so nobody would see what kind of oxen we were really producing. Then I took the idiot's balls in my hand like this. At first it made him feel good. He thought like you, Daniel. *Su Majestad, el pinche toro. qué majestoso.* Then I started to squeeze. 'Breeding fighting bulls takes us all the way back to

Crete.' Is that what you said? I should have tried that one. But he paid top dollar anyway, and carted the animals off. They've never been back in the Plaza México."

Valparaíso turned the rabbits on the grill and closed his eyes as if to savor this memory. As he lifted the meat from the fire, he looked sober.

I should be disgusted, I thought as I looked up at the remains of Tiburón. These bulls mattered; they had standing in the world. Their bloodlines were well established. They weren't supposed to drift fatherless like I had. I should have made Valparaíso feel a little shame, and at least stop boasting about being such a criminally irresponsible asshole. But my connection to the world he was describing was too weak to let me feel anything so real as outrage.

Ellen, Jane and Angela came back into the dining room. They stopped and Angela caressed Jane's rounding stomach.

Valparaíso served us. He and I sat at each end of the table. He toasted Jane and me and our baby. For the first time ever, Angela and I talked. She seemed terribly bland, asking how I liked Mexico, how I liked teaching. Maybe she already knew that her husband was about to send her away. I remembered the party in Mexico City, and wondered why she hadn't been there.

Valparaíso talked too loudly to Jane, so that I listened to him more than Angela. After a few minutes of eating and more drinking, Valparaíso made fun of his wife for not being able to conceive children as readily as Jane. "I'm just joking," he said when the rest of us grew quiet. "Angela knows I'm only kidding." But I saw her squeeze her linen napkin.

Maybe you should have a little more respect for breeding, I wanted to say to him, but didn't. I lost my appetite, and got Jane out of the house as fast as I could. "What was that all about?" she asked in the car. She sat far away from me, and seemed upset. I was driving carefully in the dark, aware I'd had plenty to drink, and that a cow or burro might be standing sideways in the road so I wouldn't even see my headlights glint off their eyes.

"Beats me," I answered. "I guess he drank too much."

"That's not what I meant."

"What then?"

"Why'd we have to leave so early? We hardly ever go out, and when we do, we don't stay."

I blinked in surprise. "I just couldn't take him. He was picking on his wife. And he spent the whole night bragging about how he'd ruined his bulls, then tricked somebody into buying them."

"Can you just drop it with the bulls? I really don't understand why you go on and on about them."

I didn't think that I did go on about them. I usually kept my bull lore to myself. But I didn't answer her, and we rode back in slowly mounting tension.

"I'm sorry," I said when we parked in front of our house. It was dark. The maid had taken May home to sleep with her. "We'll do something this weekend."

"He's not really so bad," Jane answered. "He just shouldn't drink."

19.

I woke covered in heavy blankets and sat up shuddering. I felt pushed to my feet by the same idea I'd gone to sleep with; I would have to go to the hacienda.

I found coffee in the kitchen cabinet, the same can of CafeMex I'd brought on my last shopping trip, and when the coffee pot began to percolate with reassuring gulps, I could stand still and look out to our view of the valley.

The coffee's strong smell made the emptiness of the house less maddening. While it brewed, I went to the living room window. January is brilliant on the Mexican highlands, and rich blue sky fell as tangible as rain all around my house. The hacienda was maybe three miles away, down on the plain. A thick line of trees, cottonwood, maybe, hid the hacienda from view, but the red radio tower Valparaíso used to communicate with his world-wide empire reached high above the treetops. I was relieved to feel anger rather than terror.

"Fuck you, Valparaíso," I said as if speaking to someone in the next room. In the kitchen I took one of the thick glazed coffee cups Jane and I had driven in the rain one Saturday to buy at a nearby convent, and smashed it against the tile floor. The cup was so well made that it didn't splinter; with a dull, ugly sound it broke into three big pieces. The coffee finished percolating, but I made myself stop trembling before I reached for another cup. I wanted to feel calm before I went to the hacienda, to make myself believe that, despite the emptiness of the house which Valparaíso had rented to me, I was myself authentic, that I carried weight, that the blue of his sky wouldn't pour right through me.

I didn't want to feel like a man who broke coffee cups before breakfast, and so I was glad to find eggs, cheese, and small, oblong Roma tomatoes in the refrigerator. There was even some milk, and for a moment I felt giddy, as if I should make enough eggs for everyone. But the milk was spoiled. I washed its chunks down the sink.

A red plastic bucket flew over the gate. It bounced in our rough yard as the round, close-cropped head of the little boy who had thrown it appeared over the fence. He struggled to the top of the fence; his small, worn *gabán* bunched around him. Then he dangled from the top of the fence with both hands, his feet some four feet over the ground. I saw him look down and then back up to where his small hands clutched the top, and I wondered if he'd hurt himself in a previous jump, and was now afraid to let go.

His family lived just down the street, and every morning his mother sent him to fetch a few buckets of water from our garden hose for their house. May simply called him and his family *los pobres*.

The boy dropped suddenly; I couldn't tell if he had lost his grip or worked up his nerve, and his *gabán* puffed from the air rushing up into it. He rolled stiffly, surprisingly awkward for a child. Like a little old man he got up, then wiped his palms on his *gabán* and carried the bucket toward our hose, just below the kitchen window. The hands of the children here were already dry and hard. These kids aged right before your eyes, as if they had been born into an already told story and had to hurry to catch up to its end.

I opened the window as he turned on the water.

"Have you seen my family?" I asked.

He didn't flinch. Already a stoic, he just looked worried at the sight of me leaning through the window. He was tiny, really, much shorter and harder looking than May, with his hair cut short against lice.

"I've been away," I said, because an explanation seemed needed. "Have you seen my little girl?"

The first jet of water bounced off the bucket bottom and sprinkled the edge of his *gabán*. He looked down at the water, but didn't step away.

I resisted the urge to ask his age or name. I used to know both.

"Did they go with *el patrón*?" I asked.

The boy turned off the water, then placed both small hands on the bucket's plastic handle. He had to spread his legs to lift the bucket.

"How long ago?"

"Last Sunday," he answered, looking up at me again. "I was here for the water, and then we went to the cemetery."

I said, "Do you want something to eat?" but he turned and began staggering toward the gate. He probably had to choose between making extra trips and wetting himself in the cold. Water sloshed onto his molded plastic shoes, shoes May's biggest doll might wear.

He set the bucket down to open the door inside the gate, then let himself out. He left the door open so that when he came back he wouldn't have to climb and drop. My eggs were getting cold.

Valparaíso's radio antenna now looked like the distant tower of some boy's adventure book. I poured the last of the coffee and sipped it while standing at the sink, resolutely not picturing the armed men at the hacienda gate, nor the slight sneer with which Valparaíso would assure me that Jane was free to do as she pleased. I didn't picture Jane at all. There was a blank in my imagination between Sammy and May.

The gate door swung open and the little boy stepped in with the empty bucket. But now he meant nothing to me. I thought of Laura. Why hadn't I asked her to come with me?

I set the cup down carelessly on the sink's edge. It fell off and broke; hot coffee splashed over my socks. Now the whole gate swung open. The little boy looked back over his shoulder as he turned on the water, and Jane drove inside.

I felt the familiar jolt of the mixing of epochs as her white VW Rabbit with its Industrias Polotitlán logo on both doors zipped through the opening in the adobe walls and stopped in a little clearing in the first line of *magueyes*. Jane always parked there where the plants' needle tips almost scratched the windshield, and I had taken pictures of her car stationed just so. Volkswagen with Cactus. Cactus with Volkswagen.

I didn't move out of the window. Jane sat in the car a moment, looking down into her lap. When she got out of the car, wearing severe black pants and sweater, she looked distracted, and glanced around without seeming to see. The little boy could have been a cactus. She'd cut off practically all her hair.

He looked up as she went by. Jane had the erect, and even somehow towering posture that dance gave her, and he would have had to look straight up to see her tightly coiled hair, or the big hoop earrings I'd never seen before.

I wished she would stop walking and look up to the kitchen window. I would wave casually, and she would be confused. She would think that I had both kids down for naps.

When the door opened, I called her name so she wouldn't scream when she saw me. She was quiet, and the door didn't close.

"How about some eggs?" I said.

Still the door didn't click closed, but after a moment I heard her boots tapping down the hall, toward me, and turned to face her.

Her earrings waved as she stopped in the kitchen doorway.

"I thought I'd never see you again," she said. "I thought you would just go away."

I paused, and finally answered, "I suppose that made you happy."

"Don't feel sorry for yourself around me," she answered. "Really, it's your self-pity that I just can't stand."

She brushed at her hair, trying to remind herself what its length now was, then glanced at me. She looked strange to me. I wasn't sure if she was still beautiful.

"Why did you cut your hair?" I asked. "Where'd you get those hula-hoop earrings?"

"I bought them in Mexico City. Right after I cut my hair. What are you doing here?"

"I came to see May and Sammy. And you. I have to talk to you."

We paused. Jane glanced away from me nervously, as if something, maybe her sexless hair, had weakened her. I felt myself buzz with a strength that felt completely new, as if had just been released by my exhaustion.

"Ellen told me about her affair with Valparaíso," I said. "That's why we're getting a divorce, isn't it? You knew about the affair. But you're the beautiful one. You're the one who deserves the big score."

Jane flinched as if I'd just said the most outrageous words she'd ever heard. It was a new expression for her.

"Answer me. Isn't that why you're breaking us up? Because you knew that dull fucking Ellen had done so well. And now it's your turn. Isn't it?"

She seemed about to answer, but the words caught in her mouth. Her eyes glazed over. Her whole face glazed over, and she pressed both hands down into her pad of wiry hair. I'd never seen her so low. This was a first-round knockout, and I didn't understand.

"The money's not that important," she said, then looked me in the face. I came at her in lunges, banged her against the wall, seized her biceps in my fingers that I wished could draw blood.

"Don't lie to me anymore," I said, almost gurgling. "I am so fucking sick of your lies."

The inside of my head throbbed like it had when I fainted, and holding her arms I lifted her off the floor, as if she were my daughter, not my wife. But I didn't slam her against the wall, or drop her and bust her in the face. I set her down awkwardly then stamped back a few steps. "I want Sammy and May," I said. "I'm going to pack their bags and take them home."

"I had to do it," she said, her broken voice nearly a hiccup. "We were just too pathetic together. Sammy and May deserve more than us."

"When did you start with him?" I shouted, feeling the echo of the old explosion again in my head. The pain was terrible, I wished none of us had ever been born, but I didn't want her to see me in any more pain.

I grabbed her arm and dragged her into the middle of the living room and with both hands pushed and pulled her in a circle around me in a sort of Frankenstein *pas de deux.*

"Wasn't this house enough?" I let go of her and she stumbled away. Then I picked up one of the leather-backed chairs from the table. I held it over my head, then threw it as hard as I could on the floor. "How much of a house do you need?"

Her old elegance came back as she straightened herself. "You fucking simpleton," she said evenly. "I just couldn't stand to look at your face anymore. Don't you get it?"

I slapped her with the back of my hand, hard enough to half-turn her around. My knuckles left white blotches on her creamy dark skin.

She sobbed. Snot hung from her nose and her face collapsed in on itself.

I felt transformed into the creature I never thought I would be. And that creature was completely hollow, like the bones of my hawk. I'm sorry, I wanted to say. Forgive me. But this creature had no right to talk.

Jane was quiet on the short drive to the hacienda. She wore oversized dark glasses and drove with one hand, using the other to shift gears and occasionally rub at her hair. When we approached the entrance to the hacienda, I finally spoke. "Don't turn yet. Drive a little farther."

She shifted gears and kept going.

"I understand what you meant," I said, then turned to look at her. "I turned my face, I turned myself, into a permanent memorial to the time you done me wrong. And every time you looked at me, you had to be reminded. Who would want to live like that?"

Jane nodded. "It's not that simple," she said.

"I'm sorry that I hit you. That's a ridiculous thing to say, of course. Words just aren't enough."

"That's right. Sometimes you have to blow the side of your head off to get your message out."

"Sometimes you really do."

The armed guards were impassive as we pulled up to the hacienda's looming metal gate. "Are you afraid of them?" I asked.

"Always," she murmured.

One guard bent to look into the car as if he were a customs officer ready to ask for a bribe. As if he didn't recognize me at all, and wondered who *el patrón*'s new woman was bringing to the big house. One of the guards, maybe this same small, mustachioed man, had shot a poacher behind these walls just a few months ago. The dead man was a father to one of our students, and people said that he had showed Don Carlos no respect at all, to break onto his grounds and steal his crops—his prized hydroponic plants at that—while his own children studied free-of-charge at the *patrón*'s school.

"*Está bien*," Jane said to the other guard, but the first man stepped into the guard stand and began talking on the phone.

"Why are they calling?" I asked. "You already told them we were coming."

"Maybe they think you're going to kill him," she said. "The funny thing is, you could. You're so good with guns."

I was pretty sure she was mocking me for failing to kill myself, and for fainting during Sammy's birth, for that matter.

The guard nearest her waved us on, and we passed through the gates and onto the long caliche road. A light white dust rose behind us. We drove through Valparaíso's experimental gardens, trees he had imported from all around the world, and the trees and plants he raised in bags of water. As ignorant as I am of botany, the trees had seemed vaguely intimidating back when I used to jog around his grounds.

Jane turned on her radio, and picked up a salsa station from Toluca.

No armed guards met us when Jane parked on the cobblestones in front of the hacienda. Jane walked in front of me. After she had stepped through the big wooden door, always open from dawn to sundown, I followed, pausing for a moment to remember how I used to admire the door's worm holes and the thickness of its wood. Jane had disappeared into the house by the time I entered the front room. There I stopped to look at the framed but informal portrait I had shot of Carlos and his father. The jowly old man sat at the table beside the pool, and Carlos stood behind him, hands planted firmly on his father's shoulders. With the thin man standing behind the heavy one, they had a sort of pyramid shape with the father at the base, and the son on top. Carlos' thin-lipped mouth was the altar where the sacrifices would be offered.

I went through another empty room. There weren't any servants around. Then I heard the cries of my children, and some splashing in the pool. I stepped into the tinted greenhouse light of the pool room. May stood in water up to her shoulders, her back toward me. Sammy clung to the wall with one hand, and reached out to May with the other.

"*Ven*," she said, and Sammy jumped toward her and reached her back. He wrapped both arms around her neck.

Jane stood near them, at the water's edge. When she saw that I'd come inside, she said, "*Mira. Mira quien está aquí.*"

"Daddy!" May cried. She let go of Sammy and his head slipped under the water. But he still had his arms around her, and he pulled himself back up.

"Careful, May," I said as I walked toward them. "Don't drown your brother."

She carried Sammy over to the water's edge. "Let go," she said. Then Sammy called me too. They pulled themselves out of the water at almost the same time, and came running toward me. I hurried toward them, afraid they'd slip on the tiles, then dropped to my knees as first May, then Sammy ran against me. I scooped them up and stood holding one in each arm, and water ran through the clothes that Laura had given me. May's long hair drenched my face, and Sammy dug one foot into my pants pocket and started to climb me.

When I had imagined this scene, I'd seen us laughing hysterically. But now we were all three deathly quiet, except for the occasional grunt they made as they wriggled to get a more secure hold. I finally lowered them and myself to sit on the damp tiles. With their feet on the ground, they pushed against me so hard that I was forced flat on my back, then they burrowed down into me as if they were two sopping moles. I let them try to dig through my chest, to bury themselves inside.

When I opened my eyes, Jane stood over us, eyes wide, as if she hadn't expected this scene.

Valparaíso arrived while I lay beside his pool. He dressed the same for work as for golf. In fact, he often got up at 4 A.M. to play nine holes in his backyard. His knit shirt, snug against his chest and arms, showed that although he was nearly as thin as me, he had better muscle tone.

"Want to dry off?" he asked blandly. "Humberto, get Daniel a towel."

I wasn't sure what I felt, but it was neither the fear nor the anger I had expected. I felt on stage, rather, and that despite the reality of my children, knowing my lines was the only thing that mattered. And of course, I didn't know what to say. I didn't feel as humiliated as I had on the basilica plaza, though.

"It's good you came," Valparaíso said. "Your children ask about you often. Jane does too, for that matter."

"I'll be leaving, just as soon as Sammy and May get packed."

"They're not going anywhere," Jane said. Then she said to the children, "Let's go to your room."

"Stay the night," Valparaíso said. "Your old room is open."

"No, thanks," I answered.

"Let me show you something," he said. He turned and without looking back walked toward the outer door. I hesitated, and glanced back to Jane. The kids had run on ahead and she stared right through me. I didn't know if it was her anger and remorse that I felt, or simply my own. She turned and walked away.

I set out after Valparaíso and wondered if he had a new mounted bull's head, maybe one killed by Belmonte.

Back out in his cobblestone parking lot I saw only his Mercedes and the usual bodyguards, well-fed, bored-looking men, and a couple of his scrawny uniformed guards, carbines slung over their shoulders.

Out on the stones Valparaíso turned suddenly, stared into my eyes and clamped a hand onto my shoulder. "You used to work for me," he said, "and you did a good job. So I'll let you walk away. But never come here again without an invitation."

"Sammy and May—" I said, but he cut me off.

"You have the phone number. Call Jane when you want to make an appointment."

We stood frozen a second. I waited for the impulse to say fuck you to pass, and for my body to stop trembling under his hand. When it wouldn't I reached up and pried his hand off.

"I'm taking my kids," I said, not knowing where these words came from.

Valparaíso pressed his thin lips together, then eased his fore-arm out of my hand and stepped away.

"It's my right," I said. *Mi derecho.*

I had just a glimpse of the rifle butt coming into my face, just above my eyes. Before I could move I was already falling back, thudding against the cobblestones. The guard stood above me, his rifle at port arms. He looked at Valparaíso.

"*Patrón?*" he said quietly.

My forehead burned as if a torch were pressed against it. I thought, I have to get up, but I could only stir feebly, like an overturned beetle. The other men stepped forward, and Valparaíso leaned over me. He's going to spit on me, I thought.

"Don't make trouble, Daniel," he said.

"Jane," I murmured, and felt I had no control over my mouth, my tongue, any workings of my head. I managed to roll up on an elbow. My head began to pound and the stones moved away from me, then back again.

I was shaky on my feet. "Eleazar will give you a ride to the bus stop," Valparaíso said.

I lifted my hand and meant to swing it. I hoped a guard would shoot me properly, and that one day my children would know I had died for them. But the cobblestones shifted again, moving Valparaíso out of my reach, and I fell without any help from his men.

20.

At the crossroads where Valparaíso's men dumped me, I let the first few buses pass. I felt buried alive; the rifle butt had driven me deep inside my skin. It was a cold day, and so hazy that I could not see the jagged ridges of El Nevado de Toluca, only forty miles away.

When a half-full Flecha Roja pulled up, I finally commanded my body to move, and mentally supervised my every step up into the bus and then to my seat. I rode with the window closed, but didn't notice the lack of air. I could only feel the welt the rifle butt had left, a sort of rubbery blister across my forehead.

The ride into the capital seemed both to take forever, and to not happen at all. Once in Mexico City I floated off the bus, my head just now starting to throb. I realized that my hearing was bad, but I was too dazed to worry.

I rode the subway to the stop nearest Pierre's, but when I walked up out of the Insurgentes station into its bowl-shaped plaza, the roundness of the space confused me. I saw streets, cars, and people, floating like myself in every direction. I took a few steps one way then another, trying to remember the way to Río Ganges, then gave up and wandered back to the bowl's center. When I touched any part of my head, my fingers seemed far away, as if I were touching the thought balloon of a comic book character.

Even if I had known which way to go, Pierre's house was a good fifteen blocks away. It might as well have been in Texas.

The benches around the plaza were all filled, so I looked for a clearing somewhere on the concrete where I could stretch out, just for a minute. But Insurgentes is a busy stop, and people bustled everywhere, thronging in and out of the shops and *taquerías* that ring the station. I would have to lie down right there where I stood. My head gave a series of throbs, as if trying to force me down. I sank to one knee, and put my hands on the pavement, testing it for comfort, and the sleep that I felt coming on seemed to rise up from inside me like a puff of smoke. No, not a puff. A stream of smoke. But stream didn't seem like the right word.

I heard my name, but paid the voice no mind until I felt the stab of long fingernails in my shoulder.

"Daniel," Jorge sang out, pulling me to my feet. "*Qué haces?*"

I was dimly happy to see his eyes and the skin beneath his light facial powder, and floated toward him.

"*Por Dios,*" he said as he slid a hand onto each of my shoulders and looked wide-eyed into my forehead. "What happened to you, baby? You look like a space alien."

He seemed to speak emphatically, but I could scarcely hear him, and my tongue felt too heavy to move. Some parts of my body felt sketchy, and others as if made of granite.

"I can't talk," I managed to say. "I need to sleep."

"No, *señor,*" Jorge said, and he shook me by the shoulders. "You've hurt your head, only God knows how. You must not go to sleep. We have to walk."

He got beside me, thrust a shoulder into my side, and wrapped an arm around me. Then he turned us in a circle, found the direction he wanted, and marched us through the pressing crowd.

As we entered the Zona Rosa, I felt light against his shoulder, but I knew this was an illusion, that he must be struggling beneath my weight as we passed the Benetton store and the Calvin Klein. What was this commerce doing in Mexico City? What had happened to the old temples? What had happened to the lake the city was built over? To the water itself? The city made no sense to me, and I told Jorge so as we stumbled past El Instituto Bilingüe.

He only responded, "You're not as light as you look, *gringo flaco.*"

We drifted past the French bookstore and the hotels along Reforma, and then we stood at the edge of the great avenue itself, cars streaming by in a kind of river. That explained the water. The lake had become a river of cars. The streets where Jorge and I lived were named for rivers, after all. We lived on the purifying pavement of Río Ganges.

"It'll be hell to get you across the traffic," Jorge said. "We're moving too slow."

I leaned more heavily against him, tried to take all the weight off my own feet. He stumbled, then pushed me back down. The María Isabel towered in front of us.

"I used to know somebody who lived there," I told him. "The ugliest woman I ever saw. She wants to know if I love her."

"Laura the scar-face?" he asked. "She came by looking for you last night, and stayed for dinner. Follow me."

He led me a long block south toward the Ángel statue. The avenue narrowed there and was easier to cross. I looked up at the golden angel as we passed under her. "The Angel of Victory" was her name, but here in Mexico which victory could they mean?

"She told us about you, about how crazy you were acting. We were all very worried."

We passed a big, glass-walled vegetarian restaurant. I could see the people inside eating.

"You must be crazy," Jorge said, "if you'd rather make love to her than to me."

I laughed, and thought I might be coming out of this spell, but a violent throbbing in my head almost knocked me down.

"*Cuidado*," Jorge hissed as together we reeled.

At the next corner an Indian boy played the accordion while his baby sister stood beside him holding an upturned straw hat for donations. The accordion was as big as the boy, and his concentration looked very severe as he pumped with his left hand and pushed the accordion buttons with his right. We stood beside them but I could only make out a few words as he sang, "*Me caí de la nube...*"

That's me, I thought. I fell out of a cloud, too.

"I can't hear," I said.

"Shut up, baby," Jorge answered.

We were on Río Nilo now. Pierre's would not be far.

"My God," Laura said after Jorge opened the narrow door and pushed me into the foyer, where she sat in Pierre's best chair. Her cello stood between her legs, its neck nearly pressed against her patchy right cheek. She opened her eyes wide at the sight of me, and I blinked back at her.

"*Dios mío*," Pierre echoed her. He sat behind the crumb-littered table on the sectional couch. A half-empty bottle of Sauza stood on the table between him and her. His tamped down white hair clung to his head and he looked groggy, as if

216

Laura had woken him on the couch when she carried her cello in.

"We're all together," I said, and felt loose in the knees.

"What happened? Your head looks broken," Laura said.

"He's trying to go to sleep," Jorge told them. "We can't let him."

"Take some tequila." Pierre gestured toward the bottle. "Sit down and listen to Laura. She knows Tavener, 'The Protecting Veil'. Such a dramatic monologue for the cello, and she plays with a beautiful emotion."

"Make some coffee," Laura said as she stood and leaned the cello against the table. I was sorry that my hearing was so weak, that I hadn't made out her music from the street. That dim hopeful light had returned to her eyes, which shone as she approached me and lay her fingertips across my forehead.

Her fingers hurt me and I turned away, then saw my reflection in the small mirror above the curved end of the couch. I pulled away from Laura and Jorge, then leaned forward to get nearer the mirror. I had to climb up and kneel on the couch's crumpled white sheet to see clearly in the dim light. My hair stood in all directions, but who would notice mere unruly hair when my forehead bulged as if some kind of visor had been implanted in my skull? I leaned closer and imagined I could make out the rifle butt's woodgrain. I felt the sofa give beside me, then Laura's face appeared in the mirror too. I looked at the scar across her forehead, and back at my welt. I expected her to say again that we were the perfect couple, and I spoke before she did.

"I don't know Tavener," I said. "Will you play something for me?"

217

"That's what I was practicing the other day when you took my picture."

"It's a song for the Virgin," Pierre said, his voice weak and distant. "For the veil she has laid over us all, to protect. Just as she saved me in the forests of Vietnam."

"Ah." There was too much in the world that I did not know, and now that I was losing my hearing, would never learn. I flopped onto the couch and wanted to sleep, but Jorge, Pierre and Laura tugged at me. When I wouldn't budge, and did feel almost gone, Jorge splashed a little hot coffee onto my neck. I jerked up and groaned.

"You left me no choice," Jorge said defensively, but no one criticized him for burning me.

"Take me to the hawk," I said. "I want to see my bird."

"We have had some interesting development with the hawk. With our paraclete," Pierre said. "But first you should see a doctor."

The three of them agreed among themselves and pulled me up. Laura led me toward the door.

"I know a clinic that stays open late," she said. "I'll take him."

She led me out to Reforma, then we turned and walked alongside the traffic toward the towers of el centro.

"Alone at last," I murmured.

She talked but I did not listen. I think she was telling me the story of her face. Why then, I didn't know. Maybe it was my disfigured head. I heard something about her father. His wealth, his women, his men, his cocaine, his persistent drinking and driving, his remorse.

It was dark now. A steady flow of car lights gleamed beside us. City lights reflected back down from the pollution. "Look," I said, pointing up at the filth. "The protecting veil." But now she did not seem to hear me. Maybe I was losing speech too.

I started to feel a little stronger and was able to walk without leaning on her, but still I followed her lead.

"We're almost there," she said into my face.

We got off Reforma and tramped in the direction of Plaza Garibaldi with its *mariachis*, tourists and whores.

I rubbed my arms. "I'm cold," I said.

Laura smiled. "You're going to be all right," she answered, and I could hear her pretty well. "Everything's going to be all right."

"I liked you better dead," I said.

My senses partially returned as we walked. The throbs came from inside my head rather than from far away, and when we reached Garibaldi Square I recognized some of the *mariachis'* songs. I couldn't enjoy them because of the pain, and I waved away the singers in their black spangled suits when they approached to see if we would pay for a tune. It wasn't hard to make them ignore us, given our looks.

But when the physical world, which just this morning had fallen away, began to return, my memory turned real again. When a frog-faced *mariachi* turned his thick *bajo sexto* guitar toward me, the bulky instrument seemed ready to batter me. I had to resist the urge to cover my face, and when I closed my eyes I saw the rifle butt coming at me in slow motion, and Valparaíso standing over me, and the blue sky above him. I saw Jane too, her earrings jangling against her neck as she sneered. But that was not right. She was not there when I fell.

As the *mariachis* bawled—surely a lover's lament—I shuddered in pain and fear. I saw the rifle butt again and my anus tightened, as if Valparaíso's guard was going to ram his barrel up my ass. I shook harder. Laura took my arm and said, "Come on. Let's keep moving."

I closed my eyes and felt a motion inside my gut again, but this time it didn't feel like smoke. It came up from the pit of my stomach like a creature of prey, and carried with it a picture of Jane with her snotty nose, and a white handprint on her face. The image made me wobble, and burn with humiliation.

"I have to go," I said, and pulled my arm free.

"You need help," Laura said. "It's just two more blocks."

"No," I said. "I don't need any help." The throbbing in my head met the beak in my gut and together they sent me groaning through the empty streets, the most dangerous *gringo* in Mexico City. The wanting to kill rose behind my eyes and pushed against my skull, and I started running as best I could back toward Pierre's. I heard my name, as if a woman were calling me from far away, *Dan, Dan, Dan,* but never looked back.

I made it to Pierre's house and let myself in, feeling like I was breaking apart, like the crack in my head was finally giving way and that the inside thing was finally coming out. I closed the door behind me so Laura couldn't get in, then climbed the stairs in absurd leaps and in my room pulled open a drawer and tossed out my underwear and t-shirts out until I found Pierre's pistol. But where was the clip? I had carefully hidden the clip.

I yanked a drawer out of the chest and turned it upside down. Books and coins and little skeleton figures poured out onto the floor, but no clip.

"What's happening?" I barely heard a voice behind me say.

The voice belonged to Richard, the bald Asian idiot whose one long lock hung uncombed to one side. "What happen to your fucking head, man?"

I turned away from him, opened another drawer and grasped at the clip. I stood holding the pistol in one hand, the clip in the other, and clumsily tried to jam the bullets into the butt of the gun. Richard's eyes widened when my weapon snapped together and I held the gun barrel-up in front of my face.

"Where's my hawk?" I said.

Richard waved his arms spastically. "With Pierre," he wailed and jumped back away from me. "In dining room."

I ran downstairs to start my killing with the bird, holding the pistol above my head like a machete.

But when I threw open the dining room door, the mouth of the parrot cage gaped open, and Pierre sat to one side, surrounded by mounds of newspapers, a book open on his lap, the hawk perched on his gloved forearm. A tiny, orange leather hood covered the bird's eyes. Pierre had gone to the falconry shop. The hawk had gotten outfitted.

Pierre's eyes gaped in amazement at either my entry or his proximity to the hawk. But they narrowed at the sight of the gun.

"That is my pistol, Daniel," he said, then glared across the room to where Jorge sat on the floor, leaning against a stack of newspapers.

"He made me give it to him," Jorge said to Pierre, who gestured with his arm, as if he might send the hawk flying into Jorge's face.

Then he stopped and slowly turned the hawk in my direction. "God forgive me," he said, "But I want to see this." He pulled off the hood, the hawk blinked once, and I lifted the gun.

Any of the three would have made a good target. Father, son or divine parakeet.

Pierre shook the stand, attempting to launch the hawk, who

finally lifted its wings as if to flap. Pierre threw the hood in my general direction. But the bird froze with its wings poised, as if it were the most highly trained hawk in the world. I looked at it, and pointed the gun toward its breast. The hawk looked through me.

I squeezed the trigger and as the head-splitting roar bounced off the walls of the small room, the bird flapped and burst forward with such speed that the motion itself hurt my eyes. I squeezed again, repeating the terrible sound as the hawk bowed its head and lifted and crooked its talons and focused its eyes without having to widen them. I felt the wind of it as the hawk was in my face and then behind me flying out of the dining room door.

Smoke curled up from the pistol as I lowered it. Jorge sprawled across the floor, hands over his ears, but Pierre was coming at me. I let the gun hang at my side.

"It flew through me," I said.

Richard screamed behind us.

Pierre bounded past me and I followed him up the stairs. He cried, "I see him," and raced past Richard who had collapsed, his one long lock pinned beneath his head. Pierre sprang down the hall and through the open door of my room, where the window stood open. We hit the window almost at once and looked out into the empty dirty sky.

"He's gone," I finally said, and turned toward Pierre who trembled in what I assumed was rage for his loss.

"He was my hawk," I said.

Then Pierre gathered himself, and I felt his stillness. I offered him the pistol, handle first. But he just shuffled past me back into the hall, where Richard gasped, "Fucking bird want to kill me."

Mascara streaked Jorge's cheeks. He turned away, avoiding my eyes, and closed the door behind him. I touched my face, through which the hawk had apparently flown. Finally, I had been on the winning end of a miracle.

I felt the hawk's wind pass through me again. It loosened something inside my head. I touched the short brown whiskers of my taut face. I touched the first of my gray hairs too. Underneath all that growth lay the forgotten sweetness of my flesh.

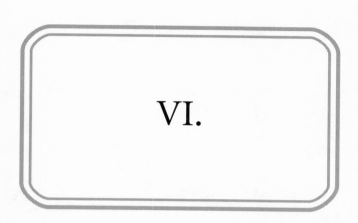

VI.

21.

_____

For days, the pain in my head woke me early. So I was lying in bed, but already wide awake when Jorge knocked at my door one morning.

"There's a woman here for you," he said from the hallway with exaggerated coolness.

Laura, I thought as I threw on her husband's clothes. The idea of her coming for me first thing in the morning excited me, even though my brain throbbed.

But it was only Ellen, slightly disheveled, and puffing on a cigarette. I hadn't been thinking clearly. Jorge would have said, Laura the scar-face.

Ellen smiled sadly, baring her big, gapped teeth as I came down the stairs.

"*Qué milagro,*" I said when I reached the floor. "What brings you here?"

"Do you still want a job?" she asked. "You can have mine." She squinted at me. "What happened to your head?"

I was sorry that I could not hear with perfect clarity, and that my feeling of having been knocked slightly off the world's rotation persisted. Distraction and deafness would be serious problems for any teacher. But I grabbed the big woman in a mechanical but sincere hug and said *sí, sí, claro qué sí.*

Six hours later, Ellen, having once again been disillusioned in love, was on a plane headed for a teaching job in Ascención—I doubted she would ever see Dilley, Texas again—and I was in her bland Instituto Bilingüe classroom, a copy of *Living English* pressed to my chest.

Her students, my students, glanced at my purple forehead as they entered, but they did not say anything. The class filled with eighteen souls, mostly young women with dark eyes, rouged cheeks and carefully sculpted hair. Bilingual secretaries in training. They were improving themselves and their prospects, and they would be diligent students.

My students looked at me with a mixture of idle curiosity and potential alarm. I might have looked a little crazy since my head was slightly swimming, and the clarity of my hearing rolled in and out. I could not control the motion inside my head no matter how hard I blinked.

I set the text down on the desk and scanned the room, careful now to control my blinking.

Be like the hawk, I told myself.

"You're probably wondering what happened to my head," I said in English. When they did not respond—this was the first day of intermediate *inglés*, after all—I tapped my forehead and repeated, "My head. What happened to my head?"

22.

The welt faded gradually, and my students stopped gawking at me. Still, on the day of my first paycheck I went into the Zona Rosa market to buy a Panama hat whose brim I could bend over the discoloration. I also bought one new set of clothes, khaki slacks and a long-sleeved *guayabera*. Black, so that it would not change colors in the grimy air.

After the hawk escaped, Pierre seemed to age. He had never been so very active, but he had seemed capable of getting off the couch and staying off if he really wanted to. His workers did finish welding his hawk paraclete sign, and Pierre had Jorge hang it over the front door, but Pierre never mentioned the brotherhood, or the Desert Fathers. One day Jorge ran inside excited, and told us he had seen the hawk land on the roof of a tall apartment building just down the street.

Slumped on his couch, Pierre lifted his hand. "Possibly," he sighed. "The hawk can live in the towers of great cities."

The pain in my head died down. It seemed to drip back into my body to lie and wait for its next chance. My hearing stabilized at a rather low level, and my ears generally either buzzed or rang, which made teaching tricky. And I could not totally shake the feeling that the rifle butt had knocked me loose from myself.

I happened by the little church across from Parque Sullivan during its Ash Wednesday service. On a whim I entered and

joined the short quiet line of urbanites who wanted their re-
minder of death.

The priest, pale-skinned and elegant, recognized me as a
gringo, and as he massaged the ash into my bruise he repeated
the formula in an English that echoed inside my ringing ears:
"Remember you are dust, and to dust you shall return."

I had known as much for years, and had even tried to speed
up the process, but hearing the words for the first time as an
adult somehow cheered me up. A moment later I sat on a park
bench and watched children scramble over the playground toys,
and felt that somebody had finally told me the truth.

Back in Pierre's house the Swedes gaped in astonishment at
my ashes. "You've become a religious fanatic," Anders said.

"Remember you are dust," I answered, and went up to my
room.

But I did not give anything up for Lent. The following Sunday
I knocked at Laura's door and nodded in satisfaction when she
answered. Her face was patchy and hard, but her eyes were alive.
Purple bougainvilleas framed her door and her face, and her
spiky gray hair looked like the latest do.

"I don't love you," I said. "But I'd like to go to the bullfights."

"What a creep you are," she said, almost without moving her
mouth. Then she went inside for her purse.

This was Manolo Martínez' retirement day, the day he would
cut his bullfighter's ponytail. Or unclip it, rather, since the fighters no longer grow their own topknots. Martínez never made it
big in Spain; he was gored almost to death in one of his first
fights there, so maybe he lost his nerve for Madrid and Sevilla
and Bilbao.

But in Mexico City nobody could touch him, not even his
splendid Mexican rival, Eloy Cavazos. Martínez' colossal arro-

gance sometimes made him lazy out in the provinces. I had seen him indifferent in Morelia, and eaten alive by the crowd-pleasing Cavazos, who loved to fight from his knees, and, as a swordsman, killed like cancer, as the saying goes. I don't know how honest Martínez was with the sword before his eighteen gorings began, but now he entered to kill with such reluctance, creeping up on the bull from the side, rather than throwing himself in over the horns, that I sometimes expected him to bring a peon out to finish the bull. Of course, if the afternoon had gone well, and he expected to be awarded a pair of ears or a tail, he would ease in between the horns and risk putting in half a sword. Otherwise he seemed determined to avoid that nineteenth wound.

But with his *muleta* he could give exactly what I wanted from the bullfight. He could make the bull move so slowly with a sweep of his right hand that he and the bull together seemed to open a hole in time, and let a shaft of eternity beam into the ring, and then we onlookers could see the motion behind the motion, the time behind the time. And in the Plaza México, the world's largest and ugliest bullring, Manolo Martínez was *el patrón*.

That should have offended me, I suppose.

It should have made me root for the bull, in good *gringo* fashion. But in the bullring my sense of values and decorum became inverted. I could tolerate arrogance only in a great bullfighter, and I did not pull for the underdog.

Sunday afternoon before any *corrida* is a great time outside the Plaza México—the city never seems more focused and alive—but on this momentous day the streets outside the massive concrete bowl absolutely roiled with ticket scalpers and taco sellers, and the vendors with their books on bullfight history and their racks of children's bullfight costumes all shouted with unusual vigor. The magic name Ma No Lo echoed from the streetside cantinas. Children sold silk reproductions of the fight poster. The Grandiose Farewell of Manolo Martínez. But I could not enjoy the excitement.

I wished that my hearing would come back, and that I felt more grounded inside my body. That I had my sense of myself back, a better, more informed self than the one I had before would be helpful.

"Do you want something?" Laura asked.

"I want to want something," I answered, then put my hand to her forehead and traced its lumpy scar. I ran the back of my hand across the brownish patch on her cheek. She narrowed her eyes and I dropped my hand.

"I'm going to buy a souvenir for my kids."

On our last trip to the Plaza México I had bought May a hat, suit of lights, cape, and plastic sword, which she took to her bed three nights in a row. That day Martínez was carried out of the ring on the shoulders of the exultant crowd, a bull's tail in his hand. Now I looked at a pair of *banderillas*, to complete May's collection. But they were not made of plastic. They were real sticks with the real metal harpoon tips which the *banderilleros* sink into the bull's humped back. The sharp points were topped with cork plugs, but if you pulled them off, the sticks could poke out an eye.

"I'll get these for myself," I said, and my own voice seemed distant and caught up in the general echoing. I would hang them on some wall, somewhere.

I made a little show of pushing Laura's money away and pulling out my own. "I've got a job," I said. Then I carried the *banderillas* inside the arena, trying to enjoy the jostling of the crowd as Laura and I wedged inside.

We picked our way down into her wonderful seats, seats I would never have bought for myself, just ten rows up from the arena's surrounding wall.

"What are you going to do with these things," Laura said, holding the *banderillas* after we sat. "Roast wieners?"

That made me laugh, but the sound felt dirty in my mouth, as if I were breathing in too much bad air. Remembering that I was dust, that I was pollution, was not enough.

"I'm glad you turned up," Laura said. "I've been thinking about going back to Chicago. To see my father. But not before this fight."

I had missed her bitterness, and how her insistence on my death had made me feel alive. Then the big clock atop the plaza's parapet showed 4 P.M., and the crowd's great and soulful *olé* shook me. I had always counted off the last minutes so that I could join in the cry, but I had missed it this time.

The fighters paraded in with their usual pomp. The stocky Manolo looked almost absurd in his tight suit of lights. He was too arrogant to worry about his weight, but his scowl defied you to laugh at his middle-aged gut. In a fight I saw in San Luis Potosí, he received that eighteenth *cogida*, a horn in the left side of his belly, and had to be carried out in the arms of his *peones*. He was too old and fat to bounce back the way he used to, and I had wondered if that would be his last fight. But he'd come back strong.

I used to wish I could photograph Manolo nude and use his bulging body as a backdrop for the scars that must line his thighs, his knees, his chest, his belly. I wanted to show that photograph to the Frida-loving bullfight haters I had left back in Austin. But today I felt far from my camera.

Manolo got off to a slow start. His first fight did not happen in slow motion. It did not really happen at all. His bull would not charge, neither fast nor slow, and so he finally killed it in terrible, almost cowardly form, attacking from the side and puncturing its lung.

But the crowd was there to cheer him, and the people required Manolo to walk around the ring twice while they rained flowers and hats and wineskins on him, instead of boos and dismissive whistles.

"It's a career achievement award," I said, but Laura was too busy applauding to respond. When everyone sat down I caught a flash of blond hair fifty feet to my right, and two rows down. I stood and saw Valparaíso and Jane. He did not like the fights, but today of course he was here. He and Manolo were probably drinking buddies.

"What's wrong," Laura said. "You look sick."

As the next bull was released into the ring I pulled the tip off of one *banderilla* and tested its point against my palm. I peered through the crowd and saw Jane slip her arm around Valparaíso's waist as he bent forward, pretending to be interested in the fight. The *banderilla* was sharp enough, all right. I could slip up behind them and slam the harpoon into the back of his head. I had one for her too.

Valparaíso looked at Jane and laughed. She shrugged her shoulders, downplaying whatever joke she'd made. Maybe it was about me. About how I was probably here in the bullring, sitting in the cheap seats.

They both laughed now. The *corrida* was lost on them.

"This one looks dangerous," Laura said. "See how he hooks to the right?"

I grunted, but didn't look at bull or man. I dug the metal tip into my palm, enough to redden my flesh, then Laura grabbed the *banderilla* and tried to take it out of my hand.

"Watch the fight," she said.

I took the *banderillas* in both hands and broke them over my knee. But with the blades' newly shortened handles, they were in fact better, more easily concealed weapons. I could hold the handle like a knife, and I imagined the harpoon tip breaking through Valparaíso's blond head, and through Jane's short black kinks. My head throbbed for the first time in days.

"I'm going," I said.

"Are you crazy? It's almost time for Manolo's second bull."

I stood and pushed the cork back onto the points, then put the *banderilla* heads into my *guayabera* pocket. Now I could see Jane and Valparaíso clearly. He was talking to the man to his left, while Jane looked down at her hands. She did that when she was sad or thoughtful, when she had something on her mind that she simply wasn't going to say. Then she leaned across Valparaíso's lap to talk to the man beside him. Valparaíso rested his hand between her shoulder blades.

Behind me someone whistled for me to sit. "I'm sorry," I said to Laura. "You stay. You can tell me about the bull."

"Of course I'm going to stay."

I nodded, then pushed past our neighbors and began trudging up the steps, not looking down at the chubby *torero* who on a good day could make time stand still. I wanted time sped up now; I wanted to get to its end.

But I was not going to plunge *banderilla* points into the back of anybody's head, though if I killed Carlos Valparaíso it would make an excellent story. Will would hear about it back home, on the San Antonio television news. I dropped the harpoon points into a trash can, then stepped into the enclosed area of the beer stands and milling people. I could not see the ring, but I could hear the crowd shout its first proper *olé* of the afternoon. It was soon followed by another louder and more unified cry. Martínez would be using the big cape now, to start the fight. He would be making some of his slow, sweeping veronicas, and the bull would be turning quickly after each pass, kicking up dust, to charge back into the cape.

The beer line emptied as the customers ran to their seats to see Manolo fight his last bull. So I bought myself a drink without any waiting, then sipped it as I stood inside the concrete structure which echoed and rumbled with the crowd's pleasure. I could only see inside myself, and there I found Valparaíso and Jane.

I was suddenly sick of myself and them too, and poured my beer out on the ground, then stepped back out into the seats, standing at the top of the steps which led down to Laura's box. I only then noticed that the air was black, even on a Sunday. How did the bulls find enough oxygen to keep charging?

When I looked down at the ring I saw that the bull, Último was his name, 517 kilos, black with huge white splotches and white pointed horns, was in fact winded, and that the out-of-shape Manolo was breathing heavily too. He stood some ten feet from his animal, his *muleta* hanging down in front of his knees. The ribs of both bull and man heaved for air.

After a moment Manolo raised his *muleta* and gestured with it decisively. The bull lowered its head and lumbered past him. Exhausted as it was, the bull bent quickly back into the cape and Manolo drew the animal into the orbit of his slow right hand.

It was happening. Manolo Martínez was happening, and I picked my way through the onlookers seated in the aisle and pushed back in beside Laura.

"Thank God you're back," she said. "You don't know what you're missing."

Manolo stopped the action again so that he and the bull could rest. Much closer now, I could see how they both opened their mouths wide, and rhythmically sucked in dirty air. Their ribs pumped in unison as if their two hearts beat mightily for each other. These were my best seats ever. I could see the sweat glinting on Manolo's forehead, and the shine above his lip. I could see the strand of slobber dangle from the bull's square bottom lip, how it stretched earthward until it broke. Either face would have made a great shot, but I was glad I did not have my camera. I was glad to see their exhausted heaves with my own eyes. And to see more as well; the bull's black whiskers; Manolo's thick brown eyebrows; the bull's blank stare as it waited for Manolo's call; the concentrated light in Manolo's eyes, their—yes—hawkish concentration as he panted for air. The smear of blood across the belly of his pink suit.

"This is bullfight history," Laura said. "They're both going to die of heart attacks."

She took my hand and I held onto her as Manolo gulped and raised his own right hand, then gestured precisely with the small red cloth.

As the exhausted crowd pushed out of the ring, it carried Laura and me in the direction of Jane and Valparaíso. I tried to squirm away from them, but Laura put her weight into my back and shoved me forward. I had almost reached them by the time Jane turned to look behind her, and there I was, holding onto Laura.

An immense smile withered on Jane's face, and Valparaíso turned to see what was keeping her. We stood just five feet apart, and the crowd pushed us closer, even though I tried half-heartedly to dig my feet into the pavement. Around us jubilant *aficionados* whistled in imitation of birds of prey, and small groups chanted *Ma No Lo, Ma No Lo.*

A goon stood behind Valparaíso, and another was to the left of Jane.

"I didn't think you liked the fights," I finally said, nearly stammering, essentially to Valparaíso.

He opened his thin lips and showed his teeth. "I like any good fight," he said. Then he turned to Laura. "I was sorry to hear about Guillermo's death."

"It was a tough break," she answered.

Like an idiot, I started to introduce Laura to Jane, then stopped at the sight of what was either disgust or terror in Jane's eyes.

"Maybe you know each other," I said.

"Of course," Laura said. "I'd recognize you anywhere."

Jane looked at me, and for a moment I forgot about our companions. The jostling of the crowd helped me to concentrate on her. But not to talk. I had nothing to say to her. Her mouth moved, but she was quiet too. Then I saw her gold necklace, stunning against her dark creamy flesh.

"You were already beautiful," I said, surprised at the calmness of my voice, "Without that fucking necklace."

"What are you doing with her?" Jane finally snapped. I felt the pressure of some craziness building up behind my eyes. Maybe it showed because Jane suddenly turned away. But I grabbed her arm. Her goon stepped toward us.

"I'm coming for the kids," I croaked. "You'll have to kill me. Do you hear me?"

She jerked her arm loose. The goon came between us, and

then everything inside me sagged when I remembered hitting her.

Valparaíso looked me up and down, grinned, and bounced lightly on the balls of his feet. "Speaking of killing, I want to hear about Guillermo some time," he said, glancing at Laura. "Did his brother really shoot him? Over you?"

With both hands she took his baby blue jacket's lapels and pulled him straight into her face. He made a gagging sound and his eyes opened wide when their noses touched, and she kissed him on the mouth, then the bodyguard pulled him away. Valparaíso almost tripped as he jerked free.

"Fucking monster," he shouted and waved his fist at her. "Guillermo was out of his goddamn mind."

"You're such a little man, *patrón*," she said.

Valparaíso gritted his teeth as he spun away from us and pushed into the crowd, knocking jubilant passersby out of his way. Jane followed without looking back.

Laura took my hand to stop my shaking, and it worked.

"Jesus Christ," I finally murmured. "You scared me."

"No," she answered, and we took our first steps away from the bullring. "I scared him."

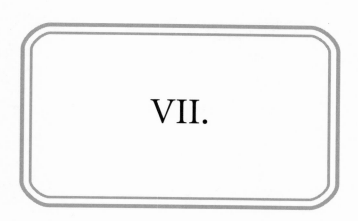

VII.

23.

The cabdriver looked surprised when I asked him to take me to Polotitlán.

"I don't know what to charge for a trip that far," he said. "It's what, 150 kilometers?"

"I have plenty," I said. "Let's just go."

Cars circled the golden angel as he looked at me. Finally I pulled out a fold of bills. Some of the money was mine, some was Laura's. He nodded.

We looped around the Ángel, then went straight down Reforma. Cars pressed around us as we drove through Chapultepec and the Lomas, Laura's and Valparaíso's neighborhood.

"You live in Polotitlán," the driver said, looking at me in his mirror. "You must have tried the famous *maguey* worms."

"No," I said. "I never got around to the worms."

He grinned into his mirror. "*Hombre*, you haven't lived. Better eat them before they get us."

"That makes sense," I said, then looked at the hack's license attached to the back of his seat. Its photo confirmed his Indian features, the roundness of his face, the wide cut of his mouth. His name surprised me. I've seen Mexicans named after all kinds of tongue-twisting gods and heroes, but never the war god Huitzilopochtli, hungriest of the Aztec deities. His name barely fit on his license.

"This must have been a hard name for a child," I said. "I can't even pronounce it."

With a long sigh he said his name, sounding it out as if the many syllables were boulders in a stream, and he a weary traveler leaping from one to the next.

"I was the youngest," he explained, "Cuauhtemoc and Moctezuma were already taken."

I tried to silently mouth his name, to jump even clumsily between its clipped sounds. But I couldn't, not without hearing it, so I began to speak it, softly but still falling into its cracks.

Huit-zil-o-po-cht-li.

Then I noticed a card depicting Guadalupe was taped to the back of Huitzilopochtli's headrest, so that she was right in my field of vision. The Virgin is everywhere, of course, in Mexico, and after a while you stop noticing her. That a man named for the Aztec war god was also a Guadalupe devotee was scarcely worth commenting on, so I didn't.

My plan came to me as we passed Toluca. Once in Polo, I would wait until nightfall, maybe drinking coffee at the little roadside café not far from the hacienda's entrance. Once it was *muy noche* I would climb the fence that ran along its border, and run through the moonlight toward the house. Long ago I used to jog through those fields; I knew the terrain, the locations of the trees and crops.

I pulled Pierre's pistol out of my bag, felt its weight in my hand, then laid it on the seat beside me. Once I relaxed, sinking down into the backseat's cracked upholstery, I could begin to see myself running across the hacienda's parking lot, stepping lightly on the paving stones. I am going to be so nimble, I thought. I know the hacienda so well. I had photographed so much of it for Valparaíso.

I would run along the long front wall of the house, past the chapel that had been put in by the previous owner, a celebrated bullfighter, then turn the corner and find the door that was never locked.

As Huitzilopochtli maneuvered us along the bumpy road, I could see everything that I had to do. Everything that was going to happen.

I would have to be very quiet. I would leave the door open to let in the moonlight, which barely illuminates the mounted heads of bulls.

I tiptoe through the dull light, and move deliberately. I push gently at a door, and slink into the hall. In the dark I always bump into furniture, but this time I am as agile as a ghost.

Huitzilopochtli asked, "How much farther is it?"

When I pass Valparaíso's bedroom, he and Jane can be fucking and I won't care. Pistol or not, I haven't come for revenge, or any dark passion. I'll only use it if I have to.

The kids' room will be just beyond theirs. I can only pray that May and Sammy sleep in the same room.

They do. My luck is changing.

The children look just as they did when I left them. May, with her high forehead, sleeps with her thumb in her mouth. Sammy is bunched up as if halfway through a hard fight.

I have to wake them before I pick them up, so they won't scream. I go to May first, and stroke her forehead, and pat her face, and put my fingers into her thick hair. Her eyes start to open slowly, then pop wide when they see me. I have to put my hand over her mouth and hush her. She throws her arms around my neck.

"Daddy," she whispers. "You came."

"I'm going to take you away," I say.

She shows me where her clothes are and I help her dress.

Sammy's things are in the same chest of drawers. He wakes more easily than May, and embraces me just as she had, and then I dress him. We creep past the master bedroom; I hear the master snore. They may want to ask about their mother, but I hush them.

"Are you all right?" Huitzilopochtli asked.

I didn't answer right away. Then I said, "Will you drive us to the border?"

"Which border?"

The car vibrated lightly beneath me. A thin rain had begun to fall. Huitzilopochtli turned on his wipers which thudded against his cracked windshield. I wished I were back at Tepeyac, crawling toward Guadalupe, making promises and petitions, bleeding at the knees, clinging to Laura.

I looked at Guadalupe, the Queen of Heaven, taped to the seat in front of me. Her face was smooth, soft, indifferent, Aztec. Not the least bit angry. I could ask Huitzilopochtli to turn around and take me to her.

Pierre's gun wasn't loaded. I dropped it onto the floor.

I carry Sammy and hold May's hand as we cross the paving stones. After the first line of trees, designed to keep the house unseen from the highway, we begin hurrying through the fields. The caliche road runs like the white bed of a dead river to our left, but I hear a guard's soft voice and veer into the trees. Sammy's head bounces against mine as I run, and May begins to drag on my hand.

"I'm tired," she says.

Of course she is. I pick her up and to my delight I can run as fast as before, over uneven turf, through moonlight and starlight, with the voice of the guard coming closer and softer.

When we pass the hydroponic gardens, the vegetables

Valparaíso has wrapped in plastic bags and sunk in water, I know we are halfway to the fence.

"I'm hungry, Daddy," May says, and before I can protest that it's 4 A.M. and not time to eat, Sammy says that he too is starving.

We have reached the grove of foreign trees and hybrids, the vegetation Valparaíso wants to introduce into Mexico. I am panting now, and hearing the guard's voice, and remembering the names of the trees. Of the bushes, even. I have finally learned something.

We run through the myrtle, with its arrow-shaped leaves, and the sorrel which is as homely as lettuce. We pass the coriander and the fig tree, and I want to stop and eat, but there is no fruit. Gasping for breath, now famished myself, looking back for the guard who murmurs my name, I carry my children past the carob plant, and the castor bean vine, and the wormwood plant and the apricot tree and the persimmon, but still we find nothing and the guard whispers my name.

We reach the pomegranate tree, with its many thin trunks rising from a single root, each trunk leaning away from the other, and we can't help it, we do stop and eat of its fruit.

"Thief," says the guard.

I take a long look at my children, at their faces stained red with juice. This look will have to last me, so I eat them with my bleeding eyes.

"What about the worms?" Huitzilopochtli said. "Are we stopping for the worms?"

24.

The cab pulled in front of the gate to Valparaíso's hacienda, raising a fine gray dust that the wind caught and tossed over the stone wall. The guards looked at the car, their carbines slung over their shoulders. I didn't see the guard who had clubbed me. I didn't recognize these men at all, which made it easier to open the car door.

Huitzipochtli turned and spoke to me over his shoulder.

"You want out here? Don't you want me to take you to the house?"

I considered the question with one leg out of the car, then said "no, thanks" and counted out some bills. I got out empty-handed and approached the guards. I had left my bag with the owner of the bus stop café just down the road, and I let Huitzipochtli drive away with Pierre's pistol on the floor of his car.

This was becoming a bad hearing day. The sound of the small rocks crunching beneath my feet didn't register, so I seemed to float toward the gate.

"Is Don Carlos expecting you?" a guard said as he stepped into my path.

"He'll know why I'm here," I said.

The guard turned stiffly and retreated to the guard box, where he lifted a phone. He spoke for a moment, then grew silent, and responded to whatever he was being told with brisk nods. The phone still in his hand, he turned to me and said something. I saw his mouth move into the precise positions that Spanish vowel-making requires, and heard a clipped burst of sound, but couldn't understand him, so I came closer.

When the guard slipped his free hand down to the butt of his carbine, I stopped and asked him to repeat himself.

"Don Carlos is not receiving guests. He and the Señorita Jane are having breakfast."

"Tell him I'm walking to the house. That they'll be finished eating by the time I arrive."

The guard's brow bunched slightly, then he spoke again into the black phone. The wind gusted behind me and the second guard, standing in front of the gate, lifted his fingertips to the brim of his quivering hat. The first guard extended the phone toward me.

I was afraid that with my hearing problem, I wouldn't be able to understand what was said on the phone, that I would have to ask the speaker to repeat himself and so appear addled and ridiculous, but Valparaíso's annoyed, guttural voice came through just fine.

"Daniel, you're not looking for trouble, are you?"

"No, just my children."

"They are Jane's children too."

I paused, and thought about how little he must care about Sammy and May, one way or the other. Even if he had traded in his wife because she couldn't give him children. Then I said, "Let me talk to Jane."

"You can talk when you get here. I'll send a car."

"No, thanks," I said. "I'll walk."

"Bullshit. Just wait there."

I hung up the phone and told the guards that *el patrón* had given me permission. The silent guard opened the gate, while the other almost made me jump when he squatted at my feet and began patting me down.

I stepped through the gate, helped forward by another blast of air. In the distance I saw Valparaíso's red antenna poking up through the trees. Polo mountain rose behind the tower, its top covered by a cloud. There wasn't much pollution out here, of course, but the wind picked up the eroded soil and tossed it in handfuls, and the air could suddenly turn gritty. I set off walking on the white caliche road, beginning with my longest strides, then lengthening them as my legs loosened.

I tried to concentrate my mind as I walked, to picture Sammy, May and me together somewhere, but instead I remembered how Ellen and I used to jog along this road when we first arrived and were guests at the hacienda. Jane, the dancer, found exercise for its own sake utterly idiotic.

I couldn't hear the shuffling of my feet, but I saw how white wisps of dust rose with every step, and how the wind gathered my dust together with the darker dirt of the fields and blew it all forward toward the sleeping volcano which framed my vision. Which now filled with Jane's image.

I imagined I was taking one step for every day that I had spent with her. When I reached the hacienda, that time would be up. We would be free of each other.

I remembered her in our first days together. The miracle of her early attention. How I suffered on her ambivalent days. I remembered my unexpected happiness at fatherhood, which came at the same time as her first unhappiness. May's birth had turned her inward; Sammy's almost killed her. In between the two, I had peeked out from behind my camera and started to lose her. But why would that be so? Jane was utterly strange to me now, not just exotic. Compared to her, Laura was a benevolent sister.

I saw a white cloud rise and advance through the trees nearest the hacienda, and in a moment the olive-colored jeep Valparaíso had sent for me appeared around a curve.

It roared up toward me, driving down the middle of the road. I kept walking, then stopped and forced myself to look as it skidded to a halt, bathing me in small white stones as it turned sideways to block the road. The driver, one of Valparaíso's bodyguards, grunted something, then spit out the cigarette that had been stuck in the corner of his mouth. I saw myself reflected in his sunglasses and remembered my father, how I saw him driving away that afternoon as the bus carried me home from school. He must have known I was in that bus. He must have known my route. Why hadn't he at least looked for me as he drove by?

The driver nodded toward his passenger door.

"I'm walking, " I said.

"This is private property," the driver said. "Do as you're told."

I was glad that I couldn't see his eyes. I hoped Valparaíso would be wearing his dark glasses too, and that he would have gotten Jane a pair. I pictured May and Sammy with mirrored glasses on, and my throat went dry. Then I stepped off the road and walked around the jeep, then back onto the road. I wished I'd brought my bag along, so that my shaking hands could grip something. Finally I crammed them into my pockets.

The driver didn't respond until I'd taken twenty steps or so, which brought me from the day Jane came to visit me and my ripped-open cheek in the hospital, to the night a few weeks later when we sat quietly in our second story apartment, glad to be home and listening to our records. May had gone to sleep early. My face had stopped hurting, and we talked about the future. About maybe traveling to Mexico, which I had eventually pushed into our living in Mexico. With her safely hidden from my rivals. That's what I was really thinking when I brought her here.

I looked at a patch of *maguey* cactus to my left, and tried to remember when I had turned from photographing my wife's body to the safety of taking pictures of their long spiked arms, their pleasing green-gray color.

The jeep rumbled behind me, and came crunching up on the small rocks that broke like little bones, but I didn't look back. I quit replaying those scenes and began concentrating on the road. The jeep's grill work nudged me from behind, then began to nuzzle me as if it were a curious bull. Then the jeep pushed and I staggered forward, but kept my feet. The driver jammed down the horn and I froze at its bellow, waiting to be gored. But all that touched me was wind and dust and little white rocks as the driver jerked around me, still leaning on his horn, and rumbled toward the hacienda.

When the air cleared I could see the long low house in the middle distance. A bird that I couldn't identify rose from the grove to my right. I picked up a handful of pebbles, intending to count them as a rosary while I walked. To think about Guadalupe and pray.

But I couldn't concentrate, and I didn't know the rosary by heart anyway, so I threw the rocks ahead of me. "Pray for us O holy mother of God," I shouted at the bird, who had lighted on a branch nearby. "That we may be made worthy of the promises of Christ."

· · ·

I didn't recognize Valparaíso's serving boy who let me in and led me wordlessly toward the enclosed pool, where I knew the *patrón* took his breakfast. I didn't want to look at his heavy furniture, or at the mounted heads of his bulls, but I couldn't help myself. Everything seemed familiar. Jane hadn't left a mark.

Then I saw myself in a small mirror that hung just at the entrance to the living room, a mirror that had reflected my image in less strange days. Back then, except for my cheek scar, which I had begun to consider discreet, I had looked unremarkable. Now I was coated in white dust. Ready for the oven.

Valparaíso sat beside his pool, a newspaper spread across the breakfast table, an empty coffeepot pushed to one side. But he didn't pretend to be reading as I entered. He glared at me and showed his teeth. The burly driver from the jeep was now a bodyguard again; he sat at the servant's table a few feet from Valparaíso, the same table that I should have acknowledged as my own the first time I set foot in the hacienda. The bodyguard had opened his jacket to reveal the pistol on his hip.

"By God you're an asshole," Valparaíso shouted. "A Sunday morning asshole."

I stopped a few feet from the table, and cleared my throat as quietly as I could.

"Well, sit down," he said. "Have a drink. Looks like you could use one."

"No, thanks," I said. "I can't stay."

"You can't stay," he barked, then jumped to his feet. "Jane, do you hear? Your husband can't stay." Jane wasn't in the room, so he seemed to be talking to a ghost.

"I just want Sammy and May. Then I'll leave you alone."

"You look like a fucking scarecrow. Like a fucking *campesino*. But you come into my house and tell me what you want."

253

Valparaíso swatted the newspaper off his table, revealing a heavy, dark blue revolver.

"Motherfucker. You want Jane too, I suppose."

He began pacing in front of me, back and forth. He seemed to have forgotten that I was there, and to be ranting to himself. "You think I need my bodyguards," he shouted, picking up the pistol. "You think I'm afraid to get my hands dirty." Then he insulted Laura and her scars.

He laughed then, and wagged his pistol in front of my face. "I can kill you right now, right in front of this man. You have invaded my private property. I'll have no problems, but you'll be lucky if you don't get fed to the coyotes." He clenched his free hand into a fist, and seemed to want to hit me, but didn't.

Then he turned away, pushing his chair so its metal legs screeched against the ridged tiles along the pool, and walked off toward the bedrooms. The bodyguard stared at me. I saw a motion reflected in his glasses, and turned to find another man five feet behind me, the brim of his hat pulled down near his eyes. He showed his holstered pistol too.

I quietly cleared my throat. I wanted to blink and see the hawk, or the Virgin, or even Laura, but was afraid to close my eyes.

I stood between the two men, and couldn't see them both at once. My forehead filmed over with sweat, but I didn't move my hands which hung at my sides.

Then Valparaíso and Jane came into the room and walked to the edge of the pool. Jane stood erect and powerful beside him. Over him, even, taller by a couple of inches. Valparaíso lifted his arm slightly and slipped it around her slender waist. With the other hand he pointed the pistol into my face, and the guards stepped away.

"*Sí o no*," he said to her. "Do I kill him or not?"

I nodded in recognition of the moment. I was the one who had given her life or death power over me, and now she finally got to choose.

We stood quietly. Jane and I looked into each other's eyes, and I tried to tell her things, to send her telepathic messages. That whatever she chose would be all right, that I wasn't too attached to my life. But that she ought to think about Sammy and May, whatever she did. And to remember the times we fenced and danced and fucked, and let that count for something.

I felt my eyes narrow as I communicated these things, but I wasn't getting tired. This was my last long look into her face, and even though her beauty didn't seem quite as overpowering these days—she had really ruined her hair—I was in no hurry to turn away. Something told me that only my deepest, most peasant doggedness would save my life, and I told Jane with my eyes that I would stare at her forever if she killed me, and even more hungrily. And that part of her would always be mine, and she might as well resign herself.

Jane returned my gaze, but seemed more to be studying me than trying to communicate. I think I had surprised her, and she was trying to figure out who I was.

Finally Jane lifted her hand and set it down on Valparaíso's shoulder, but still didn't speak.

I coughed cautiously, then said her name. "Jane." Then, "I want to take the kids home."

Jane nodded, then folded her hands together in front of her womb. Her eyes went blank, and I couldn't tell what she was thinking or remembering.

"And then what?" she asked, her voice husky. She pulled away from Valparaíso.

"Then I want to keep them," I said. "They shouldn't be here."

"They should be with Laura?"

"With me."

She blinked and pressed her lips together. His pistol still pointed at me, Valparaíso looked at her, and twisted one side of his face in a grimace. The pistol wobbled. He was getting tired.

"I'm not leaving without them," I said, trying not to sound exhausted.

Jane put her hand over Valparaíso's pistol and gently pushed the gun down. She murmured. "I'll go pack their bags. You can take them for a little while, and then we'll decide."

Valparaíso's eyebrows curved slightly upward, and he stuck out his bottom lip. He turned away from Jane and with an underhand sweep of his arm threw his pistol into the pool where it splashed and immediately sank.

"I've wasted enough time," he said. "I've got things to do."

He flipped over the servant's table on his way out; the sound of its grinding against the tiles echoed over the water.

I couldn't make out Jane's next words, and I had to ask her to repeat herself.

"How are you getting to the bus? Are you going to make them walk to the highway?"

I didn't want to admit that I hadn't considered the trip back to the crossroads, where we would catch the bus to Querétaro, and then the train to Laredo.

"I'll call a cab," I said.

"Never mind. I'll drive you," she said, her voice under tight control. I recognized this voice well.

She squeezed her hands into fists, then relaxed and clenched them again.

"Sure," I said.

"Wait here," she said. "I'll get Sammy and May."

When she turned, the guards relaxed without actually moving.

I moved to the edge of the pool and dropped to one knee. With my right hand I cupped water, and splashed it onto my gritty face.

A few minutes later, Sammy and May approached on short, timid steps. May had her fingers stuck in her mouth. Her hair was shorter and more curly than I had seen it. A young, timid-looking maid walked behind them, carrying a bag in each hand. I took only one step toward them. When they got close May stopped and wiped her fingers on her new red skirt. Sammy hid behind his sister, and glanced up over her shoulder toward me. He had the darkest blue eyes I had ever seen, except for my own.

"Let's go," I said, and took their small hands.

Ramón, the owner of the bus stop café, was clearly surprised to see Jane and me walk in together with our children. When we had first arrived in Mexico, we came over often during the school's long lunch breaks, and until recently we would stop in to pick up drinks on the way home. But everyone around here knew the extent of our damage, and who Jane's new man was, so when Ramón saw us he looked nervous. A *mariachi* lament too loud to be understood began to thunder out of his jukebox just as we walked in.

Ramón was a short, barrel-shaped man who obviously enjoyed his own *cabrito*, and his own Tecate and Presidente as well. His belly extended over the table as he stood between Jane and me and asked if he could serve us. His shirt gaped open at the navel, where it had come unbuttoned. On another occasion he would have let it go, but now when he noticed his dishevelment he closed up his shirt with his stumpy fingers.

"Anything for you, Don Daniel?" he asked.

I asked for coffee. Jane tensely shook her head, and I ordered Cokes for Sammy and May. Sammy knocked over the napkin holder and pushed it halfway across the table, apparently pretending it was the train he was about to ride. "Choo choo," he cackled.

The door opened and one of Valparaíso's men came in, the one who had stood behind me at the pool. He opened his jacket, took a table near the window, and stared at us.

I turned to May, who looked across the table at me, panic and exhilaration mixed in her eyes.

"Who cut your hair?" I asked her.

May answered, "Are we going to see Grandma? And Aunt Doris?"

"That's right."

"But you just went to see them."

"No, sweetheart," I said. "That day I changed my mind. I wanted us to go together."

May glanced up at Jane, probably wondering if her mother had changed her mind too, and was now going with us to Texas.

"Why did you say 'yes'?" I murmured to Jane. "Is he getting tired of them?"

Jane rolled her narrow shoulders, whose width I could encompass by holding my hands just eighteen inches apart. Amazing how much she could fit into such a narrow space. She took off the dark glasses and set them on the table. The whites of her eyes were etched in red, but she didn't seem on the verge of tears as she looked at the dim mark on my forehead.

"I didn't know you were actually going to be hurt," she finally said. "I wanted to get away from you. Not to hurt you. Not that way, at least."

"Maybe so," I murmured as I looked out Ramón's greasy plate-glass window to the gas pumps. "Anyway, I guess that makes us even." The wind gusted again, and twisted itself into a dust devil that swirled scraps of paper and dead leaves. The cloud on the volcano was thickening, and pressed halfway down to the tree line. Valparaíso's man leaned back against the window and looked a little bored.

Ramón returned with our drinks. He had the only public espresso machine in this part of Mexico, and I took a small pleasure in the light brown foam, the color of Jane's skin, which covered my coffee.

"*Tienes popote?*" Sammy said, and Ramón answered, "*Para ti, jefe, claro,*" and then slipped a straw into the boy's Coke. I asked Ramón to turn the jukebox down a little so Jane and I could talk.

Ramón nodded, and when he stepped back from the table Jane said, in English, "I'm pregnant."

"Enjoy your drinks," Ramón said with unusual formality. "I'll see to the music."

My ears buzzed for the first time in days as I looked away from Jane, back toward the kitchen. I imagined Huitzilopochtli then, still driving toward Mexico City with Pierre's pistol on the floor behind him. I hoped it wouldn't cause any harm.

The children bent over their drinks, and Jane fingered her dark glasses on the table and stared into their lenses. Then our eyes met. Hers seemed to retreat from mine, back into their sockets. My inner buzz grew stronger, became a vibration, as if someone had snapped a giant rubber band inside my head.

"Carlos doesn't know yet," she said.

I nodded and pulled the spoon from my coffee and set it on the table. The brown film ran halfway up its handle.

"He'll run you off," I said. "He won't need you after you have it. He'll treat you just like he did Ellen. You've already offended him."

Jane set her jaw, and her eyes came toward me, hardened behind their coating of held-back tears.

"You've got it all figured out," she said. "You understand what everybody's going to do before they do it."

Valparaíso's man pulled a folded-double comic book out of his jacket pocket and placed it unopened on the table. Káliman, the Mexican super hero. The turbaned Káliman did have it all figured out. He had developed his mind to an abnormal degree. Unlike the heroes I'd grown up on, he had achieved total self control. "*Serenidad y paciencia*," he liked to say. It was advice that my students had sometimes given me, but I'd shrugged their wisdom off.

May set down her Coke and got off her chair to stand between Jane and me, as she often did when her mother and I fought. I put my hand on her exuberant curls, but May stared straight ahead at Sammy, who pulled the straw from his drink and blew into it, spraying us with Coca-Cola. Sammy laughed, then poked his straw back into the drink to draw more out. The kids need baptizing, I thought. I have so much to do.

Then, in a low voice, not wanting to scare May, I said, "This is Mexico, Jane," and looked around May and into Jane's eyes. I set my jaw to match hers.

A northbound Flecha Roja pulled up to the café, and its passengers poured out. The driver got off too; evidently they were taking a break en route to Querétaro or San Luis. The kids and I could catch this bus, or another in thirty minutes, or an hour, or whenever we wanted, really.

Now that Ramón had lowered the volume, I could make out a stanza of the song. The singer despaired unto madness. Alone with his thoughts at the end of a lonely day, with the love of his life driven away forever, maybe to her death, by his oh-so-obvious defects, he might not survive until cockscrow. But if he could somehow sing the story right, and sing it all night long, he might live to grieve another day. That was the best he could hope for, but it was something. This was a song Jane and I might each hum into the other's ear if we took that one last dance for the road I wanted to ask her for, but was afraid to.

"Quit looking at me like that," Jane said as the song throbbed to its end, trumpets blaring, the singer wailing right up to reason's edge. "Say something."

I looked at the bus driver as he emerged from the toilet. There was a line of customers in front of Ramón's counter, buying chips and *tortas*. We still had a few minutes together.

Customers filed out of the café and back onto the bus, converting themselves back into passengers. Jane didn't look at the bus, didn't give me any clues that the kids and I should be getting on our way. May stared at us, eyes as big around as hundred-peso coins. Sammy was absorbed in his Coke.

"Dan," Jane said. Her voice was jumpy.

"It's time to go," I answered.

Now Jane looked at the bus. The bodyguard turned a page of his comic.

The driver, last in line, paid for his chips, and Jane looked at me. I couldn't exactly tell what was in her eyes, but something was there. Some combination of question, fear and excitement.

I set a handful of coins on Ramón's table, then took the napkin that I'd used to wipe Sammy's Coke off my face and laid it over Jane's keys. Valparaíso's keys, that is. She cleared her throat as if she wanted to speak, but didn't. Then when I stood and picked Sammy up, Jane stood too, and took May's hand. Jane and I looked at each other just long enough, then, tentatively, as if moving through a dream, we walked toward the door. Valparaíso's man didn't look up. *Serenidad y paciencia.*

The bus was nearly full, so we had to sit near the front, almost under the mounted pictures of Jesus' Sacred Heart, and, of course, Guadalupe. I looked up at the Virgin, and wondered if this were one of her miracles. Of course, the Devil has also been known to play tricks in these parts. Once I got back to Texas, I wouldn't ask myself such questions, but for now I was thinking with a Mexican mind.

Sammy started chattering as soon as the bus pulled away, and after asking a few questions May fell into an exhausted sleep. Sammy soon joined her. Jane and I were quiet a long time. We let the parched country roll by. Then just before Querétaro, we started to talk.